"Hold the elevator!"

"Grady..." Cassie stumbled.

"Come on!" he encouraged her, running. "If we get there first, I can tell the waiter Ben's paying. He has a tab here."

The man held the door from closing as Grady ran in, drawing Cassie in with him. He wrapped his arm around her shoulders as she struggled to catch her breath. The man let the door go and the elevator began to rise.

Grady was completely unprepared for what happened next. Cassie's hands caught his in a biting grip, her fingernails drawing blood as she let out a high-pitched, ear-splitting scream. She began to shake him and point to the door.

"Cassie—"

"No!"

The other man's eyes widened as they reached the third floor and the doors parted.

Cassie gasped and ran out into a hallway that spilled into the restaurant, only feet from the hostess's podium. She stopped and drew in air, her arms wrapped around herself, her cheeks red.

She looked mortified and somehow isolated. "I'm sorry," she whispered, then added grimly, "Remember that issue from my childhood I mentioned that I still deal with?"

"Yeah?"

"It's claustrophobia."

"Yeah," he said. An inch of skin was scraped off his left hand. "I guessed that."

Dear Reader,

I was a pudgy little kid, and all these years later, nothing much has changed. I've tried every diet out there with various levels of temporary success. Having a sedentary job doesn't help, nor does the propensity to sit and read a book when everyone else is playing tennis.

The real boon of that sedentary job, though, is that I can create and spend time with a heroine who has a perfect body. I know a great body doesn't make a better person, but I've always wanted one anyway. I make no apologies.

When Cassidy Chapman formed in my mind, the third child in my Manning Family Reunion series, she was beautiful and looked perfect, but I didn't know what she did for a living. Then I thought about the perfect job for a woman with a perfect body and I let out all the stops. She's a supermodel with a great life, but she has a past she knows little about since she and her siblings were separated as children.

As *New Year's Wedding* opens, the paparazzi are on her trail after an embarrassing episode on a photo shoot, and she's running to escape them with Grady Nelson—Ben's police department partner from *To Love and Protect*.

In Beggar's Bay she finds family, answers to questions that have plagued her for a long time and love. But Grady has his own issues, so finding solutions that will allow them to build a life together isn't easy. But is it ever?

While it's true that her model's body didn't simplify her life, she looked wonderful while she struggled. I loved that.

Thank you for buying my book!

Muriel Jensen

HEARTWARMING

New Year's Wedding

———

Muriel Jensen

HARLEQUIN® HEARTWARMING

ISBN-13: 978-0-373-36850-1

New Year's Wedding

Copyright © 2017 by Muriel Jensen

This edition published by arrangement with Harlequin Books S.A.

For questions and comments about the quality of this book, please contact us at CustomerService@Harlequin.com.

Printed in U.S.A.

www.Harlequin.com

Muriel Jensen lives with her husband, Ron, in a simple old Victorian looking down on the Columbia River in Astoria, Oregon. They share the space with a wild West Highland white terrier mix and two eccentric tabbies. They have three children, nine grandchildren and six great-grandchildren. Their neighborhood is charmed, populated with the kindest people who are also the best cooks. Life is so good.

Books by Muriel Jensen

Harlequin Heartwarming

Always Florence

Manning Family Reunion

In My Dreams
To Love and Protect
New Year's Wedding

Harlequin Superromance

All Summer Long
"Home, Hearth and Hayley"
Man with a Mission
Man with a Message
Man with a Miracle
Man in a Million
The Man She Married
The Man under the Mistletoe

Harlequin American Romance

Daddy to Be Determined
Jackpot Baby
That Summer in Maine
His Baby
His Wife
His Family
His Wedding

Visit the Author Profile page at Harlequin.com for more titles.

To the Seattle Mariners and the Seattle Seahawks to whom my husband is devoted. Their games gave me uninterrupted time to write. They're also quite a gorgeous group, so my "heroes" folder is full of their photos.

PROLOGUE

THE COLD, CRISP night had begun so well. Despite the last-minute schedule change just days before Christmas, the crew had rallied for the flight from Paris to Ireland. They would make this photo shoot work. The only hitch had been Maggie, the makeup artist, who had already left on her Christmas holiday. But a replacement had been found and everyone approached the Heart and Soul perfume shoot with the enthusiasm required for success.

The palatial country home where they were being allowed to set up lights and cameras had a pillared portico outlined with Christmas lights and a tall, decorated oak by the front steps.

Cassie Chapman was cold. Her filmy red, off-the-shoulder gown was intended to contribute to the glamour of the scene, but someone stood just yards away with a warm coat to wrap around her during breaks.

She was excited and edgy. Work always revved her body and her brain, but that wasn't all. That morning, she'd learned that the brother and sister she hadn't seen since she was two years old had found her and invited her to join them in Texas for the holidays. Though feeling like a lit firecracker inside, she tried to focus on the work at hand, knowing the entire crew was as anxious to finish the night's work as she was.

The shoot began to go bad when the woman who had replaced Maggie kept running in between shots to reset the combs that held Cassie's thick hair back. Her movements were quick and understandably nervous. She was very young and it was the first time she'd worked with this crew. She jabbed blush on Cassie's cheekbones with a finger that felt like an auger, and fussed with eyelashes she'd applied earlier and that now drooped slightly on the outside edge.

Cassie had stood quietly while the woman tried to fix it, apparently not achieving the look she wanted. The stars and the lights began to spin a little, her breath coming as though having to fight its way out. Oh, no. Those symptoms usually preceded an event. She told herself firmly, "Not. Now."

But rough, anxious hands were all over her face, pushing and smoothing, reattaching a comb and scraping her scalp.

Cassie remained still. She had a reputation as a consummate professional whether she was in water, on a camel or in a tree. Discomfort meant nothing as long as they got just the right shot.

Panic began, anyway. It was mild at first because she tried to work the behavior strategy. *Breathe deeply, think about wide, open spaces and put yourself there.*

Her favorite place was Paloma Beach on the Riviera. She struggled to remember the feel of the warm breeze on her face and the sun on her limbs, to hear the surf and the laughter of other bathers.

She was anxious, though, about meeting her siblings. She could miss her flight, and travel was crazy at this time of year. And the strategy required focus and not distraction to work well.

She finally said politely, "Please stop. I need a minute to…"

But the woman went on as though Cassie hadn't spoken, determined to fix the troublesome eyelashes.

Mild panic quickly became the serious stuff of nightmares. After twenty-five years and several therapists, she still didn't know if she'd been born this way or if something she couldn't recall had caused it. Once the panic took her over, its origin didn't matter. Dealing with it was all she could do.

Now she couldn't breathe, felt the darkness coming as though someone lowered a heavy, prickly blanket over her, saw the lights go crazy as the spin quickened and she began to gasp for air. The need to jump out of her skin and run was overwhelming.

It acted like a memory that wouldn't quite form. She had a sense of something holding her tightly in place, squeezing the breath out of her. In contradiction to the imprisoning hold, she felt something silky against her face. It was always the same. Loud, angry voices, cries of pain and anguish, then a harsh, ugly noise and a moment's silence. She struggled to put a time and place to what was less a memory than an imprint on her brain without words or pictures. As always, nothing came.

When the makeup artist smoothed the eyelashes again and accidentally stuck her finger in Cassie's eye, Cassie came back to the moment suddenly, screaming. She grabbed the startled woman's wrist and held it away from her.

"Stop!" Cassie shouted at her. "I asked you to stop!" She was horrified to hear herself. She never shouted. "Are you *deaf*?" she demanded.

The cruel question was spoken in exasperation rather than anger but she noted that the woman's eyes were on her lips. When they rose to meet her gaze, they looked mortified, stricken.

Several members of the crew closed in to try to help, but that was the last thing Cassie's claustrophobia needed. Though she felt as though a breath was trapped in her lungs, she managed to free a high-pitched scream. She dropped the woman's wrist, pushed away the coat someone tried to wrap around her, picked up the skirts of her dress and ran away. The scream seemed to fill the night and follow her.

CHAPTER ONE

CASSIDY CHAPMAN HELD Grady Nelson's hand in a death grip as they raced across the tarmac toward her father's private jet. Footsteps pounded after them.

"Cassie!" a rough male voice shouted from behind them. The rest of what he said was drowned out by the sound of the growling jet, ready for takeoff. The smell of diesel and grass filled the warm, south-east Texas air, making the Christmas carols coming from the terminal some distance away seem out of place.

"Almost there!" Grady encouraged her as they continued to run.

"Thank goodness," Cassie gasped. "I feel like my feet are wearing through the soles of my shoes."

"If you weren't such a celebrity, you wouldn't have to keep dodging the press."

They ground to a stop at the steps leading into her father's plane. The copilot waiting for them directed a passing security guard to stop the pursuing photographer.

"Drew," she said as she ran past the copilot and up the steps, her small tote bag weighing a ton after that run. "Thanks for being so prompt. But I thought Dad was sending the helicopter."

"It's our job to be prompt, Miss Chapman," he called after her. "Like the Boy Scouts, only we fly. And I was closer than the 'copter."

The small Gulfstream G450 was luxurious yet comfortingly familiar with its white-and-gold tapestry-covered armchairs around a low table. Several Picasso prints decorated the bulkhead. She'd accompanied her father on business on this plane many times. Flying with him had been part of her therapy. There'd been a point when she'd thought she'd licked all those old problems, but recent events had shaken that belief.

Grady stopped just inside and looked around in apparent astonishment. She hustled him forward so Drew could pull up the steps and close the door. She stowed her bag and took Grady's from him.

"Ah…" he said, frowning as his eyes went from the Tiffany lamp on the table to the art prints. "I guess we won't have to worry about legroom."

"Nice, isn't it? It's really hard to fly commercial airlines when you've gotten used to this." She pointed him to the two traditional passenger seats facing forward and put his bag in an overhead bin. "We have to sit here for takeoff," she said, taking the aisle seat. "Do you mind sitting by the window?" She nudged Grady toward the window seat as she asked the question.

"Happy to." He sat and buckled his belt, peering out the window, and then looked around, his expression still one of disbelief. She didn't blame him. He was probably wondering how a trip to spend Christmas with his friend in Texas had turned into a mad chase with her to the central Oregon coastal town where he lived and worked and was a friend of her family's.

"Are you beginning to regret helping me escape?" she asked, buckling her own belt, the small Chloe suede cross-body bag she still wore across her chest.

"No." He turned to smile at her. "But I do admit to feeling a long way out of my element. I seldom have reason to fly, much less in a private plane. My life is so much… smaller than this. And I like that."

Was that a message? she wondered. *I rescued you this time, but don't get used to it. This isn't going to be one of those cop-rescues-model-in-distress stories with a romance-movie ending.*

If so, that was fine with her. She had too much to repair in her life, and that required her complete attention. Like the panic she always felt when flying. And the fact that she may have just killed her career with a major meltdown in the middle of a shoot in Ireland. Both were related to an issue she couldn't explain, except to wonder if it was left over from her nebulous childhood. She'd done a good job of keeping that to herself, so, to the world at large, she just looked like a white-knuckle flier and to the crew in Ireland, a spoiled brat.

Added to that, she'd been reunited with her siblings after most of a lifetime spent apart, only to have to escape their Texas reunion when the paparazzi appeared.

She'd dreamed of getting her brother and sister back for most of her life. She barely remembered Jack; just an impression of gentleness and a comforting voice.

But she and Corie had corresponded for a while when she was twelve. Then Corie had run away and they'd had little contact since. Until they'd met in Texas.

As though that wasn't enough to keep a woman up at night, at age twenty-five, she suddenly had this undefined longing nothing seemed to satisfy. It wasn't related to men because her life was filled with them, and though she enjoyed their friendships, she felt no desire to spend the rest of her life with one. She did not need one more complication. She needed...*something*.

She patted Grady's hand where it rested on his knee, just to be able to touch something strong and solid. "Well, don't worry about it. I'll be out of your hair as soon as we get to Beggar's Bay. Your car's at the Salem airport, right?"

"No. I drove my mother and my aunts to Reno before I flew to Texas. I flew from there to meet Ben and Corie, expecting to fly back to Reno. And then you came along."

"Oh. Then I'll rent a car. But how are you getting the Jeep back?"

"Ben will drive me down to pick it up. It's not that long a drive from Beggar's Bay."

"Good."

Drew's voice came over the speaker. "Ready? We're off to the great Northwest, where we'll be greeted by—big surprise—wind and rain! Temperature is 42 degrees."

Cassie braced herself for takeoff. Wind and rain. She could deal with them, of course, but she was a hardcore Riviera rat at heart, not for its elegance and famous visitors, but because she loved blue skies and sunshine dancing on the azure Mediterranean. She closed her eyes, unconsciously tightening her grip on Grady's hand. The weather was the least of her concerns right now.

GRADY TURNED AS her fingernails dug into his knuckles, saw that her porcelain profile was set as though she was in pain, and concluded that she didn't like to fly. Seemed odd, since she must have to do it often. But fear was tough to conquer. He turned his hand to hold hers.

He had to tell himself again that this was really happening to him; he wasn't dreaming. And while it was true that he didn't regret a moment of the last few hours, he was seriously out of his comfort zone. As long as she looked desperate and lost, he was carried on the tide of rescue. The cop that lived inside him, that most days defined his very being, would move heaven and earth to get her to safety. Not that the pursuing paparazzi had threatened her with physical harm, but escaping them seemed very important to her, so he would do his utmost to help her.

Otherwise, this kind of opulence made him uncomfortable. He'd never traveled among people who appeared on the covers of magazines, or who could move airplanes around as her father had done. In fact, Grady came from a social circle that believed rich people didn't live real lives and were, therefore, not real themselves.

He hadn't learned much about her on just two days' acquaintance, except that she was the most beautiful woman he'd ever seen. She had long, loosely waving hair like a stream of moonlight, perfect ocean-blue eyes framed by long lashes, and a small feminine nose and chin. Her skin was flawless, a creamy shade of alabaster.

He squeezed her fingers. "You all right?"

Her reply was breathless. "Yeah."

Obviously not true. He tried to distract her with conversation. "Ever been to Oregon before?"

"I was born there, actually."

SHE HAD TO think about something other than her need to scream.

Looking into his eyes did provide a distraction. The irises were blue, a shade paler than hers, with rims around them that looked as though they'd been made with a felt-tipped pen. There was a comforting quiet in them that belied the sharp-witted, quick-thinking way he operated. She guessed that was critical for a cop.

She observed his face with professional interest. He was handsome. Not the kind of handsome she saw every day in the men she modeled with or the actors or other celebrities she'd dated. He was stunningly real, his burnished gold hair without product to thwart its tendency to fall on his forehead. It had no artfully applied highlights and was no thousand-dollar cut. It was simply thick and a little too long all over.

He was focused on her, waiting for her to go on. For a moment she couldn't remember what they'd been talking about. Even her encroaching panic had receded a little. Right. Oregon.

"Ah…my sister, Corie, was born there, too. My brother, Jack, was born in California and was just a toddler when our mother moved to Oregon."

"I didn't know that."

Grady had a strong, straight nose, a nice mouth that smiled a lot, and a square jaw with just the suggestion of a cleft. He smiled at her now. "It's great that you're all finally together again. Jack's wanted to find you and Corie so badly." He quirked an eyebrow. "I'm still not sure why we left your family behind in Texas when the press descended. I thought celebrities loved publicity."

She wondered whether or not to tell him about what had happened at the shoot in

Ireland but then decided against it. She'd have to explain her backstory and he really didn't have to know all that.

And everyone was coming home tomorrow to quickly put a wedding together for Corie and Ben, and she wouldn't cast a pall on that for anything. Besides, she wouldn't be in Oregon long enough that she even had to explain what had prompted this escape.

So she lied a little. "Publicity, yes. Paparazzi, not so much. I'm so tired of their constant presence. It's interesting to me that you can get a restraining order against a man who is always in your face or hiding in your bushes, but put a camera in his hand and it's suddenly a freedom-of-speech matter. When I saw that press caravan pull up in front of Teresa's…" She hesitated, unable to describe how surprised and horrified she'd been when the press had appeared at the foster home where her sister had spent her teen years and where'd they'd all gathered to spend Christmas. Word must have gotten out about the scene she'd made in Ireland. Though Grady hadn't known about that, he had seemed to understand her need to get away.

She felt a sudden burst of gratitude for this man who'd come with her without question. "I can't tell you how much I appreciate—"

He stopped her with a shake of his head. "No need. Ben's been my partner on the force for five years. He's like a brother to me. Since his family adopted your brother, Jack, and Ben is about to marry your sister on New Year's Day, I think it makes you and me family—sort of."

She had to agree. "True, but a thank-you is in order, anyway, because we were all having such a nice Christmas holiday."

"We were. I'd expected to have a grim Christmas until Ben invited me to Texas."

She smiled empathetically. "Yes, I heard about your girlfriend. You know, I really can't believe she left you. Why did she?"

"I guess I just wasn't the right man for her, after all." He shrugged. "She didn't want to talk marriage with me, yet she ran off to marry someone else after knowing him three weeks."

"Well, then, who needs her? You tell me what you're looking for in a woman and I will fix you up. I have friends all over the world. You want an heiress? An adventuress? An activist?"

He laughed at her business-like approach to matchmaking. "Thanks, but I'm off women for the moment. Tell me more about you. Ben said you were in Ireland when your father called to tell you your siblings were looking for you."

She didn't want to talk about Ireland.

"We were shooting a perfume ad."

"Corie said you've been on every notable designer's runway and you're the face of six or seven major ad campaigns. And all that time she'd admired you, she didn't realize you were her sister."

"She hadn't seen me since I was two, except for a photo when I was about twelve. Besides, I go by Chapman, my father's name, and I had dental surgery to cover a gap between my front teeth when I began to model. You knew our mother had three children from three different men?"

"Ben told me a little about your situation. Must have been hard on everyone."

"Well, Corie and I were sent to our fathers when our mother went to prison. Jack's father had died in a plane crash and

Ben Palmer was his best friend, so he was adopted by Ben's parents."

"That's a nice note in a sad story." He shifted in his seat with a sudden smile. "It seems to be turning out well, after all. Back to you. Are you spoiled and demanding? Like, only red M&M's when you do interviews and only classical music on the sound system when you're modeling?"

"Of course." She replied with a straight face. "Except yellow M&M's rather than red, country-western rather than classical, and only dark-haired men in the shot with me."

"Because the contrast shows off your golden goddess looks?"

Golden goddess. Was that a compliment, she wondered, or an accusation? She couldn't tell. "No. Playing the diva is never in the interest of the work. It's just my personal preference in men."

"Of course. I presume you have character and spirit standards, as well? Because, you know, hair color doesn't really tell you anything."

She ran a smiling look over his old-gold hair and blue eyes. "You come closest to those."

Uh, oh. He realized it would be wise to withdraw even as he leaned toward her. She wasn't at all what he'd expected of a fawned-over celebrity. And the moment she'd turned to him for help, he'd run away with her. It was unsettling to know she'd had such an effect on him. He was as fun-loving as the next bachelor, but he wasn't a thrill-seeker as a rule, or particularly reckless. He'd had a sick father; had to quit school. Life had been hard, but that had made him a practical man. "Well, no man worth his salt—even one with the wrong hair color—can resist a beautiful woman in distress."

She stared at him an extra minute then pointed at the window to the heavy clouds around them. "I understand it rains all the time in Oregon."

"Not all the time," he corrected. "Just October to April, but climate change has made every year less predictable than the one before. Of course, I have only five years of Beggar's Bay weather history to go by. I'm a transplant from Idaho, and we lived in Europe until I was in high school. My parents taught at American schools there—mostly in Italy and Spain. We went to Paris once, though I don't remember much about it. But I've never been to New York, except at the airport. I'm happy in Beggar's Bay."

"I have seen many of the world's most beautiful places—big cities, natural wonders, postcard views—and they're a feast for the soul. But the heart needs something else."

He kept his surprise to himself. The heart? Of course, supermodels had heart. He'd seen her in Texas with her rediscovered family and the children at the foster home in Querida. But this observation seemed to be about something else; something very personal.

"Your heart's searching for something?"

"Isn't everyone's?"

She closed her eyes and turned her head to the side, away from him. Hmm. Interesting woman. Impulsive and trusting, but holding a few secrets?

Well. Not his problem. After the wedding, she'd probably go back to Paris or New York or wherever the next shoot was and it would be as though their paths had never crossed. Just as well.

It was dusk when the pilot's voice came over the speaker to tell them they were beginning to descend and asking that they fasten their seat belts. She'd been fidgety and restless most of the flight and had just dozed off a few moments before. He reached out to fasten her belt rather than wake her. The small movement woke her. She looked into his eyes and said sleepily, "I didn't dream this. You are here." Her grateful look pinned and melted him.

"I am," he said easily, as though he ran off with supermodels every day.

DARKNESS HAD FALLEN when they began the drive home in a rented gray pickup he'd thought would handle the road better than the luxury car she'd suggested. It was raining hard, water from the winding, poorly lit road splashing around them.

Cassie imagined tomorrow morning's articles.

Popular 25-year-old supermodel Cassiopeia, AKA Cassidy Jane Chapman, was killed on Highway 101 on the central Oregon coast when the car in which she was a passenger swerved off the wet road and into a tree. Before the scene in Ireland that might have ended her career, she was the face of Eterna Beauty, Belle Face Pharmaceuticals, Heart and Soul Perfume, as well as many other products. Clothing designer Josephine Bergerac of the award-winning Empress line of eveningwear wept as she told CNN, "There will never be another body like Cassie's for my clothes. I am done."

All right, so maybe Josie wouldn't give up her work if Cassie died, but her friends and family would miss her. Her father would be devastated.

Grady slammed on the brakes as something large with four legs ran across the road just feet in front of them. Water flew around them as he skidded, and they finally came to a stop in the other lane. His bright lights illuminated a break in the trees through which the animal had disappeared. Cassie got a quick impression of a large brown body and a white rump.

"You okay?" he asked, catching her

shoulder until she turned toward him. He looked her over.

"Yes." Her voice was breathless, her heart hammering.

He expelled a breath then checked his rearview mirror as she watched the road for oncoming traffic. They seemed to be alone. Then a smaller version of whatever had raced past them loped across the road and into that break in the trees. This time she saw the first buds of antlers on a beautiful young head.

"I didn't realize deer were so big," she said as he turned back into their lane.

"Those were elk," he replied. "Roosevelt Elk. When a doe goes by, there's often a young one behind her. The Oregon Coast is full of them."

"Do you see them in Beggar's Bay?"

"I do. I live in an A-frame in the woods. They're a little shy, but they like to eat the salmonberries on the other side of my backyard."

She, on the other hand, didn't live anywhere. At least, not tonight. Her hasty departure from Texas had left several details about the next few days unresolved. "When we get to Beggar's Bay, can you just drop me at a motel, please? I'll buy you dinner as a thank-you if there's a restaurant nearby." She made a face when she heard her own words. "Not that dinner could repay you for helping me."

He shook his head, dismissing that idea as he turned onto a long, straight stretch of road. "We don't have a motel. We have a couple of B and Bs, but they're probably full because of the holidays."

She hadn't thought of that. "What about the next town?"

"It's another ten miles. Why don't you just stay with me? I have a spare bedroom and a bath. You'll have privacy until the wedding. You know you're safe with me because your brother would kill me if I let anything happen to you." He was quiet for a moment and then he asked, "What *are* you going to do? I mean, ultimately. You can't hide from the press forever, and you must have jobs lined up."

"Workwise, I have a couple of months off, but I promised to do a charity show in early January," she said. "Maybe I'll travel around a little after. I've worked hard so I could pull together some weeks to relax. Turns out my timing was perfect. Meanwhile, the whole family's flying home tonight on the red-eye, so it's possible I can bunk with one of them." She nodded gratefully. "But I'd appreciate staying at your place tonight if you're sure it's all right."

"I'm sure. Just relax. We'll be home in half an hour."

Relaxing didn't seem to be an option. Used to sitting in the back of a limo or a taxi, she was a little unnerved by the bumpy ride. The in-your-face view from the passenger seat was filled with tall trees and deep darkness, except for the path of his headlights and an occasional light suggesting a house some distance off the highway.

Grady drove with calm competence despite the near accident, and she kept quiet, appreciating his need to concentrate.

The headlights finally picked out a sign that read Welcome to Beggar's Bay. Population 8,912.

The edge of town was heavily forested, but lights and signs of habitation began to thicken. Finally they drove through three blocks of a brightly lit downtown. He turned up a road and pointed past her to a construction site where a three-story building was going up. "That's the assisted-living facility your brother Jack's wife, Sarah, is heading up. I'm just another mile this way."

Lights became spotty again and trees crowded the road.

He eventually turned up a side road for a short distance, then into the driveway of a tall, brightly lit A-frame house. It was trimmed in Christmas lights. She smiled in surprise. "When you said an A-frame, I imagined something simpler. The lights are beautiful."

Grady's home had a rustic façade with a central fieldstone chimney and high, wide, wedge-shaped windows on either side. Stilts supported a wraparound deck and, to the left of the house, terraced bricks held large pots with green plants.

"I got it for a steal when I moved here. It had been vacant for a year and a half, and the owner was anxious to get out from under two mortgages. I didn't get a tree up before I went to Texas."

He groaned as he pulled in beside a red-and-white Mini Cooper. "My mother's here." He turned off the car and gave Cassie a rueful smile. "I was hoping she'd still be in Reno. She'll want to know all about you."

Cassie smiled. "That's okay. I have nothing to hide." Mostly. She unbuckled her belt with a philosophical shrug. "While my father is kind and caring, he's made poor choices in women in the past. I imagine that's how I was born. It'll be nice to meet a real mother."

"Yeah." His tone was doubtful. "You're such an innocent, Cassie," he teased, then frowned at the simple dress she wore. "I don't suppose you have rain gear in your luggage?"

"I don't. I was expecting to stay in sunny Texas. But I'll be fine. It's not that far to the front door, is it?" She peered through the windshield. "Where *is* the front door?"

"Halfway back on the left side. Just run for the shelter of the deck overhang. Here." He yanked off the white cotton sweater he wore and held it over her head. She put her arms into the sleeves and he pulled it down. "It isn't too much protection, but better than nothing."

She was surrounded by the scent of male

and something dry and spicy with a suggestion of pine. The cotton was warm from his body. "Thank you," she said. He let himself out of the truck.

The rain was torrential—and cold. It struck her face and bare legs when she hesitated to get her bearings. Grady caught her hand and pulled her with him as he ran for the shelter of the overhang. She blinked against raindrops and followed, slowing as he did halfway up the walkway at the side of the house. A door flew open.

Cassie caught a glimpse of a woman in the doorway who was probably in her late fifties. She was wearing a beige turtleneck sweater and dark blue pants. She held the door open as Grady passed her in a rain-soaked T-shirt.

"Hi, Mom," he said, pulling Cassie inside.

"Hi, Mrs. Nelson." Cassie smiled into the woman's suspicious expression as she tripped in after Grady.

Grady's mother had permed gray hair without much style, brown eyes and a slightly pointy nose and chin. Her skin was beautiful and only lightly lined around her eyes.

"Hello," she replied, frowning at the

large sweater she must know to be her son's. Then her eyes went to Cassie's face—and stopped—and widened. She finally said in a stricken whisper, "Oh! My! God!"

They were in a sort of foyer. Cassie looked worriedly at Grady.

"You're not, are you?" his mother asked Cassie. She stepped a little closer, staring at her, closed her eyes and then opened them again.

Cassie wasn't as used to this kind of re-action as someone might think. In most situations, she was surrounded by other celebrities, famous—or notorious. She re-fused to shrink away.

"You *are*!" Grady's mother answered her own question.

Grady kissed his mother's cheek. "Mom, this is Cassidy Chapman. Her sister, Corie, is marrying Ben on New Year's Day, so she's come to the wedding. Cassie, this is my mother, Diane Nelson." Then he took Cassie's arm and led her through a door-way into a bright kitchen decorated in blue and white.

Grady's mother followed. "Thank God you made coffee, Mom," Grady said as he went to the coffeepot on the counter. Cassie turned to face his mother, guessing by her grim expression that something bad was coming. She braced herself.

"You've recovered quickly from your nervous breakdown," Diane said. As Cassie stared at her in disbelief, she added, "The screaming scene you made at that Irish mansion was on SAN—*Stars at Night*—just a few hours ago. Somebody took a cell phone video."

CHAPTER TWO

"MOM!" GRADY CAME back to Cassie as she struggled to find a sense of equilibrium.

Come on, she told herself. *You do it for the camera all the time. What's happened to you personally is hidden behind whatever the camera needs from you. And you had to know this was coming. Just not so soon.*

"I...I had a bad moment there," she said, simplifying an explanation. "It's a long story."

"The reporter speculated that you were upset because Fabiana Capri got the cover of the *Sports Illustrated* Swimsuit Edition and you didn't. She thought maybe it was just a temper tantrum."

Cassie was speechless.

"I'm a celebrity news junkie," Diane said a little smugly. "SAN had the whole story."

Sure. Entertainment news paid a lot of money for the inside skinny about celebrities. There'd been enough technical people and assistants at the shoot that one of them was bound to find the money appealing.

Unused to being so disliked so quickly, Cassie fought for composure. She met Diane's condemning brown eyes calmly. "They may have had the story, but it wasn't accurate. I guess that comes from speculating instead of getting the facts."

"What are the facts?"

Grady came to stand between them and handed Cassie the cup of coffee. He frowned at his mother. "Cassie is a guest here for a few days, and I'd appreciate it if you would be polite. You know, like you taught *me* to be?" He added that last with emphasis.

"It's all right," Cassie insisted, transferring the cup to her left hand and offering her right to Diane. The woman did look like a grassroots sort of mother, the kind who would see that you ate from the food pyramid, got your eight hours of sleep and were polite to your elders. And would kill any predators that came near you. Cassie had dreamed her entire life of having such a mother.

"If she saw me acting like a crazy woman on television, she probably fears for your safety." She sent Grady a wry grin then smiled at his mother, who looked a little surprised but still suspicious. "I assure you I'm a very sane, ordinary woman who's been working too hard for too long. I snapped." Everything inside her shuddered as she remembered that moment, but she struggled to look like the normal woman she insisted she was. "I had just learned my brother and sister, whom I hadn't seen since I was a toddler, were in Texas, and I sort of lost it while trying to finish the shoot before I could join them."

His mother shook her head. "Shouldn't you have gone to be with them instead of agreeing to work?"

"I agreed to work just hours before my father called me with the news. That shoot was expensive, and all those people were away from their families during the holidays to get it done. It would have been selfish of me to leave them all there and ask them to come back again later. To incur all that expense a second time."

Diane granted her that with a reluctant "True."

"So I was anxious to get it done quickly while still doing a good job, but the designer had insisted on false eyelashes and the makeup artist was having trouble with them and I was tired and antsy and sort of lost it."

"Sort of?"

Cassie ignored that and went on. She was glad she'd missed *Stars at Night*'s report on her behavior. "We were having a wonderful time in Texas until the press descended. I had to get away or ruin the holiday for everyone. Grady helped me get away out the back, drove to the airport and…" She spread her arms as she looked around her at the comfortable kitchen. "Here we are. You have a lovely son."

From behind her, Grady questioned, "Lovely?"

His mother studied her as though she were a lab rat. She answered grudgingly, "He is a nice boy."

"Boy?" Grady again.

CASSIE HAD HAD a nervous breakdown? That surprised Grady. Or maybe that information was just wrong, considering it was Hollywood gossip. Except for the occasional moody withdrawal, Cassie seemed very together. Though she had appeared a little tense on the plane.

Grady frowned at his mother, though he understood her bad manners. She loved him. She wanted what was best for him. She just had trouble understanding what that was or that it was up to him and not her.

"We've had a long day, Mom. Thanks for coming to welcome me home." He wanted to add, "You can go now," but was hoping she'd take the hint.

Instead she pointed toward the living room. "Your aunts and I had a lucky streak in Reno, so I bought you a little something to thank you for driving us down. It was delivered this afternoon."

"You did? What's that?"

"An armoire for your television."

Cassie spotted it through the open door into the living room and took off to investigate, probably anxious to escape the tension in the kitchen. He didn't blame her. He tried to follow her but his mother caught his arm.

"What are you *thinking*?" she demanded.

He struggled for patience. "About what?"

"About that girl!"

"She's not a girl. She's a woman. A very nice woman."

"A nice *crazy* woman. And what do you think she's doing with you?"

He growled. "I explained all that. She's here for Ben's wedding to her sister."

"Oh, Grady." His mother put a hand to her head as though it throbbed. "She's using you to escape reality. Apparently she freaked out because she can't deal with her life." She lowered her hand and rolled her eyes. "Has to be hard, right? Millions of dollars in income, on the cover of magazines, dating super jocks and movie stars, and when she doesn't get what she wants—like the cover of *Sports Illustrated*—she has a tantrum. Do you really need that? I mean, given what happened with your last—?"

"Mom," he interrupted firmly. "Her sister is Ben's fiancée. Jack's been trying so hard to put his family back together since he came home from Afghanistan. Now they're all going to be together for the wedding on New Year's Day and Cassie is staying with me until she goes back to work. It's going to be a happy family time for all of them, and no one is going to spoil it. Got it?"

"Sort of. What I don't get is what a supermodel is going to find to do in Beggar's Bay. With you."

He tipped his head back in exasperation. "I wish you'd stop saying that as though I have no right to be in the same world as her."

She blinked, maternal concern alight in her eyes. "I meant that she doesn't have the right to be in the same world as *you*."

He was still annoyed with her but put his arm around her. That was mother-love. A supermodel who made millions and was known the world over wasn't good enough for Diane Nelson's son. "I'm a trained police officer, Mom. If she decides to run off with my savings or try to kill me in my sleep, I can take care of myself."

"Don't be smart. You know how you are."

"I'm not sure I do. How am I?"

She opened her mouth to answer then fluttered her hands, seemingly at a loss for the right words. "I don't know. You're always everybody's problem-solver." Then she followed the direction Cassie had taken to the armoire. He took a cup of coffee and fell in behind her, stopping beside Cassie, who stood several feet back, admiring the gift.

He made every effort to mask what he felt. It was the ugliest thing he'd ever seen. It was seven feet high, with doors two-thirds of the way up and two drawers at the bottom. It was painted to look rustic in a flat, medium blue, and was covered in colorful, primitive-style floral designs. It looked like a gaudy weed among his simple furnishings.

His mother asked from the other side of Cassie, "Do you like it?"

He poured coffee down his throat. "It's wonderful, Mom." He was grateful she and his aunts hadn't tried to disconnect his television to put it inside the cabinet. When he'd moved into this place, they'd connected his set while he was helping move in the sofa and, for reasons no one could understand, he got Korean television.

Cassie took a step forward and ran her fingertips over one of the painted flowers.

"This is milk paint, isn't it?" she asked his mother.

"It is. And these are lion-mounted ring pulls, right out of the early nineteenth century. A little much for this piece, but some folk artist might have saved it off a more elegant dresser. I have a small but interesting folk art collection."

"I love it. It has so much enthusiasm."

"How long are you staying in Beggar's Bay?" his mother asked with no attempt to fake politeness despite that civil exchange. She wanted to know when Cassie was leaving.

Cassie seemed to get that but smiled, anyway. "My brother and sister are flying in overnight, so I'm hoping I'll be able to stay with one of them until I go home."

His mother seemed appeased. "Good. Well, I should go. I left a casserole in the refrigerator for you for tomorrow's dinner."

"Thanks, Mom." Grady walked her around the front to her car.

"I like the armoire," he said to his mother's back.

She turned and gave him a knowing look. "You didn't like it until you saw that she liked it. And how do we know she didn't say that just to get in good with us?"

Rain fell in sheets beyond the protection of the overhead deck, and the night air was perfumed and cold. "Mom, that's paranoid and completely unfair. I'm sure her bank account is fifty times larger than mine. What reason would she have to ingratiate herself with you to get to me?"

In a sudden loosening of her severity, his mother patted his cheek. "Because you're such a sweetheart and, according to *ET*, she hasn't had a lot of luck with men. That meltdown suggests she's troubled about her life, and you are like a stockade wall."

A stockade wall. Tall timbers lashed together to form a barrier, their tops hacked to a point to prevent a breach. He wasn't sure that was flattering.

She gave him a quick, strong hug. "That's how it felt to me when you came home from school to help me with Dad. Like we were safe behind *you*." She pushed him back. "Now, go inside. I won't bother you again unless you need me. Or want to invite me to dinner, or come over to put up the pergola for me like you've been promising."

"I painted it, didn't I?"

"Last July. And you did such a lovely job that it should be in my garden and not my garage." She smiled sweetly then hurried to her car. She took a few minutes to get settled inside, then started to back up.

Grady watched her turn around, keeping a careful eye on his basketball stand; he'd replaced it twice already thanks to her lack of skill in Reverse. He waved her off and ran back inside.

Cassie sat at his breakfast bar, her veil of hair shining under the overhead light, soft, weary blue eyes looking up at him as he walked into the kitchen. She appeared fragile suddenly, not at all the athlete who'd raced across the airport tarmac with him, who'd put up with the chilling rain and his unwelcoming mother.

"You look about to fall asleep," he said, helping her off the stool. "Come on. I'll show you to your room then I'll get your bag."

"I can get my things," she said, stifling a yawn. "In my job, sometimes it's expedient to be waited on. But, here, I can fend for myself."

"You can do that tomorrow. Tonight you

need some sleep." He pointed her into the foyer and up the stairs.

"You get your hardheadedness from your mother, don't you?" she asked over her shoulder. "I'm sorry if my being here upset your homecoming. She seemed very disappointed that you weren't alone. She really doesn't like me."

They stepped up onto the fir-wood floor of the bedroom. "She thinks you're toying with me for selfish purposes. I kind of like the notion, so I didn't try too hard to set her straight."

"Grady."

"Okay, I did try. You're right, though. She is a hardheaded woman, but that's helped her a lot in her life. And she's a great person, when she's not acting like a mother bear."

"You're lucky to have someone care that much about you." She turned her attention to the room. It was a big space with lodge-style furnishings that looked like they hadn't been disturbed since they'd been placed. "It's beautiful up here. Thank you. I'll try not to get too comfortable."

He went to the small bath in the corner

and reached in to flip on the light. "You might *want* to get comfortable. I've been thinking about Jack's and Corie's situations and, much as I'm sure either one would love to have you, Jack and Sarah are in the process of packing to move to a house nearer the assisted-living facility, and Ben's got a great condo, but it has only two bedrooms, and he's bringing home two kids— a boy and a girl. So you'd probably end up on the sofa."

THAT WAS TRUE. She'd had no choice in Querida but to escape the press or let them intrude upon her reunion with her family. But she made a mental note to remember that even in moments of great distress, she had to plan ahead a little. Every step she'd taken so far would have been off a cliff if it hadn't been for Grady.

She had to smile. "Your mother would hate that."

"True, but she'd adjust. Look around, figure out if there's anything you need that isn't here, and I'll go get your bag."

"Thank you. Grady?" She felt she had to say something about the meltdown. He had to be wondering. "The scene I made that ended up on television and probably all over the internet…"

"Is nobody's business but yours."

"I'm not like that—temperamental and hysterical and…"

He grinned. "I don't know. Yellow M&M's, only dark, handsome men…"

She gave him credit for the continued calm that so defined him, and that he could joke despite what his mother had revealed about her. "I just didn't want you to think you ran off with a lunatic."

"Nothing to worry about. I took off with you because I wanted to. That part's on me. I'll get your bag."

As she heard his footsteps going down the stairs, she tried to shed her worries and focus on the quiet comfort his home offered.

The large room was decidedly masculine. A king-size bed with big pillows and a brown suede bedspread and a simple iron headboard stood against the wall. Rustic wooden bedside tables held brass lamps that looked like lanterns. She went to the triple mirror on the wardrobe door. Inside the closet were four levels of shelving about four feet wide. The other ten feet of closet had nothing in it but a hanging rod with three empty hangers.

She closed the doors then went into the smallish bathroom. It was white with a pedestal sink and a tall cabinet made of planks. It held several white and brown towels, paper products and other supplies.

A walk-in shower with a sliding door looked serviceable. On the wall next to it, clear of furniture, was a two-dimensional, three-foot-wide carving of a pirate ship, sails billowing, Jolly Roger flying. She laughed lightly at that, thinking it seemed out of character with the rest of the house and what she knew of the man who owned it.

"Ben gave that to me."

She turned at the sound of Grady's voice.

He stood in the doorway. "On my last birthday. He thought my life needed more adventure."

If they were in New York, she thought, finding herself completely distracted by him, she could get him modeling jobs. He was the perfect height, had a nice face with interesting planes and angles, and an easy look in his eyes. She could picture the camera's tight shot of his face. For a Drakkar Noir ad, or one that featured a pair of Ray-Bans slipped down his nose.

She drew herself back to the moment. This wasn't New York. This was Beggar's Bay, Oregon, and she had to stop thinking about work.

He stepped aside to let her pass. "Doesn't the life of a police officer provide you with enough adventure?"

"It has its moments, but as Jack is always teasing Ben and me, mostly it's about animal control and fairgrounds parking."

As she went to the bed where he'd placed her bag, she noticed for the first time the waist-high carved railing that ran across the room, affording her a view of the great room below with its vaulted ceiling and the magnificent windows that looked onto the dark night.

She looked over the railing. "I had my back to this when we came up the stairs and I didn't even notice it."

He showed her that the fold-out shutters expanded from either side of the railing and met in the middle. "You can close these for privacy."

"Great."

"Is there anything you need?"

"I don't think so. But, if I do, I can probably pick it up tomorrow."

"All right. I can take you wherever you need to go. I'm off two more days, then Ben and I are giving two weeks' notice."

"Jack told me. You and Ben are going into business together. Private investigation, isn't it?"

"Right."

"That ought to give you more adventure than you need."

"It should." He backed toward the door. "Sleep well. Just shout over the railing if you need anything."

"Okay. Thanks, Grady. I'm not sure what I'd have done if you hadn't come with me. Somehow all the little details of running off escaped me."

"Happy to help. See you in the morning."

"Good night."

Finding her toiletries bag, she took a quick shower, slipped on a midnight blue, silk nightgown, a gift from a lingerie designer after a shoot that had earned her a very large order from Neiman Marcus, left the bedside light on, and climbed into bed.

Snuggling into a soft pillow, Cassie thought about what she would need in the way of clothing to survive the next week in this rainy world. But she fell asleep before a plan could take shape.

CHAPTER THREE

GRADY SMELLED COFFEE and something sweet. He wondered what was cooking. And who.

He sat up in bed, expecting to see the simple beige wall from the B and B in Querida with its poor print of cowboys around a campfire. Instead he saw the lush conifers outside his window in Beggar's Bay, a pewter-gray sky and local geese flying at a low altitude in a ragged vee toward the bay.

He was home. He felt a weird sense of loss at the realization. Not that he didn't love his home, but he'd had a really great time in Querida. He'd spent a couple of weeks there, helping Ben put up a play set for the kids, getting to know Corie, Jack's sister, and helping Ben solve a few mysteries Corie was involved in.

When Ben and Jack's parents arrived in

Querida to spend Christmas, it truly became family time. Then he had answered a knock on the door when everyone else was busy, and a supermodel had begun to introduce herself—then fainted dead away in his arms. Two days later she'd pleaded with him to run away with her. He had a rental vehicle and she didn't, and her need to get away had seemed desperate.

A supermodel. Cassidy Chapman was asleep upstairs in his loft. Or, based on that wonderful smell, maybe she wasn't. He got to his feet, pulled on his jeans, yanked a Seahawks sweatshirt out of a pile of things still on the chair from his unpacking and went barefoot down the hall to the kitchen.

He needed a moment to pull himself together. Cassie was working at the stove in a dark blue silky thing that skimmed her bare feet. Over it, she had pulled the sweater he'd lent her last night to get from the car to the house. She held a spatula, but her head was turned toward a television at the end of the counter.

He finally opened his mouth to shout a good morning over the sound of the TV and then closed it again when he realized she was watching the infamous video of her meltdown. It had apparently made the morning news.

On the screen was a sharp image of everyone involved in the shoot gathered on the grounds of a palatial country home with a pillared portico. They all pressed around Cassie, who stood in the middle in a fluttering red dress. Someone adjusted her hair while someone else seemed to be fitting something over her eyes as yet another person leaned in to make an adjustment to the neckline of the dress.

Without warning, a scream was heard, the tableau erupted, the circle around Cassie freezing in place—except for that dedicated makeup artist with her hands at Cassie's eyes. Cassie screamed again and grabbed the young woman by both wrists.

The woman's arms hung in Cassie's grip with what looked like a spider in one hand and a tiny bottle in the other, her mouth an O of astonishment.

"Stop!" Cassie's voice was high and shrill. "I asked you to stop! Are you deaf?"

For an instant both women stared at each other, then Cassie dropped the woman's wrists, picked up the long skirts of her dress and ran.

The video over, a female reporter appeared on-screen accompanied by a cohost and a beautiful dark-haired woman Grady thought looked vaguely familiar. They sat at a table in the studio.

"I'm sure you all recognize Fabiana Capri," the reporter said, "the spokeswoman for the new Tesla smart car, and Cassidy Chapman's good friend. What do you make of that behavior, Fabiana?"

The model, dressed in yellow, shrugged an elegant shoulder. "I'm not sure what happened," she replied with a look of concern. "Cassie disappeared right after that and no one's seen her or talked to her since. It could be that it had been a very long day for her. She works very hard, gives every job her all, in sometimes very uncomfortable circumstances. When we did the *Sports Illustrated* shoot, the temperature was 57 degrees and the water was freezing. I got to pose on a rock, but Cassie stood in cold water up to her knees for an hour before the photographer felt he'd gotten it right."

"*Stars at Night*," the reporter said, "thought she might have been upset because she'd wanted the SI cover and you got it."

The model laughed. "I doubt that seriously. Last year she had the cover and I didn't. But we're all adults. We're in competition for the big jobs, but you win some and you lose some. It's the same in every business, even fashion." She leaned forward, expression earnest. "What you should be talking about is the trust Cassie set up for poor women needing clothes and transportation so they can look for work."

The reporter ignored that. "But *you've* never imploded during a shoot."

"Sure, I have. I was just lucky enough that none of the crew sold me out to the press."

"Maybe when you grab the young woman doing your makeup and yell at her for not hearing you when she really *is* deaf, your adoring fans should know that about you."

Fabiana waited a beat, obviously straining for patience, then said, "In Cassie's defense, the woman was a last-minute replacement because it was the holidays and the makeup artist who knows about...who Cassie's used to working with, had already left to be with family in Alaska. Cassie didn't know the woman was deaf. How many times have we all said that when people don't respond to us the way we think they should?"

Again the reporter let that go. "You said Cassie disappeared. Do you have any idea where she went?"

Fabiana knew something; Grady could see it in her eyes. "I don't, but I'm sure she'll turn up in February to do the fund-raiser for Designers United Against Hunger."

Apparently a reporter's instinct was as strong as a cop's. "You hesitated there. You do have a clue where she is."

Fabiana smiled and shook her head. It was the smile she used in the Tesla commercial, capable of selling anything to anyone. "No. It's Cassie's life. She'll come back to it when she's ready."

The reporter thanked her and announced a station break. Cassie aimed the remote at the television and clicked it off. She groaned as she turned back to the stove.

"Good morning," Grady said. "I wouldn't worry about that too much. Tomorrow some politician will say something stupid and they'll forget all about you."

"Hi, Grady." She glanced at him with a half smile and flipped a pancake. "I couldn't find an apron to protect your sweater. Do you have anything?"

Worried about her bare feet on the cold floor, he went to the thermostat first and turned up the gas heat. Then he opened the bottom drawer in the stove that held a barbecue apron his mother had given him that he'd never used. He handed it to her. She slipped her head through the neck hole and tied the strings behind her. Born to Barbecue was printed in rough red lettering above a caricature of a man in front of a barbecue, his chef's hat on fire.

She looked down at herself and snickered. "Now here's a look for the catwalk. Sit down. I'll get you some coffee."

Two places were set at the breakfast bar. She'd found two placemats he never used along with dark blue cloth napkins stored in the same drawer.

She poured coffee and brought him a

cup. "This might be a little girlie for you. It's Colombian coffee with dulce de leche flavor. I have a pound in my bag whenever I travel."

He took a sip. "Definitely girlie, but good." It was wonderful to have coffee ready when he got up. Even girlie coffee. Since she clearly didn't want to talk about the news, he observed, "You're making pancakes?"

"Crepes," she corrected. "Fewer calories. I found frozen blueberries in the freezer, cooked them down with sugar and made a compote for topping. Is that all right?"

He leaned his forearms on the bar and looked into her bright eyes. Her hair was pulled into a high ponytail. She looked remarkably fresh, if sad.

"No," he replied with a straight face. "I want the same old, dry fruity flakes and past-the-pull-date milk I always have in the morning."

"No!" She pulled a plate out of the oven. "Tell me you don't really eat fruity flakes."

"I would, but it would be a lie. I'm sure they have nothing of nutritional value in them, but then, the bad guys don't really care how trim I am, and I have a maple bar midmorning to keep up my strength."

If she thought that was a bad idea, she kept it to herself and brought him a plate of crepes and a steaming pitcher of compote. Butter was already on the bar. The aroma made him salivate.

"You can cook, too," he said in wonder, pouring blueberries on the crepes and passing the pitcher to her as she sat beside him with her own plate.

"I grew up without a mother," she said. "My father was gone a lot and nannies aren't always good cooks. I loved my cooking class in high school, and I watch food shows. It's amazing what you can pick up."

"Are models allowed to eat this stuff?"

"There are antioxidants in the blueberries." She elbowed him. "I'm on a break. After the wedding, I'll go back to fasting."

"Sorry. You hear stories, you know, about how you guys eat only lettuce and lemon juice and work out six hours a day."

"Exaggerated."

"We'll go to the market and get whatever kind of food you want."

"Actually, I *have* to go clothes shopping.

Doesn't have to be fancy, but I have nothing for underwater living." She pointed to the kitchen window beaded with rain, the trees beyond it swaying in the wind.

He turned to her. "Winter in Oregon. Some people adjust to the wet and some people don't." He cut a bite of crepe with the side of his fork. "It'll probably be harder for you…"

She frowned at him over the rim of her cup. "Why? Because you think I'm used to bigger and better things, and take pleasure in abusing all the 'little people' in my life? That isn't true."

"That's not what I—"

"I'm the first to admit I live a very good life, but no one escapes problems."

"That's for sure."

"You're wondering what kind of problems a model could possibly have."

Now she was acting a little like a diva. Or maybe she was just upset by her appearance on the news. Who wouldn't be in her position?

He smiled. "Well, all that mind reading you're doing has to be a problem, for one thing. Can you read everybody's or just mine?"

Her eyes ignited. "You're laughing at me."

"Just a little. Anyone who presumes to know what someone else is thinking is fair game."

Sipping at her coffee, she met his eyes, but the easy camaraderie they'd shared since they'd escaped Querida together wavered.

"I'm sure one of the problems," he said, trying to defuse her anger, "is that everything in your life, however private or personal, can be recorded, replayed and streamed for all the world to see. That's pretty awful."

She relaxed a little, heaving a sigh before she said, "It doesn't matter that the interpretation of what happened is incorrect, entertainment and internet reporters put the most salacious or embarrassing spin on their news. I've avoided much of it, but they seem happy to have a juicy tidbit now." She shook her head at him.

"*Were* you upset about the *Sports Illustrated* cover? I mean, there has to be more prestige in being on the cover than just inside it, right?"

"My behavior had nothing to do with the *Sports Illustrated* cover!" she shouted at him. She stopped a moment, drew a breath and went on in a measured tone. "I'm sorry. I...I don't know if you know that just before I went to Ireland, my father was stuck in Bangkok during a coup and we had no idea if he was all right or not. The pictures on the news were scary. He'd gone there to work on the computers for the government. On special jobs, he always goes himself. That's what built his reputation as one of the best IT men in Europe. I was terrified."

"Yes. That had to be awful for both of you."

"Well, I'd just learned the day before that he was all right. And the following day he called to tell me that my siblings, who I've been separated from most of my lifetime, were in Texas and wanted me to join them."

"Yes."

"I had to finish the shoot before I left, but the makeup artist was making me crazy." She tipped her head from side to side self-deprecatingly. "Clearly, I wasn't looking my best, the wind was blowing my hair, and she was determined to make these false eyelashes fit and stuck her finger in my eye. She wouldn't stop."

He looked empathetic.

She put a hand out in front of herself about three feet away. "Here in the US, the three feet surrounding you are considered your personal space. You feel challenged and a little touchy when people invade it."

Unsure where she was going with this, he nodded to assure her of his attention.

She continued. "Okay. So, try to think of yourself as a model. Hair and makeup people are always right in your face—" she fluttered her fingers an inch from her cheeks "—touching you, pushing you here and there so they can work on you. I know it isn't their fault because you're sort of their canvas. So you're like a *thing*, not a person, to them in that moment. Designers fitting you into their clothes don't even see you as a person, you're just a place to hang their clothes and they're always turning you, pushing you, ignoring *you* and see-ing only the clothes. I've been modeling since I was sixteen, so most days I accept it's just part of the process.

"But, when I'm tired, worried, frightened, they're like some buggy invasion and I feel like I'm going to go insane..." She sighed and pushed her plate away. "Or say something awful. Like, 'Are you deaf?'" She put her head in her hands and groaned. "Of course, I didn't really know she was deaf. I ran away so I wouldn't go over the edge before I got to meet my family."

She dropped her hands and looked at him with a wince. "It's all part of a bigger problem I've had most of my life, and modeling just exaggerates it." Without clarifying, she continued. "I did go back and apologize to everyone involved, particularly the makeup artist. I wrote a note to her and then tried to explain face-to-face. She seemed to understand. I bought the crew's dinner that night before I took off for Texas. It would be nice if SAN would report *that*."

"You have the comfort of knowing you have a good friend in Fabiana. She did her best to make that reporter understand."

She nodded. "I do. She's as wonderful a

person as she is beautiful." She slipped off the stool. "I'm going to get dressed."

"I've got a raincoat you can borrow."

"Thank you." She started away then turned back to add, "I'll take care of the dishes when we get back."

He pointed to the dishwasher. "It's all under control."

WHEN CASSIE AND Grady met at the front door twenty minutes later, she wore a pair of dark blue pants with a gray cardigan pulled over a cotton shirt. It was wrapped tightly around her. She wore boots and carried a small folded umbrella.

He tried not to laugh. "Mostly, we don't use umbrellas around here because the wind's usually blowing and you end up with a mouthful of metal ribs." He held out his serviceable green, hip-length, hooded jacket.

She looked at it doubtfully but allowed him to help her into it. He pulled up the hood. With a jolt, he noticed how gorgeous she was even lost in the dung-colored fabric.

Her height provided him with a different perspective on the feminine face. At six-two, he was used to looking down on the top of a woman's head, on the curve of her eyelashes, the shape of her nose. With Cassidy close to six feet tall, he looked into fathomless eyes that looked right back into his and somehow seemed to see more deeply than he was comfortable with. He watched the subtle movement of her beautifully shaped lips, covered in pale and glossy pink. Those lips now inverted in a frown.

She gasped her disapproval and pinched the leather on the arm of the ancient bomber jacket he wore. "Let's swap," she said, the tension between them from breakfast seemingly put aside. "I can wear your jacket, and you can wear this."

"Not a chance, Blondie," he replied with a grin. "This jacket has been with me through college, nature hikes, pickup football..."

She held out her arms. "And this has been with you through putting out the garbage and covering tomato plants against the cold. It has absolutely no style."

"Do you want to be warm and dry, or do you want style?"

"Life should allow you both."

He turned her around and opened the door. "I'm sorry, but today it doesn't. Let's go."

GRADY WAS AMUSED, even charmed, by watching Cassie shop. The Beggar's Bay Boutique had to be far less interesting than the places she usually patronized, but she really seemed to be enjoying herself.

The clerk, a twentysomething whose badge read Molly, ran to the dressing room to take garments Cassie handed out and then brought her more pants, dresses, sweaters. She scoured the racks with avid intensity while Cassie shouted suggestions from behind the curtain. "The jeans are still too short!" Cassie called.

"That's the longest I've got in women's! What about the smallest, longest pair from the men's department?"

There was a moment's hesitation then, "Sure."

Cassie emerged twenty minutes later with dark jeans from the men's department that were sparely designed but seemed to fit well. She'd pulled a bright yellow sweater over them and dropped everything else on the counter. She stood still while the clerk cut tags off her outfit.

"Why didn't you buy a jacket?" Grady asked. "Or slippers?"

"The jackets are all too short for me. So, it's back to the tomato plant cover. And my feet are too big for the size range here." She pulled on the green raincoat, looking bright and happy. That made him feel better. She grinned. "Good thing I brought my boots along."

"You going to wear those to the wedding?"

"No, I'm going to have something sent to me One-Day Air."

Of course. Whatever her problems were, getting whatever she needed wasn't one of them.

The clerk took Cassie's card and swiped it. Then as she studied the card, her fingers began to tremble. She looked up at Cassie in astonishment. "I *thought* it was you," she breathed.

Cassie smiled as he imagined royalty would smile. "Thanks for not outing me. It was fun to shop in peace."

"No wonder you seem to know what you

want. And can pull it together out of odds and ends and look fabulous."

Molly packed everything into two shopping bags, and Grady took them.

"Thanks, Molly," Cassie said, leading the way to the door. "You were so much help. You're an excellent sales associate."

The young woman beamed.

CASSIE OPENED THE door for Grady, who walked out ahead of her.

His phone rang. "Do you mind getting that?" He raised his left elbow so she could reach into his hip pocket to retrieve it.

She ignored the warmth of his body through the pocket and took out the black iPhone. Ben's face lit up the screen.

"It's Ben," she told Grady.

He moved toward the truck. "Ah, they must be home. Answer it. My keys are in the right side pocket. Want to get the door?"

She answered the phone as she dug for keys.

"Grady's phone. This is Cassie." She was distracted again by how warm he was. For someone who was perpetually cold when the weather dipped below 70 degrees, she felt the absurd desire to crawl inside that cozy pocket.

"Cassie!" As she aimed the key remote to unlock the car, she heard Ben's voice as he apparently handed off the phone and said, "Corie, it's your sister."

"Hi, Cassie. You escaped the press?" She loved the sound of the word. Sister. She *had* a sister. She *was* a sister. Cassie opened the truck's passenger door and watched Grady put her bags on the seat. She wondered for a minute if she was going to have to ride in the truck bed.

"We did," she told Corie. She swallowed and asked, "Did you see me on the news?"

"Yes. How cool that you've started a trust for women needing clothing and transportation to job interviews. I can contribute clothes."

Cassie couldn't help the little glow that started in her heart. Sisterly support. "I meant the scene—"

There was a smile in Corie's voice. "I know what you mean. I've made a few scenes myself, so it's hard for me to criticize anybody else's. Don't worry about it. Nobody cares."

Except for the millions of people who probably now saw her as a bratty diva and an abuser of the deaf. "You're not embarrassed?"

Corie laughed. "No, we're not embarrassed." Cassie heard Ben's laugh. "Listen, we're all meeting for lunch at someplace called...uh..."

"The Bay Bistro," Ben shouted into the phone. "Grady knows it. Can you be there in ten minutes?"

Cassie went to Grady, who was now placing her packages in the jump seat. "Can we be at the Bay Bistro in ten minutes?"

He straightened and tried to smooth his hair, mussed by the tight quarters in the back of the truck cab. "Sure."

"Sure," Cassie relayed, helping bring order to Grady's hair with her free hand. It was thick and coarse. She resisted the impulse to run her fingers through it one more time.

His gaze collided with hers, seeming to ask her to. She dropped her hand and had to look away to concentrate on what Ben was saying.

"Great. Tell him he's paying," Ben said. "See you then."

She smiled at Grady. "He says you're paying."

"Tell him he still owes me for the night I went into the river after a DUI and he *watched* me."

She tried to but Corie had reclaimed the phone. "Cassie?"

"Yes."

"We all think it's fun to be related to someone the press is making a big deal over. So don't worry."

"But it's a *bad* big deal."

"This family will turn it into something good. It's what we do. See you in ten."

"Right." Well, right on the "seeing her in ten" part. Turning this press nightmare into something good was going to require a miracle.

GRADY DROVE THE three blocks to the edge of downtown, then turned down a side street to the old mill that had been converted into shops and a restaurant. The Bay Bistro was on the third floor. Cassie, he noticed, looked worried.

"Forget the news," he advised gently. "They're your family. They don't care."

She turned to him with open disbelief. "That's what Corie said, but of course they care. How can they not? When I met them in Texas, I kept everything to myself, hoping it would just go away. I didn't know then that someone had recorded it."

"Again, I'm sure it's not a big deal to them."

"Jack has to be disappointed. He worked so hard to get us all together again, and his little sister turns out to be a monster diva who yelled at a deaf woman! And the whole world knows about it!"

"Big fuss over nothing."

She huffed a breath. "Grady, I'm the piece of the family that's been missing and I…"

He heard something in her voice somehow deeper than the words she was saying. He turned to her as he pulled into a spot right in front of the mill and shut off the engine.

"What if I'm a disappointment? What if they've been waiting all this time to get me back, they're impressed to learn than I'm a model, then find out…I have all these… issues?"

"You have nothing to fear here, Cassie. The Mannings and the Palmers are the best people you'll ever meet. Everybody's got their issues, so they're all tolerant of everyone else's. Jack came back from Afghanistan with nightmares. Corie's life was sometimes so awful that she became a thief. Just relax. All they care about is that the three of you are together again. Come on."

He went around to her side to help her out, then caught her hand and hurried her so she wouldn't have time to relive the cell phone video that had taken up permanent residence in her head.

He escorted her before him into the old mill's elegant downstairs with shops off of a central atrium, then caught her hand again and ran for the elevators, doors closing as they hurried. If he could get her upstairs before the family arrived and distract her with the spectacular view and a glass of wine, she might get over her nervousness.

He was vaguely aware of her pulling against him as he shouted to the lone man inside to hold the elevator. But he thought she was just having trouble keeping up in her boots.

"Grady…" she said.

"Come on!" he encouraged, walking quickly. "If we get there first, I can tell the waiter that Ben intends to pay. He has a tab here." He warmed to that thought above all else. "He'll hate that. Ha!"

The man held the door from closing as Grady hurried into the car, drawing Cassie in beside him. He wrapped his arm around her shoulders as she struggled to catch her breath. The door closed and the car began to rise.

He patted Cassie's back as she gulped in air. He was happy with the day, glad to have the opportunity to help her relax before her family got there. He was anxious to see his friends, anticipating all of them around the table, talking and laughing while sharing the bistro's outrageously delicious food.

So, he was completely unprepared for what happened next. Cassie caught his hand in a biting grip, her fingernails drawing blood as she let out a high-pitched, ear-splitting scream.

She began to shake him and point to the door. "No! No! No!"

"Cassie—"

"No!"

All right. No. No, what? He wasn't sure, but it didn't take a genius to figure out she wanted out of the elevator. The man who'd held the door for them did so again, his eyes a little wider this time as they reached the third floor and the doors parted.

Cassie gasped and ran out into a hallway that spilled right into the restaurant, only a few feet from the hostess's stand. She stopped and noisily drew in air, her arms wrapped around herself, her cheeks crimson.

She looked mortified and somehow isolated. Her hands shook. "I'm sorry," she whispered, then added grimly, "Remember that issue left over from my childhood I mentioned that I still deal with?"

"Yeah?"

"It's claustrophobia."

"Yeah," he said. An inch of skin was scraped off his left hand. "I guessed that."

CHAPTER FOUR

THE METHODICAL PART of him was remembering her tense behavior on the plane. That small space you couldn't escape without a parachute had to be even more frightening than an elevator car you knew would stop in seconds. He regretted attributing her tension to a more normal fear of flying.

But deep down he knew some fears could not be explained or wished away, and he put both hands on her shoulders, saying quietly, "Just relax. You're out now. We're about to go into this big, airy room with views of the river, so there's nothing to confine you or to be afraid of."

While people wove around them into the dining room, her eyes were huge and turbulent, as though the emotional storm she'd just endured wasn't quite over.

She nodded, expelling a deep breath. "Right. I'll be fine in a minute."

The elevator's second set of doors opened and he glanced up to see most of the Manning-Palmer family. "Good," he said quietly, "because here they come."

"Please don't say anything. Nobody knows."

He dropped his hands and said firmly, "Don't worry. Our secret."

CHAOS REIGNED FOR a good ten minutes. Love, energy, laughter and pre-wedding excitement raised the decibel level in the corridor to deafening. There were hugs among the women, back-slapping among the men, and the children jumped up and down in joy. No one would have guessed that they'd all seen each other less than twenty-four hours ago.

The Mannings and the Palmers snaked through the dining room in a long parade as the hostess led them across the room to a table in a far corner set up for ten.

Sarah, Jack's wife, began to suggest that couples sit opposite each other, but the children had already chosen places. Soren, a slender, fair-haired ten-year-old, grabbed a frosty pitcher of water and started filling glasses. Rosie, a year younger, with glossy black hair, wide brown eyes and a busybody attitude, took a basket of rolls and distributed them to the bread plate at every place.

Ben suggested to Soren that he not fill the glasses to the top and Corie handed Rosie the small tongs that rested beside the basket. "At the foster home," Corie explained as they sat, "everybody helped put the meal on the table." She smiled at the children. "Good job, guys."

Cassie felt a new sense of comfort at being part of this warm, loud group, but also a new insecurity she hadn't experienced when she'd been with them in Texas. Then, she'd thought her old childhood bugaboo had been beaten. Now, as she watched how confident everyone seemed, she realized she was a little broken. Jack and Corie had had more difficult lives than she'd led, yet she was the one with a leftover emotional tic.

"Hey." Grady pulled a chair out for her and guided her gently down. "They're much less alarming than the noise they make," he said quietly, about to take the chair beside her when Jack shouldered him out of the way.

"You had her company all the way over on the plane," he said, pointing him to the chair on the other side of him. "And I understand she's staying in your loft."

"She is. Turns out, she's a great cook. I had crepes with blueberry compote for breakfast."

Jack laughed. "Saved from your own bachelor cooking until the wedding. Thank you." Jack accepted a menu from a formidable-looking fortyish waitress with a crisp black-and-white uniform and dyed red hair styled in a topknot and bangs. She distributed menus like she was dealing cards, listing off the details of the salmon special. She looked around the table and asked gravely, "Who poured the water?"

Soren raised his hand worriedly. "I did."

She nodded. "Well done." And walked away, promising to be right back to take their drink order.

Everyone laughed at Soren's relieved smile. Ben ruffled his hair and caught Corie's eye. She sat with Rosie at the end of the table on the opposite side. Their shared look spoke of love and happiness.

Cassie looked away and found Jack struggling for composure. He must have caught the look and was probably overcome to see his sister so at peace. She watched him reach for his glass of water, already empty, and handed him hers.

"Here," she said.

But Soren had already foreseen the problem. "I got it, Aunt Cassie," he said, coming around the table to lean over Jack, reach for the pitcher and refilling his glass.

Jack pretended to frown at him. "Am I going to have to tip you?"

Soren, his blue eyes alight with the teasing attention, spread his free hand as though the answer should be obvious. "Corie said I did a good job, and the waitress said 'well done.' And she's a professional."

Laughter erupted again and Jack grabbed him and gave his shoulder a gentle noogie while he giggled. Grady reached out to save the pitcher.

The waitress returned to take their drink orders. Soren went back to his place beside

Ben and everyone got serious about studying the menu.

During lunch, Sarah, a slender woman of medium height, with light brown hair and blue-gray eyes, held up her Caribbean-blue napkin.

"Is this the shade you were talking about for the wedding?" she asked Corie.

Corie nodded, opening her napkin. "It is. In silk. Or charmeuse, it's even more beautiful, with a softness you can't quite get in paper. I wish we had time to make dresses for all of you. I think the best thing to do is just wear your favorite dressy dress. I'm wearing one I made for myself."

"That pretty pink one with the quilted look?" Helen asked. A comfortably plump woman with a warm smile, she was Ben's natural mother and Jack's adopted mother.

Corie shook her head. "I've been designing a new line, something different—less street chic and more…" She smiled as she thought. "More…elegant. The two of you can just wear whatever dressy dress you have that you love the most. I'll have to find something for Rosie. The guys are renting suits because neither has one!

Helen knows the owner of the rental place and set up an appointment for them in the car on the way over."

"I'll try to find a dress in this color," Helen said. "It's so pretty." She stuffed the napkin in her purse. "What else can we do to help? You must be overwhelmed with just a few days to plan while adding two children to your household."

"I am, a little." Corie sat quietly, everything about her remarkably calm. Cassie thought she seemed too small and fragile to be able to deal with so much, but she knew her sister had lost her father at twelve, escaped a cruel and negligent stepmother shortly after that, and finally found serenity because of an accidental meeting with a woman who ran a foster home and took her in.

Corie had spent the time since then working as a waitress while studying to be a designer, and helping her foster mother stay afloat financially. She so deserved to be happy.

"But," Corie went on, "life with Ben is so much more wonderful than I ever thought I'd know. And the kids are going to be an adjustment for both of us, but I know it'll work in the end. They're both great." She laughed lightly. "I hope you don't mind that your dinner rolls were manhandled. Or rather, Rosie-handled."

Helen dismissed that with a shake of her head. "Of course not. I think we all grew to love both of them while we were visiting you in Texas. They're precocious and seem happy with their new lives. But they're not going to leave you much time to get ready. Seriously, how can we help?"

"I'm not sure where to start," Corie admitted. "I thought knowing I had a dress to wear was a forward step."

Sarah took a notebook and pen out of her purse and smiled from one to the other. "You're right. The dress is very important, and I love that it's one you designed yourself. So why don't Cassie and Helen and I divide the rest of the duties?" She made a few notes in her book. In her management persona, she was impressive, and they all waited quietly for her to give instructions.

"How many people?" she asked.

"Fifty, tops," Corie replied. "Some friends

of Ben's from the police department. Some neighbors. That's it."

"Good. That's manageable. Have you thought about where to have the ceremony?"

Corie made a face. "I called the church while we were still in Texas, and they're already booked. And there's so much going on in most of the venues around town because of New Year's Day."

Cassie got a sudden inspiration. "What about Grady's house?"

Corie's eyes widened. "I haven't seen it. And, anyway, would he want an invasion of fifty?"

"It's gorgeous," Cassie said feelingly, remembering the comfort she'd felt in it last night, despite his mother's dislike of her. She loved the lodge-like atmosphere, the log walls, the standing columns in the living room, the vaulted ceiling and the loft's turned railing. She explained all that to her companions. "What would be more perfect around here than a wedding in the woods?"

Sarah looked enthused. "What do you think, Corie?" She turned to Cassie. "Since you're right there on the spot, Cassie, would you be in charge of decorating?"

She frowned, as though having second thoughts. "Shouldn't we ask Grady first?"

"Ask me what?" Grady, Ben, Jack and Gary, Ben's father and Jack's adopted father, grouped together at the other end of the table, had been talking architectural restoration. Construction was Gary's business and restoration was Jack's. Grady, leaned around Jack to find out what was happening.

He looked from woman to woman, his expression growing more concerned as their smiles widened. "What?" he asked warily.

"Can we have our wedding at your house?" Corie asked him with a little trepidation. "The church and every other venue in town is booked for New Year's Day." When he stared at her in surprise, she added, "Cassie says it's gorgeous."

His eyes went to Cassie, who met them with a smile in hers. "Well, it is," she insisted. "Can they?"

"Ah…sure." At the resultant cheers and applause, he added quickly, "But it's just a log house. Pretty basic. No frills and fussy stuff. Only two bathrooms." He turned to Ben. "Aren't weddings all about frills and fussy stuff?"

Ben shrugged. "Don't know. Never had one before."

"They're not." Sarah placed her notebook on the table and her pen at an angle on top of it. "They're about having a cozy place where the wedding couple can surround themselves with family and friends and really enjoy the day. After all, they're promising to spend their lives with the person they love the most, come hell or high water. We can bring in a few Porta Potties."

There was a moment's silence when she'd finished. Then Soren asked Ben, "Hell or high water? What does that mean?"

"It means if you have bad times, you'll still stay together."

"Oh. But, hell? I mean, if you go to hell, you're already dead, right?"

"Sometimes things can feel so bad," Corie said, "that it's like hell has come to you while you're still alive. But you know that you'll get over it if you stay with the people you love."

"And high water is like a flood," Rosie put in, always sure of what she knew. "Because people get really discouraged when a flood comes and gets their house all messy.

But if they clean up together, it's not so hard."

Sarah nodded. "I couldn't have said it better." She smiled across the table at Grady. "What do you think?"

"Wouldn't you like to see it first?" he asked.

"It is a beautiful place," Ben said. "Of course, I've mostly played poker there and not paid attention to how 'gorgeous' it is." He emphasized Cassie's word. "But, maybe you *should* see it first, Corie."

"I'd like to," Corie said. "But if it's gorgeous to Cassie, who's seen some of the world's most gorgeous places, then I don't think there's any question."

Grady cast a glance at Cassie that she couldn't quite read. But she guessed it suggested payback later. "Good," he said. "We'll go after lunch."

Before they left the restaurant, Helen volunteered to be in charge of food for the reception.

"Perfect," Sarah said. "And we can all help with that. Can you make that sausage and pasta casserole Ben and Jack love so much?"

"Of course. I'll put a menu together and we can all go over it and add or subtract."

"Great. I'll get invitations out by email and phone and, together, Cassie and I can arrange for flowers."

The major questions answered, Sarah closed her book and set it aside again just in time for the arrival of lunch.

"I DIDN'T CLEAN up the breakfast dishes," Cassie whispered to Grady as they walked out to the car. The family had split into the groups that had ridden together.

"I did." He aimed the key fob at the truck to open the doors.

"We can make coffee, but do you have milk for the kids?"

He pulled open her door and replied with what sounded like slightly strained good humor. "No. But had I known eight people were coming back with us, and that you were going to volunteer me to host a wedding, I'd have tried to be better prepared."

She stopped before slipping onto the passenger seat and tried to analyze the look in his eyes. "Are you angry?"

"I'm never angry," he replied. "But I'm

not crazy about surprises, particularly those that involve something like a wedding."

"It's for your best friend in the whole world. You said you were as close as brothers." She added with a small smile, hoping to rid him of that remote expression, "And that it made you and I almost related. So, I'm sorry I mentioned it without asking you first, but we're family, so to speak. That's what you said."

SHE WAS WORKING HIM. That was an unusual experience, and he couldn't help the inclination to let the moment stretch to see how far she'd go. Celeste had never bothered with feminine wiles; she'd either planned things her way without explanation or apology, or she'd simply ignored what he'd wanted to do. This blatant attempt to manipulate had a certain charm.

"I know what I said," he replied, having a little trouble keeping a smile off his face, but he felt it was important that he try. "But it is my home. You might have consulted me first. It was hard to say no with your entire family waiting for an answer."

"Did you want to say no?"

He had to answer honestly. "No. If you don't get in the truck, they're all going to get there before us."

She grinned as she stepped up gracefully. "I doubt they'll break in."

He pushed the door closed, walked around the hood and climbed in behind the wheel. He didn't want to notice that the new yellow sweater gave her a golden look, and that her scent made the truck smell like a flower shop.

Everyone was standing around, looking up at Grady's house, when he and Cassie arrived. He pulled onto the grass beyond the driveway so their guests would be able to back out again.

They were all smiling. He took a good look himself, trying to see it with new eyes without considering what it meant to him on a personal level. It looked large and strong, simply constructed, tall firs gathered along the sides, a shelter in the mysterious woods. The property opened onto a deep meadow in the back for about a hundred yards, then the forest closed in. It was the last place he'd have thought of to have Ben and Corie's wedding.

He unlocked and threw his door open, holding it to let everyone pass through.

He followed them into the great room, where Sarah, Corie and Helen stood in the middle and looked around.

"Isn't it magnificent?" Cassie asked. "I mean, imagine what we can do. What if we got a few floor chandeliers to make a walkway for the bride, then, maybe, a hanging one right above where you'll exchange vows?" She moved forward to stand under the loft railing. "Maybe about here. Then tulle or something gathered like bunting on the railing and down the stairs. And we can trim everything with flowers."

Corie clasped her hands beneath her chin. The warrior woman who'd done so much to save her foster mother's home and the children in it now looked younger and less troubled than he'd ever seen her in the few weeks he'd known her.

"Oh, Grady," she said on a whisper. Had he wanted to resist hosting the wedding, the tone of her voice would have changed his mind. When Ben went to stand behind her and put his arms around her, both of them looking around delightedly, he knew it had to be the best wedding ever held in a log home. With noble self-sacrifice, he accepted that he was probably going to hate the process but he'd do his part to make it perfect for them.

He leaned toward them. "It rents for a thousand a night, a couple hundred more if you want chairs and whatever those chandelier things are Cassie talked about."

Cassie turned to smack his arm. "Stop it," she said. "Standing chandeliers. Instead of hanging from the ceiling, they're on a stand. It'll be so beautiful."

"Where are you going to get all this stuff?"

She gave him a superior smile. "I have connections. I can have it all here in two days. I'll make the calls tonight, and it'll all be delivered the day after tomorrow, One-Day Air being more like two days from Europe."

Corie turned to her with a pleat between her eyebrows. "Cassie, it doesn't have to be extravagant. I don't want you to go through all that tr—"

"It's no trouble." Cassie cut her off as

Sarah closed in to put an arm around her shoulders. "Let me do this for you. Since Grady's in agreement, we'll make it memorable. I mean, how many times does a woman get married?"

"Three. Four," Grady answered without making eye contact.

This time Helen swatted his arm. "Once, if you're as much in love as Ben and Corie." Then she tucked her hand in his arm and hugged it. "Oh, Grady, this is going to be wonderful. It's so nice of you to offer your home."

It was on the tip of his tongue to remind her that he hadn't been the one to make the offer, but he loved Helen and this wasn't the moment for any more jokes. The Manning-Palmer family seemed to be in a sort of wedding reverie, still looking around the great room and envisioning something he couldn't see.

He patted Helen's hand. "Happy to do it." He sent a glance Cassie's way, wondering if she could, indeed, do all she claimed she could. He hoped so. He now seemed to be in partnership with her in this whole dreams-come-true, happily-ever-after fantasy.

Sarah put his concerns into words, but not in quite the way he'd have framed them. She was clearly willing to believe. "I can't wait to see how you pull this off," she said, giving Cassie's shoulders a squeeze. "Wow. What a holiday. What a reunion!"

"Should we get together tomorrow to make sure we're on track?" Helen asked. "I'm a little worried about the flowers. Our flower shop is small and…"

"I can get those, too," Cassie said. She seemed to have a sudden surge of internal power because her eyes were brighter and her cheeks were glowing. "Just decide what you want, Corie, and let me know. Sometime tomorrow for sure. We can have them sent to your florist and ask her to work with us."

The women stared at her openmouthed. She brushed away their shock with a casual backhanded gesture. "It's fine," she said. "The whole world of modeling revolves around glamorizing products and people and sites. We'll make it happen. But, what do you want to do for music?"

"What?" Grady asked. "You can't get the London Philharmonic? Or Beyoncé?"

She sent him a scolding look, but before she could reply Ben said, "Why don't we ask the Wild Men?"

Cassie frowned, clearly fearing for the plan. "Who?"

While the rest of the family applauded the idea, Grady explained. "It's a singing group Jack and Ben belonged to as teenagers. They all went to school together. They recently did a fund-raiser talent-show thing here and brought the house down."

She smiled and expelled a breath. "Great. Can you ask them?"

"Yes." He grinned. "I'm sure they'll love to do it."

CHAPTER FIVE

GRADY AND CASSIE stood side by side in the doorway, smiling and waving as the family left. The moment they were out of sight, she turned to him. "Thank you for agreeing to do this. I apologize that I didn't ask first. But, Corie seems to love the idea, and that's very important to me."

"Sure," he said, following her into the foyer and closing the door. "I hate this sort of thing, but I'll do it for Ben."

She looked at him over her shoulder on her way into the kitchen, an eyebrow raised. "What sort of thing? Weddings?"

"Fuss," he replied, opening the dishwasher door while she filled the sink with water and added soap. "All that glamour that trips us in to an unreal place."

She tried to justify her feelings about it. "I haven't seen my sister since I was a toddler, and she's been through so much. I can help make this wedding beautiful for her, and I'd like to do that. Glamour isn't about pretensions. It's just giving your best attention to the moment because it's important."

With the tray in the dishwasher only half-full, he pushed it in and closed the door. He carried the frying pan she'd used that morning and placed it on the counter beside her. He smiled, but his blue eyes were judgmental.

"Then I guess you should, but I doubt that she needs you to turn her wedding into something that would be held at Notre-Dame Cathedral. She just needs you to be her sister—and in this case, her maid of honor."

"If you recall," she said, dropping the skillet into the sudsy water, "I was photographed abusing a deaf woman and having a meltdown the world saw on television. I'd like her to remember me for something else." She plunged her hand into the water and turned her back on him.

He came to stand beside her and lean back against the counter while she worked. "Is that what all this extravagance is about? You're trying to make up for the Ireland thing?"

"No!" She gestured with a soapy hand and accidentally flung suds onto his cheek. She gasped in apology and brushed the suds from his cheekbone with a dish towel. "No, it's not about that. It's a wedding. They should all be beautiful, but I have the ability to make it absolutely fabulous."

"That's not going to make the marriage last any longer."

Now she was tempted to throw suds at him deliberately, but she drew a breath instead. "Of course it won't. But it'll enrich the moment and go just a little way to paying Corie back for all the hard times she's endured. Don't you believe in weddings?"

"I believe in marriage," he insisted. "Just not weddings that make us believe the more money we pour into things, the more fuss we make, the better it'll be."

Another dark look. "It isn't going to cost you a dime."

"I'm not worried about that. I just hate the…the…"

"The fuss. I know. You've said that a couple of times." She pulled the pan out of the sink and rinsed it under hot water. "Don't worry. I'll keep it under control."

He sighed heavily and took the pan from her. She wondered if he feared for his safety. "Let's just call a truce and try to coexist in harmony until after the wedding. Okay?"

She grinned at him. "Afraid of me, aren't you?"

He grinned back. "Little bit," he admitted.

Later, once she was dressed more comfortably in a hooded red sweatshirt pulled over her jeans, she sat in the middle of her bed, making notes.

Castle Props in London had the floor chandeliers she needed, and the one that would hang from the loft. They promised to ship them tonight for either late delivery tomorrow or the morning of the following day.

For tulle and ribbon, she called Louise, a seamstress for Josie Bergerac, her favorite Paris designer.

"You're getting *married*?" Louise asked excitedly.

"No, my sister is," she replied, and heard the sigh of disappointment. "I need yards of tulle and Caribbean-blue ribbon. Can you help me?"

"Of course. How many yards?"

"Forty?"

An exclamation of amazement crossed the Atlantic. "Are you decorating Madison Square Garden?"

"Ha, ha. No, Lulu, but a pretty large living room in a log home. It's going to look spectacular."

"I'll send it in the morning. Cassiopeia?" Louise used the name the fashion press had given her early in her career.

"Yes?"

"I believe it's the tradition in romance novels for the maid of honor to run off with the best man."

"Believe it or not," Cassie said, "I've already done that. Actually, he's one of the groomsmen. And he helped me leave Texas when the paparazzi descended."

"Texas?"

"It's a long story. The log home is his. But I'm afraid we're not the stuff of romance novels."

"Well, that's disappointing."

She had no idea.

"This will ship in the morning," Louise promised.

"You're a doll, Lulu."

MELANIE STORM, THE REALTOR, was short and plump, with dark hair in a short, feathery cut. She had freckles in abundance, cocoa-colored eyes and a gamine face that, along with her height, made it a little hard to take her seriously. Her services had been a gift to Grady and Ben from Jack and Sarah as congratulations for starting their PI business.

When she began to take Grady around to locations she thought might be appropriate, he forgot that she was short and freckled. She knew every detail of every location, and suggested some pros and cons he wouldn't have thought about.

By the fourth location, an office space in the same building as the Bay Bistro, he admired her style.

"This is a little smaller than the other places we've looked at, but there are two offices, two restrooms, a small area that would be a waiting room, and a small kitchen. Rent's a little higher, but it's recently been re-carpeted. I know everyone's doing hardwood floors now, but in the kind of business you're going into, warmth and quiet are good things. The building has Wi-Fi, but I suppose by the nature of detective work, you'll want your own system. Here we are." They stepped off the elevator and he couldn't help remembering his earlier experience that day with Cassie, and the serious fear in her eyes.

Melanie turned right off the elevator, rounded a corner and unlocked an oak door with a window trimmed in clear, leaded-glass squares. She ushered him in before her and stayed near the door, checking her phone while he wandered.

"The building was restored years ago," she said, following him slowly as he walked around the first office. "But they kept the crown molding and the chair rails." She chuckled. "It'll give you a sort of Old World detective atmosphere."

He smiled at that, looking around the office that was maybe ten by ten. Through the window, he saw the lot next door, a day-care center with toys strewn all over the yard. There was a very small bathroom at the back of the office.

The second office was smaller, possibly eight by eight. It also had a very small bathroom at the front. He went out across the hall and found a long, narrow kitchen with a row of cabinets and a small refrigerator. "Last tenant left the fridge. I can't vouch for how well it works."

"Well, I like it," he said, taking another walk-through. "But my partner has to see it and he's getting married on New Year's Day, so this is probably second in line in his priorities." He took out his cell phone. "I'll take some pictures so he has some idea."

"Oh, don't bother." She handed him a sheet of paper with all the space's specs and the address of a website that showed the place in detail. "He can look it up online and take his own tour. I don't have anyone else interested right now, so we can wait until after the wedding. If I do get a nibble, I'll let you know."

He was impressed by her eagerness to accommodate them. "That's very kind. Thank you."

Well, that was a relief, Grady thought as he drove home. The office space at the mill seemed like a definite possibility to him, if Ben agreed, and he couldn't think of anything better than being just a hallway away from the Bay Bistro.

Being a hallway away from Cassidy Chapman was another matter. Before this afternoon, he'd been bracing himself for the minor uproar caused by simply being part of a wedding. Now that uproar was going to be in his home, and the beautiful woman responsible for all that was going to be there, too.

How had he gotten into this?

Ego, he guessed, turning up the road that would lead him home. A supermodel had asked him for help and he'd obliged without a second thought. Served him right.

The house was quiet when he arrived. He knew it wasn't empty because Cassie had no way to get anywhere. The accordion closures above the loft railing remained open. He stood in the middle of the great room and called her name.

She appeared at the railing, a polite smile

in place. "Hi," she said. "Did you find an office?"

"Maybe. Depends on whether or not Ben likes it. I'm going to email him some photos, then I'll microwave that casserole my mother left. Will you be ready for dinner in about fifteen minutes?"

"Sure."

"Coffee with dinner? Only other thing I have is beer."

"Coffee's good."

"Your dulce de leche or is that just for breakfast?"

"Whatever you have. I have to start the day with dulce de leche, but for the rest of the day, it doesn't matter."

"All right. See you in fifteen."

She disappeared into her room and he took off for the small room off the kitchen where he kept his computer and printer and other stuff that didn't fit anywhere else. He wished he could put the blue armoire from his mother in there, but he knew she'd expect it to be visible when she came. And she wouldn't be shy about asking where it was.

He and Cassie chatted over dinner. She told him she was expecting a delivery from

Castle Props tomorrow, and possibly one from a Paris designer. That news rattled the resolution he'd just made about coexisting, because standing chandeliers and French designers were so contrary to all he knew, and made him uncomfortable. But she said the words with such ease and confidence that he had to believe it was going to happen.

"Just wanted you to have a heads-up. And…" She looked suddenly apologetic. "Would you mind if Corie, Sarah and Helen meet here with me tomorrow to talk about the flowers? That way I can be here to receive the Castle Props stuff."

"Sure. Do whatever you need to do. Until the wedding, I'll just work around you. My life will go back to normal after."

"After I'm gone?" she asked.

He nodded. "Right. I have Java Chip ice cream for dessert."

"Java like coffee?"

"Yeah. With chocolate chips."

"Sounds heavenly."

He got up to get it and pulled down two bowls. "You're going to have to fast for weeks when you go back to your normal life."

She shrugged as though it didn't matter. "I've done that before. Once I modeled ski clothes and forgot that it had been a couple of years since I'd skied. I broke my femur. I went home to recover and the nurse my father hired was a wonderful cook.

"And another time when I was seventeen, Paul Preston dumped me right after I went with him to the Grammys."

"Paul Preston the rock star?"

"Yes."

"Wasn't he too old for you? I mean, he's forty now, so when you were seventeen, he was…"

"Thirty-two. Yes. But I was scared by the new world I'd entered as a model, and he was big and sure of himself and I was flattered by his attention."

He got that. Same thing had happened to him when she'd picked him out for her rescue.

"Anyway, after that, I drowned my sorrows in macarons."

"If I wanted to drown my sorrows, it wouldn't be in coconut."

She put both elbows on the table and watched him scoop ice cream, a memory smile on her face. "Not macaroons with a double *o*, but macarons…" She gave it a French roll of her tongue.

He went a little weak.

"It's like a cookie cake with a flavored cream center. They make all kinds of them, but my favorite was salted caramel. Oh, my! They're hard to describe."

He carried the bowls to the table. "So you OD'ed on macarons?" She laughed when he tried to copy her accent.

"I did. But two weeks later, I learned that Eterna Cosmetics wanted me as their spokeswoman. I quickly recovered and went to the gym. I was myself again, maybe even better, before shooting began the following month."

"So, all it'll take is a couple of weeks in the gym to erase all the signs of Texas and Beggar's Bay?"

Her expression sobered slowly and her blue-sky eyes became as dark as dusk. "Nothing," she said, picking up her spoon, "will ever erase Texas or Beggar's Bay."

CHAPTER SIX

IN THE MORNING Grady went to rent wedding clothes with Jack, Ben, Gary and Soren while Cassie made a coffee cake with streusel topping for her meeting with the Palmer women. Corie brought Rosie, who seemed delighted to be part of the feminine proceedings.

"I've been thinking about this," Cassie said as they all gathered around the kitchen table, Rosie tucked in between her new mother and her new grandmother.

Sarah stabbed her fork into the coffee cake and said with a shake of her head, "I can't believe you just whipped this up before we got here. It's only nine thirty. You are going to be a marvelous addition to this family." She put the bite into her mouth and groaned in approval. "Wow. Did you learn to make this in Paris?"

Cassie laughed. "I think it's in the Betty

Crocker cookbook. Nothing brilliant about it. You add butter and brown sugar to anything and you've got something swoonworthy. So, back to the matter at hand."

Sarah turned to Corie with a haughty expression. "She's going to be marvelous but bossy."

Corie made a so-what sound. "She's a Manning. You're married to one. You know what they're like. Well, she's a Manning-Chapman, and Jack's a Manning-Palmer, so they've compromised a few gene pools, but they are all the same. Please give her your full attention or she'll take away our coffee cake."

Corie put an arm protectively around hers. "Go on," she said to Cassie.

"I was thinking," Cassie said again, "that maybe I don't have to send for flowers. We'll see what you think about this idea, then we'll call your local florist and see if she can do it. It's pretty basic, but beautiful. Even the simplest flower seems to raise an occasion to an elegant event."

They were listening, except for Rosie, who was eating all the streusel off her coffee cake. "What about dark pink Gerbera daisies, pink roses and delphiniums, maybe, for a little blue to coordinate with your Caribbean blue? It's not even close in shade, but that's better, because it won't look like we tried to match it and failed."

Corie opened her mouth to speak but Sarah put a hand on her arm. "I have the perfect solution!" she said. "To the blue, I mean."

Everyone leaned toward her. "When I was living with Ben and Jack after my apartment caught fire and Jack had just come home, I dried some gorgeous blue hydrangea that are now the most amazing shade of gray blue with pink in it. They'd be perfect with pink roses and Gerbera daisies. In fact…" She dug her phone out of her purse and scrolled through her photo album until she found the flowers.

"They're on the mantel in the guest house Jack and Ben's parents rent out to Helen's writing friends." She showed the photo around the table. There were oohs and aahs of approval. Cassie smiled across the table at Sarah. "Well, how brilliant of you to have done that. Did you have some prophetic knowledge that Corie was going to need them?"

Sarah laughed lightly. "At the time, I

thought I was the one who needed them because I thought they'd be beautiful in the room Jack had just remodeled. Just proof, I guess, how closely connected we all are." She turned to Helen. "Is it all right with you if we take that arrangement apart for Corie's flowers? I'll buy another bouquet for you."

"Of course you can take it. We'll find something else to put there."

"Then, if we're in agreement," Cassie said, "I'll call the florist right now to make sure it'll work."

They nodded. Sarah shooed her away. "Go make the call. We're going to split your piece of the coffee cake while you're gone."

A very helpful woman named Denise at Beggar's Bouquets assured her that she could have Gerbera daisies and pink roses in abundance.

Cassie held the phone to her chest and turned back to the table. "Three bouquets for us, a little basket for Rosie, a corsage for Helen, and four boutonnieres for the guys and Soren. Then loose flowers to string into the bunting, and bouquets for the tables?"

They all turned to Corie, who raised her

hands in surrender. "I leave it to you. It sounds wonderful."

Cassie held the phone to her ear and repeated all that, then asked, "For the bridal bouquet, can you do that swirling silver wire around the flowers that's so popular now? Maybe with a few pearls in it?" She listened for a moment. "Wonderful. I think wrapping the boutonnieres in wire would be great, too. I'm expecting the ribbon to arrive tomorrow. Can I bring that to you? Perfect. Thank you, Denise."

With a smile of victory, she carried the phone with her to the table. "That's taken care of. I ordered the standing chandeliers and the tulle to make a sort of bunting to go around the loft railing and maybe a few of the columns. What else do we need to do? Some kind of favor for the guests?"

"There's no time for that, sweetheart," Helen said. "Otherwise we'll all be going crazy rather than being able to focus on the next few days."

"I have to go shopping in the morning for a dress," Sarah said. She turned to Cassie. "What are you going to wear, and try not to look too spectacular?"

"I told you to wear something you already have," Corie reminded Sarah. "Don't go buy anything."

"I never had much in the way of dressy clothes when I did home health care," Sarah said. "It'll be fun to have something that makes me feel glamorous."

"I hadn't packed that much to go to Ireland, and I left in a rush." Cassie looked around the table, wondering if her family was expecting her to explain. They didn't seem embarrassed or in any way upset, so rather than skating past an explanation, she brought it on. "Do you want to know what happened?"

Corie said gently, "Only if you want to tell us."

"'Cause we really don't care," Sarah added. "We don't know you all that well yet, but we're sure there had to be some kind of misunderstanding."

Cassie told them what she had told Grady, how the entire incident had come about, without explaining that the invasion of her personal space had to do with her claustrophobia. She explained what she'd done later to apologize, and how the makeup artist had forgiven her.

They were comfortingly indignant that the news story hadn't shared her side or that she'd done her best to make amends and been forgiven.

"My point is," she said, "that I don't have anything to wear, either. I picked up some things yesterday at the little Beggar's Bay Boutique, but I wasn't looking for more formal things, so I didn't notice if they had anything."

"They do," Sarah said. "That's where I'm going. Why don't you come with me?"

"We'll come, too." Corie smoothed Rosie's rich, dark braid. "I have to find something for Rosie. Helen, want to make it a crowd?"

GRADY BROUGHT THE guys home with him after their fittings, planning to order a pizza. He had beer in the fridge and milk for Soren. He was surprised and vaguely disappointed to find the house still filled with women. He loved them all but felt a pang of longing for the simplicity of his old bachelor lifestyle before he'd been invited to Texas.

Now Jack had married, Ben was getting married, and he was sharing space with a woman who completely disrupted everything he knew to be familiar and sound.

Those thoughts were softened just a little by the fact that Cassie and the Palmer women had apparently expected their return and had raided his fridge to make everyone lunch. Cassie had sliced his stash of sausage and cheese onto crackers, and someone must have run out for vegetables because he didn't remember having yellow peppers, cucumbers, tomatoes or green onions.

He went into the kitchen to pour a glass of milk for Soren and found Cassie slicing apples and pears, something else he didn't remember having.

She was pink with...well, he wasn't sure what it was, but it gave a depth to her natural glow. She was happy. Apparently she loved the hubbub of a house filled with people and the low roar of several conversations going on at once. Pitched a little higher was the sound of children laughing on the stairs to the loft as they played with an electronic game.

"Hi," she said with a very genuine smile he didn't want to crush despite his wavering mood. "Sorry there's so much fuss, but I thought if they stayed until the Castle Props stuff arrives, we'll have help unpacking it. And I'll replace all your food. I'm going shopping tomorrow for something to wear to the wedding. You guys are renting suits?"

"Yes. We're going to look spectacular."

"I have no doubt." She looked out the kitchen window at the swishing tree limbs. "Wind's picking up out there."

"Yeah, that's pretty much an all-winter thing around here. Lots of windstorms. I like the sound of it."

She looked up, interested. "It sounds a little like the decibel level in here. I'm surprised the noise doesn't bother you." Then she nodded as though she suddenly understood. "That's because it's natural, isn't it? Not something man-made in an attempt to be glamorous."

"Don't be smart," he scolded with a grin.

"It is natural. They use the sound in relaxation tapes."

"True. And that would work if you don't think about the destruction wind can bring about. Roofs blown away, buildings toppled, crops destroyed."

"Now you're being deliberately argumentative. I'm talking wind, not hurricanes or tornadoes. Anything under twenty-five miles an hour."

She grinned back. "I'm just making the point that even natural things have the potential to do damage. Wind's ability to destroy can make glamour look pretty good."

He wondered how a woman could be exasperating and charming at the same time. "So, when are you leaving, again?" he teased.

"Not sure. I guess I'll stay until it ceases being fun harassing you."

"Thanks. I have to work the next couple of days, so I'll have crime and criminals to distract me. You want this on the buffet I noticed you set up on the credenza?"

"Please."

He turned with the plate and stopped in surprise when his mother appeared in his way, a large, square, food storage box balanced on the flat of her hand. Sure, why not? The day was already far beyond his control, anyway.

"Hey, Mom," he said. "What's going on?"

"I made a chocolate sour cream cake." She went around him to place it on the table. "I didn't realize you were having company. I'll just leave it right here and be on my way."

"No, Mrs. Nelson." Cassie hurried from the sink, drying her hands on a towel. "Please stay. Would you like a cup of coffee? This isn't company, it's my family. You probably know my sister Corie's getting married and we've gotten together to plan her wedding on New Year's Day. We're expecting a heavy package delivery anytime now, so the guys are hanging around to help bring it inside."

His mom looked reluctant but Cassie poured a cup of coffee and put it in her hand. "Actually, you're just in time, if Grady doesn't mind sharing your cake. We're having finger food for lunch, but I have nothing for dessert."

"I do mind," he teased, trying to stop his mother from removing the cover.

"Grady Joshua," his mother said, pushing his hands away. She turned apologetically to Cassie, a little softening in her manner toward her. "I'll cut it for you, but I don't think Grady has enough small plates."

"I've got a stash of paper plates for poker night." Grady went to the cupboard to pull them down and placed them on the table near the cake.

"I'll get you a knife." Cassie went to the utensil drawer as Grady delivered the plate of fruit and vegetables.

When he returned, Diane had taken the cover off to reveal a thickly frosted single-layer cake. Suddenly both children appeared in the doorway. "I smell cake frosting," Soren said. He looked up at Diane, his manner frank and friendly. "Who are you?"

Diane laughed and crossed the kitchen to take the knife from Cassie. "I'm Grady's mother," she replied, slicing expertly into the cake. "Who are you?"

The boy pointed to himself. "I'm Soren." Then to his new sister. "This is Rosie. She's my sister now. We just came here to live."

"Oh?"

"Corie and Ben are adopting us," Rosie said. "We don't have to call them Mom and Dad until it feels right."

"Well, that's very nice." Diane put two slices of cake on plates as they sat eagerly at the table. "Welcome to Beggar's Bay."

Ben appeared in search of the children. "Ben!" Soren said then amended with "Dad! Look what we've got. This is Grady's mom. She brought cake!"

Ben smiled and went to Diane, his hand extended. "Yes, I know Grady's mom. She's made dinner for Grady and Uncle Jack and me a couple of times. And she makes the best peanut-butter fudge."

"Maybe she should make it for the wedding," Rosie suggested, chocolate already on her upper lip.

Ben frowned at the children. "Did you have some lunch?"

Soren made a face. "There's a lot of vegetables out there, so we came in here and found the cake." He held his fork poised over the cake, waiting for approval.

Groaning, Ben said, "Okay, on the principle that life is short so we should eat dessert first, it's okay."

Soren and Rosie cheered.

"Thank you," Ben said, accepting a slice of cake from Diane. "Can you come to the wedding? We don't have time for invitations, so we're just making phone calls and emailing. I know it's rude, but time is short. New Year's Day. Five o'clock. Right here. And you don't have to make fudge."

"Well…yes, if I'm not intruding."

"Of course not." Ben backed as far as the doorway and shouted into the main room, "Guys, Grady's mom brought cake. Corie, come and meet her."

In a moment the kitchen was packed with ten people who clearly subscribed to the "life is short" philosophy, all talking at once.

Grady was surprised how warm, if a little uncomfortable as the center of attention, his mom seemed.

He closed his eyes for a minute at the cacophony in the kitchen then opened them again and allowed himself a very small smile.

Cassie went to him with a piece of cake

and a fork. "Here you go. I think this is a matter of, 'if you can't lick 'em, join 'em.'"

"Thank you." He took it from her. "She does make amazing cakes."

Cassie shrugged. "I wouldn't know. My family has eaten it all. This was the last piece."

"Ah." He forked a piece and held it out to her. "You have to experience this for yourself."

CASSIE WAS SUDDENLY very aware of his closeness. Her gregarious family in the tight space and Jack gesturing with his fork as he explained to Corie his plan for restoring something. The sounds around her faded as Grady's eyes focused on her mouth while he guided the fork to her lips. She caught the scent of his aftershave, felt the warmth of his energy and the touch of his little finger as he poked her chin with it.

"Hey," he said, puncturing her distraction. "Open before I get chocolate all over you."

Still ensnared by his nearness, it took her a moment to part her lips. He put the fork gently inside then withdrew it and she

closed her mouth around the bite of cake.
On one level, she was aware of the taste of
the thick chocolate icing, then the succu-
lent cake, but on another, nothing existed
but his eyes looking into hers with a sweet-
ness that had been missing in him since
he'd discovered she was all about glamour
and fuss.

She drank it in, unafraid of what he
would think because she was staring at
him. He darted a quick glance beyond her,
probably because of the sudden silence she,
too, noticed. Looking behind her, she saw
everyone watching them. His mother was
the only one who seemed a little concerned
about what she saw.

Cassie was saved embarrassment by the
arrival of the delivery truck.

Grady heard the air brakes and knew it
had to be a vehicle from out of town. The
driver started toward the side door with a
clipboard and stopped in his tracks when
eight people and two children swarmed out.

Cassie approached him. "I'm Cassidy
Chapman," she said. "You're delivering
from Castle Props?"

He looked relieved. "Yes. Are you staging a revolution or do all these people live here?"

"They're my family," she said, feeling a small thrill at the sound of those words. "We're having a wedding, and they're all anxious to see what the standing chandeliers look like.

"Thank you for being so prompt," she said, walking with him to the rear of the truck.

He opened the back, lowered a ramp and disappeared inside to reappear with a tall, wide box on a dolly. He guided it carefully down.

"Can we help you?" Jack asked.

He shook his head. "Insurance covers you while I'm delivering, so it's best to let me do it. If anything happens, it's my fault."

Jack stepped back. "Makes sense to me."

After the seven chandeliers had been delivered and the driver sent on his way with a plate from the buffet, the women stood aside. The men gathered around the one box Cassie had asked the driver to place in the middle of the room.

Jack produced an impressive knife and opened the smaller end of the box.

"Please be careful," Cassie said. "Under all that padding is crystal."

"Did you buy these?" Soren asked, standing beside her.

"No, I'm renting them," she explained. "We'll use them for the wedding and send them back."

"Wow," Rosie said again. "You're the coolest aunt to have."

"That's for sure!" Soren agreed.

She laughed and put an arm around both children. "Thank you, both of you. You're the coolest niece and nephew. Let's just hope nothing's broken."

"What happens if it is?" Soren asked worriedly.

She shrugged. "We fix it. We have all these smart men and women. We can figure it out."

"All right!"

Jack and Ben bore the weight of the chandelier's wide head still wrapped in cotton batting while Grady held the stand, now horizontal, so that Gary could slide the box away.

"Looks good," Cassie said, feeling a little breathless. "Let's stand it up."

The brass base was entwisted with copper and had a wide foot plate for stability. Jack held it while Ben carefully pulled off the protective batting.

Cassie approached it after the last wad of cotton hit the floor. It stood just above her eye level, somehow lighting the darkening room even though it wasn't turned on. She ran her fingers gently through the strands of crystal droplets that had been bunched together in their packaging. She straightened them so that each hung perfectly on its finding, catching what light there was.

The women closed in, gasping at the beauty of the chandelier brought down to eye level. "Imagine six of them," Cassie said, a little breathless over how right she'd been about this, how gorgeous they would be lined up in two rows of three to make a path for the bride.

"I can't believe something that delicate came across the ocean unscathed," Helen said. "I ordered a small chandelier once and you had to attach the crystals when it arrived."

"Oh, Cassie!" Corie whispered. "They're… I don't have a word."

"How are you going to light them?" Ben asked. "With our guests walking around, we can't let cords stretch across the room to trip people."

Cassie pointed to the base. "You'll notice there are no cords." She reached up and turned the battery-powered switch in the neck. "We used them on the beach in a shoot for champagne, the principle being that the level of elegance of the beverage required the same level of elegance to light the evening."

She saw Grady's eyebrow go up, but she ignored him. "Obviously there was no place to plug in, so one of the guys modified them to take batteries. Only problem is, they really eat up the power, so I'll have to be sure to have extras on hand." She smiled at her family. "So, everyone approves?"

Helen, Sarah, Corie and even Diane helped her clean up. They talked about Sarah's new job as administrator at Rose River Assisted Living, about Corie's plan to design and market a new line of clothes, and Helen and Gary's upcoming trip to visit friends in San Diego. Diane stayed out of the conversation, listening politely and contributing only when asked.

"And you get to go back to your glamorous job in Paris, or New York, or wherever your next assignment is." Sarah huffed a wistful sigh. "I'd love to see Paris."

Cassie covered sausage and cheese plates for the refrigerator while her sister-in-law wiped off trays. Corie and Helen washed and dried utensils. "Now that you have family there," Cassie said, "you'll always have a place to stay when you come."

"Are the pastries really as wonderful as all that?"

"Better than you can even imagine. Although Diane's cake was pretty amazing." She smiled at Grady's mother, who was watching her with an expression she couldn't quite interpret.

"How do you stay—" she swept a hand up and down Cassie's very slender body "—like that?"

"I walk everywhere, for one thing, and I've inherited my father's height and body type. He's as lean in his sixties as he was as a young man. And I do eat really lightly when I'm working."

Sarah sighed. "I'd never have the self-control to do that."

"I'd never have the smarts to run a senior care facility. We all have our skills. Mine just happen to be…physical."

"That's not true." Corie spoke firmly. "I remember how much fun it was to be your penpal when you were twelve. For a couple of months you were the only happy spot in my life." Her firm expression turned into a soft smile of affection. "I'm so glad we found you. And I'm so happy that life's been good to you."

It had. She couldn't deny that.

"It's going to be so good for all of you to be reconnected," Helen said. "Jack used to do his best to take care of you when your mom was…" She groped for a word then stopped trying to find one with a wave of her hand. "He talked about you all the time after he came to live with us. I'm so happy that he has his family back."

Sarah nodded. "Maybe now his nightmares will stop forever." At Cassie's look of confusion, she went on. "He used to dream about your mother being in Iraq and Afghanistan when he was stationed there.

I think his subconscious confused all the bad things in his life and put them together in nightmares about her dressed in a hijab and climbing onto the vehicle he drove."

"How awful." Cassie closed the refrigerator door and sat at the table. "I feel so badly that those times were so awful for Jack and Corie, and I barely remember them."

Corie sat across from her. "It wouldn't make it any less bad for me, if you remembered having a bad childhood, too. So don't think about it that way. After I ran away from my stepmother, I liked the thought that you were on your way to Paris with your dad and that things would be good for you there. And they finally all worked out for me, so let's just let all that go."

Cassie nodded. "I can do that."

Helen said, as though determined to put that out of their minds, "I confirmed with Father Eisley for five in the evening."

"Who's giving you away?" Cassie asked. "Didn't you say Teresa isn't able to come to the wedding?" Teresa McGinnis ran the foster home that Corie had grown up in and then stayed to help run.

"No, she isn't." Corie was clearly unhappy about that. "But she has a whole new batch of kids and their needs come first. Ben and I will make a special trip to see her in the spring." She cheered visibly. "Gary offered to give me away. I'm very honored."

Jack, Ben and Soren walked into the room. Ben said, "We're here to report that all the chandeliers work beautifully. We lined up the chandeliers in their boxes on their sides along the back wall. And we're thinking we'd better get home because the wind's picking up and the kids left their bikes out behind the condo."

Jack scrutinized the women. "You look very sad for women planning such a happy occasion."

Sarah stood and went to put her arms around his waist. "It's not sadness, it's happiness that the three of you are together again. That's seriously heavy stuff."

"That's true. But we make a promise here and now to put aside what separated us, and forge ahead to whatever awaits. And even though we have to let Cassie go back to Paris or wherever, Christmas will always be all of us together. Agreed?"

Corie and Cassie chorused, "Agreed."

CHAPTER SEVEN

BIG DROPS OF rain came with more wind as Grady and Cassie saw the family off. Grady went onto the deck to take down a set of wind chimes and carry in a pair of wicker chairs.

Cassie had followed him and looked over the railing at the potted plants below. "Are those going to be okay?"

"I think so." He pointed to the window behind her. "Want to get that shutter, please?" he asked as he closed the one nearest him.

"At home in Paris or New York, outside shutters are just decorative," she said as she closed the other one.

He narrowed his eyes against the rain that began to thicken and fall in earnest. "In the woods in Oregon, they're functional to save your windows from flying debris."

He guided her ahead of him into the

great room and closed and locked the doors. With the shutters closed, the room was dark.

Darkness was sometimes a trigger for her claustrophobia because it was impossible to be sure nothing hemmed her in or closed her off.

She flipped the light switch she knew was right beside her and the great room came to life, the boxes on the floor lined up against the wall a testimony to the success of her wedding planning so far.

She was suddenly exhausted. "I was thinking about going to bed early," she told Grady as he headed for the kitchen. "Unless there's something you need me to do."

He turned at the doorway. "No, nothing. I'm still stuffed from your buffet and Mom's cake. Do you need anything before you go up?"

She shook her head. "I'm good. The girls and I are going shopping in the morning."

She was trying hard not to look into his eyes, or at his mouth, but staring at his hair made her feel ridiculous. He even rolled his eyes up, obviously wondering what was on his head. She quickly added, "I'll get groceries. Thanks for today. I loved it. I know you must have hated it, but I appreciate that you didn't complain about my family being all over the place. Good night, Grady."

She was halfway up the stairs before he replied. "Good night, Cassie," he said.

CASSIE WOKE OUT of a deep sleep and sat straight up in bed. She remained still, the blanket clutched in both hands, and wondered what had awakened her. She hadn't been dreaming, and except for rain thumping against the windows, there didn't seem to be anything wrong. Then she realized how dark it was, that there were no illuminated numbers on the bedside clock. The power must be out.

The night pressed against her, nudging her, running a finger of sensation along her spine, whispering in her ear, "Got you now! You're all mine. And there's no one around to see or hear you." A shudder ran through her.

Well, that was just stupid, she told herself, throwing her blankets back. She was not going to fall victim to her own terrors.

Then thunder clapped as loudly as

though it were hanging from the ceiling above her bed. She was transplanted for an instant to that nebulous darkness of loud voices and noises.

She heard a cry and realized it was her own as she hurried toward the stairs, hands held out in front of her to guide her. She'd taken just a few steps when she made herself slow down.

She heard her breath rasping as she felt the end of the railing with her left hand and took a firm hold. There was no light in the great room, no night-light in the kitchen. Rain and wind slammed against the windows. For an instant, bright light illuminated the path to the kitchen, but the shutters she and Grady had closed against the wind kept the lightning from the great room. Then the light was gone, thunder crashed again, and she held the railing in one hand and forced back a cry with the other.

You're fine, she told herself. *Terrified beyond description, but fine.*

"Cassidy?" Grady called. He suddenly materialized at the bottom of the stairs, the glow of a bright lantern in his hands casting a ring of light from his knees to his shoes and the fir floor under his feet. He raised the light so that she could see his face—or so that he could see hers.

He smiled. "You okay? That was pretty loud."

And pretty dark! "Yeah." The thin quality of her voice didn't even convince *her*.

He seemed to hear that and came up the stairs, stopping a few steps below her and reaching up to take her hand. "You're shaking," he said, helping her to the bottom.

"Yeah," she said again. "I'm not crazy about the dark." Her voice quaked in rhythm with her body.

"It's okay," he said, putting an arm around her and holding the other with the light out ahead of them. "Want to sit on the sofa and I'll make you a cup of tea?"

"Please. Thank God for your gas range."

"Want something to nibble with it?"

"I don't know." She tried to joke. "I think my family ate every last crumb you had. Anyway, I'm not hungry, but tea would be wonderful."

"Watch your shins." They'd reached the coffee table and she walked carefully around the sharp edges to the soft, inviting sofa. She sat a little tensely in her midnight blue negligee, realizing now that she was freezing. She wrapped her arms around herself.

Grady yanked a knitted throw off the back and placed it over her shoulders. "Sugar in your tea?" he asked. When she shook her head, he left her the lamp and headed unerringly for the kitchen. She caught a glimpse of lightning from that direction, and this time it took a moment for the thunder to crash. She hoped that meant the storm was moving away.

She turned sideways on the sofa and tucked her legs up under the blanket, resting the side of her face against the sofa back. Her heart had stopped thudding and was now down to a steady bongo beat. She drew a breath and let it out slowly, trying to free herself of the fear as she'd been taught. Breathing in confidence, breathing out fear.

She remained a tight ball in the blanket until she heard the kettle whistle. In a minute, Grady returned with two steaming mugs. She swung her legs down and held the blanket over her lap.

Grady put the mugs down and walked

around the table to sit beside her. In a gesture she didn't want to analyze, she threw half of the blanket over his knees. She hoped that didn't scare him.

She realized that had been a baseless worry when he moved a little closer and put an arm around her shoulders. "You're still shaking," he observed.

"But not as much. I'm beginning to..." *Get over it,* was on the tip of her tongue but she bit the words back. That sounded as though she'd had a panic attack or some other frightening event. She'd been on the brink, but she didn't have to admit to it. He hated fuss.

He looked down at her face, framed by the crook of his elbow. "You look like you did when you got off the elevator," he said. "Does thunder have anything to do with your claustrophobia?"

"No." She sat up and reached for her tea. "Though I don't like loud noises, it's the darkness that's the real problem for me."

"My father used to tell Jack and me when we were children that there's nothing in the dark that wasn't there when the lights were on."

She told him with a look that that wasn't always true. "Actually, it's not fear of someone in the darkness that could hurt me, it's the oppressive nature of the inky blackness itself. It's like I'm all wrapped up and closed off. I can't see ahead, or beside me, or anywhere, to give me some sense of having space. I'm trapped in a void."

His frown was sympathetic. "Did something happen to you as a child to cause this condition, or is it just something you've always had?"

"I'm really not sure. I have sort of unformed memories of shouts and screams and other loud noises. I think I was afraid."

"If that awareness goes back so far that you have no clear memory, maybe it was from before you were separated from your brother and sister."

She'd thought about that. "Could be."

"Maybe they know what happened. Why you're afraid."

She sipped at her tea and shrugged. "Yes, but they don't know about my claustrophobia, remember?"

"You think that diminishes you somehow? Because it doesn't."

"Yeah, but who wants to go into all that during wedding preparations? It's better left alone for now." She was glad Grady sat beside her, comfortingly big.

"I suppose. Can I ask you a question about your claustrophobia?"

Lightning lit the path from the kitchen for an instant, and they were both silent, waiting for the thunder. It was loud but a little more delayed and sounding slightly more distant.

She returned her focus to the conversation. She also noticed that she felt warm and even comfortable again, and that his nearness was…nice.

"A question. Yes, go ahead."

His turn in her direction disturbed the blanket. He pulled it up over her again and leaned his elbow on the back of the sofa. "I don't get why you're frightened of elevators and darkness, but you were able to ride in a plane. I mean, I noticed you were tense. But that's got to be the ultimate nowhere-to-go scenario. Why didn't that freak you out more?"

That was tricky to understand. It didn't even always make sense to her. "First," she explained, "the plane was part of my therapy when I was an adolescent. I traveled with my father, and the therapist worked with me to make me face my fear. It's a matter of putting you in a worse situation so you have to deal with it in order to move through it and finally come out the other side."

"That doesn't sound easy."

"It isn't at all, but I did very well. In fact, eventually I thought of myself as cured—until about a month ago when all kinds of major emotional things converged to bring it all back."

"You mean the Ireland thing?"

"Yes, but before that my father was caught in a revolution in Bangkok, where he'd gone to set up the government's new computer system. For days, there was no communication from him."

Grady nodded, touching her shoulder. "I'm sorry. I heard about that. We were all in Texas at the time. That was when Jack and Corie had just located you and were trying to contact him."

"I'd noticed that I was having a minor recurrence of my fear. I usually rode the Metro all over Paris, but I couldn't anymore. I got on to go visit a friend who was no longer modeling, and I had to get off long before my stop, and almost knocked down an old man on my way out. I had to take the stairs everywhere because of my issues with the elevator, and left the light on when I went to bed at night." She was starting to feel a little agitated.

"We'll stop talking about it," he said, handing her her cup. "Have another sip of tea."

"No." She remembered her therapy. "I have to get to the end of the story. Or at least where we are now." She smiled thinly as she took her cup from him. "I'm sure this isn't the end by a long shot." She sat back, the cup held against her blanket, the other hand wrapped around it.

"I went to Ireland thinking that I always have great control when I'm working. I'd get rid of this little emotional blip and I'd be fine. But then there was all that hair and makeup stuff I was telling you about." She sounded distressed even to her own ear. "I had resolved that for myself when I started modeling. That invasion of your space can make you insane, but I'd learned to distance myself from it, to become as much of an object as the pushing, the brushing and patting and painting of me made me feel. The thing was..."

She stopped and heaved a sigh. "The thing was," she said again, "that I was different now. I couldn't just compartmentalize like I used to because now my emotions were more important, a bigger part of me than they used to be. The thing with my father really scared me. I know my brother and sister had endured so much by the time they were my age, but I hadn't. That near loss shook the world for me, and even my place in it. I'd started to wonder if I should be away so much. My father and I were all each other had.

"So, going back to work made things worse instead of better. I was emotional and edgy, and all my old tricks to maintain control weren't working. Then I got word from my father about Jack and Corie, and how long and hard they'd looked for me. While I was so anxious to see them, I was scared, too, because I was starting to feel like a fraud. All those confident stares into the camera, all those smiling struts along the runway no longer represented the real me."

He took the cup from her and placed it on the coffee table, then put his arm around her shoulders again and drew her close.

"Jack and Corie are crazy about you and very proud of you. Not because you're a supermodel, but because you're their little sister."

She leaned into him and said gloomily, "Who they think has it all together. And I don't."

"Nobody has it all together. We just try to act like it so that maybe one day it'll happen. And, anyway, look at all you've accomplished so far for the wedding. You've got everybody pumped."

"That's only thanks to all my connections." She raised her head to look into his eyes, his smile coaxing one from her. "I thought you hated all that stuff. Are *you* pumped?"

"I have to admit that I am, a little."

"But there's going to be lots more fuss." She made it sound like a dire warning.

"I'm resigned to that being my life as long as you're here."

She rested her head against him again. "Something's missing in my life. Maybe that's why I'm trying so hard."

"What's that?"

"I don't know. And I realize that's ridiculous, like I don't even know myself."

"Well, if you knew yourself, you'd have it all together, and we've already concluded that you don't."

"Thank you for sparing my feelings." She slapped his chest.

"On the chance that what your life is missing is honesty," he speculated with a grin, "I'm trying to help out."

She straightened, something suddenly clear to her.

"That really is part of it," she said, leaning on his arm, but looking into his eyes rather than laying her head on his shoulder. She missed that intimacy but wanted to say this to him directly. "When I first started having this sense of being out of sync, I thought a lot about what I do and how it's all superficial and artificial..." She added seriously, "Though, of course, it serves a purpose and I'm not condemning it, just admitting what's true." She drilled him with a look. "As someone who so values reality, you should understand what I'm saying."

"I do. And maybe you're right."

"But…to you, reality is hard work and no fun. To me, it's…" She sighed and dropped her head to his shoulder, exhausted. "I don't know what it is, so how will I ever know when I have it, or find it, or walk right by it? No, don't answer that. I'll figure it out for myself." She could hear herself beginning to slur just a little from sleepiness. "Have you noticed that it hasn't thundered in about ten minutes? You think the storm is over?"

As though in answer to her question, thunder boomed in the distance.

"It's still here, but moving away. Why don't you try to sleep?"

She snuggled into him, found a spot for her nose right against his throat, and put an arm around his waist to anchor herself.

He closed his eyes and knew he wouldn't sleep a wink.

CHAPTER EIGHT

"I JUST WANT to look at your suit and see if you need me to take it to the dry cleaner's for you. You can have it back in two days if you pay extra." Grady's mother was wandering around his kitchen, apparently conducting some kind of personal inspection.

"It's fine, Mom," he said. "We're renting suits."

"But you should look nice for the bachelor dinner."

"I'll look great, I promise." So that she would stop pacing, he asked, "What are *you* wearing to the wedding?"

Finding nothing to complain about, she dropped her purse on one of the stools at the breakfast bar, blinking at him in surprise. "I've never known you to have an interest in fashion."

He downed the last of the dulce de leche coffee Cassie had poured for him before she'd left with the Palmer women and put his cup in the sink. "Can't help myself. Cassie's a model, Corie's a designer, there's enough wedding stuff going on around here to make a man run for the hills. I can't help but absorb some of it."

"I may not even go to the wedding," she said, picking up her purse, sitting and holding it on her lap as though it were a toddler.

He poured her a cup of coffee, thinking there was something else going on besides talk about clothes. She was avoiding his eyes, looking a little uncomfortable, and that was very unusual for the woman who prided herself on being forthright and always speaking her mind. He placed the coffee in front of her and took the seat beside her. "What's going on, Mom?"

She tried to look innocent. "What do you mean?"

"I think you're here to talk about something besides wedding clothes. And why don't you want to go to the wedding when Ben's mom specifically invited you?"

"How do you know that?"

"She told me. She said she thought you

were lovely—her words—and they'd be so happy if you would join us."

She did that evasive thing with her eyes. "I'm not sure they're my…type. Or that I'm theirs."

He rolled his eyes. "Mom. There are no *types*. You like people or you don't. If you do, it's a shame to pass up getting to know them better."

"They seem so…sort of…stylish," she said, as though that defining word had a bad connotation. "A model, a designer and Helen used to be an editor. I have nothing in common with them. They live in a world we don't usually ever see."

"True. Not a lot of models and editors in our lives. But that doesn't mean you won't like them when you get to know them. And the fact that they invited you into their lives by asking you to the wedding means they'd like to know *you* better."

"Yeah…well…" She tried to brush it off. "I'm just a former teacher who became a housewife who stayed home for ten years to take care of a husband who was too busy trying to stay alive to notice how hard I worked for him and…" Her lips tightened.

She kept emotion bottled up, closed off. One day she was going to blow like shaken champagne.

"How much you loved him?" Grady guessed. "I know. Dad was a pretty simple man, who considered everything outside his experience something not worth caring about. And, when he became ill, and you were healthy, even though you lived your life in the interest of his, he sort of lost track of even you."

"Your father was a good man," she said defensively, one tear slipping down her cheek. She wiped it away as though it offended her.

"I know that." He put a hand over hers on the table. "I can be honest about him without loving him any less. He was a good father, but pretty rigid in what he thought. Not everything you know about is good, and not everything you've never seen or heard of is bad. You'll love these people. You have to give them a chance."

"I don't know. I don't have anything to wear to a wedding. And I hate shopping. I'm all…square and lumpy." She swept a hand down her sturdy torso.

He had to laugh at that. "That's ridiculous. You always look nice. Let Cassie take you shopping. She can make something out of nothing."

At her offended look he quickly amended, "She can help you find something that will make you look spectacular. I'm going to call her. She and her family are shopping right now."

"No! Grady…"

He stood and dialed Cassie on his cell phone. "Hey, Cassie. My mom's here and needs something to wear for the wedding. Are you still at Bay Boutique?"

"We are."

"If Mom meets you there, can you help her find the right thing?"

"I'd love to," she said, sounding pleased that he'd called. He was surprised by how pleased that made him feel in return. In the background, he could hear the other women's laughter. "If she doesn't see us when she walks in, it's because we're running in and out of the dressing rooms. Tell her to just follow the noise."

"Right." He smiled to himself. Considering how worried she'd been last night, it was nice to hear her happy. "She's on her way."

His mother's face was purple with exasperation as he turned off his phone. "I wish I could still ground you."

He went around the table to wrap her in a hug. "Just enjoy this, Mom. I know it's a lot of fuss and feathers, but in another week Cassie will be gone and life will be back to normal. A lot more real than we need it to be."

She frowned at him as he walked her to her car. "What does that mean?" She stopped at the driver's-side door to look up at him with a penetrating stare. "You're falling for her, aren't you?"

"I like her a lot," he corrected. "But I'm as steeped in reality as you are. Mostly. Actually, I don't know anymore. Go buy a dress. I have to get to a meeting at the station." He opened her door.

"Remember Celeste," she warned.

"Will you please get in the car?" he said a little more sharply than he'd intended. "I'm not likely to forget her." But the truth was, he seldom thought about her now. He'd thought he'd never get over the hurt, but he seemed to have done just that. And that made it all the more mystifying.

"This woman's even more highfalutin than Celeste was."

"Mom, if you don't start the car, I'm going to push you all the way downtown myself."

"I'm going. But mark my words."

"'Bye."

"I love you," she said before she started the car.

"And yet you love to torture me."

"Really. And who's sending whom to buy a dress?"

"Well, we'd both look pretty silly if you were sending me, wouldn't we?"

Mercifully, she drove off.

ROSIE STOOD BEFORE the three-way mirror and giggled over the endlessly repeated images of herself. She wore a dark blue, silky, A-line dress patterned in snowflakes. It was simple and feminine, and the line flattered her.

She put both hands to her mouth as Corie, Sarah, Helen and Cassie stood behind her. "I look pretty," she said in wonder.

"You look beautiful," Cassie said. She took one of Rosie's thick braids in her hand and turned to Corie. "Can she wear her hair down for the wedding? We can make her a coronet of flowers."

Rosie's eyes grew enormous. "Like a crown?"

"Like a crown. What do you think, Corie?"

Corie wrapped her arms around Rosie from behind. Helen snapped a picture of their reflection. She'd been taking photos all morning. "I promised Teresa we'd send her pictures since she can't be here," she'd explained.

"I think you're going to outshine the bride," Corie said to the child in the mirror.

"What does that mean?" Rosie asked.

"It means you're going to be prettier than I am."

Rosie made a face. "I don't think so."

Sarah stood behind them in a straight sheath the precise blue of the restaurant napkin they were trying to match. With her fair features and light brown hair she had a soft look that belied the smart, organized, senior-living administrator inside.

Helen had found a knit skirt and top a

shade darker than the Caribbean blue with a wide sprinkle of rhinestones around the neckline. She looked magnificent, even though still in her white tennis shoes.

Cassie's dress had a close-fitting velvet top with long sleeves in a shade of blue somewhere between Sarah's and Helen's, and a flared organza skirt that skimmed her knees. Before she'd begun modeling, she'd always chosen full skirts because they made her look shorter. Now that she appreciated what height could do for a woman's body, she wore whatever she liked. Still, she loved this dress and prayed that the shoes she'd ordered, along with the tennis shoes she could be comfortable in, arrived in time.

"Come on." Helen encouraged everyone to close in for another photo through the mirror. "Let's show Teresa and maybe the guys how gorgeous we are." They all closed in, Corie put her hands on Rosie's shoulders and they tightened ranks around her, Helen leaving a hand free to take the photo.

Then they turned away from the mirror and crowded in for a selfie. Their laughter vibrated the small room.

"Cassie?"

"Oh, it's Diane!" Helen said, parting the curtains and reaching out to pull Grady's mother inside.

Everyone greeted her warmly and she smiled in return, looking a little embarrassed. "I...I have nothing to wear," she said. "To a wedding, I mean." She laughed nervously. "And I have this awkward body."

"There's a dress or a suit to make every woman look beautiful. Let's go find something," Cassie said. Aware of Diane's discomfort, she suggested everyone else make their purchases and take a coffee break while she helped Diane shop. "We'll meet you there."

Cassie's family disappeared to a doughnut shop across the street and she led Diane out to the dresses. "What are you most comfortable in?" Cassie asked.

Diane indicated what she wore. "Pants and sweaters. I so seldom have to dress up." She put a hand to her midsection. "I need something that'll hide bulges. And if it'll make me look like a size ten, so much the better."

"We'll see what we can do. What's your favorite color?"

"I like pink or purple." She winced. "In an 18W."

"Don't wince," Cassie scolded her gently. "Curves are in. You were married a long time. Your husband must have loved them."

Cassie saw immediately that was not something Diane wanted to talk about, so she began to look through the dresses. Nothing seemed quite right, and the only pink one was sleeveless. She moved to another rack.

"Do you ever wear a suit?"

"I wore one to Grady's graduation from the police academy. But that was forty pounds ago."

Cassie found a dark rose suit with a straight skirt and a top with a V-neckline and a peplum. She pulled the hanger out of the lineup and held it for Diane to inspect. "Do you like this? V-necks are always slenderizing and flattering to your face, and a peplum takes pounds off."

"It's very pretty," Diane said, "but shouldn't it be longer to cover my hips?

Won't that little ruffle thing just accent them?"

"That's a mistake a lot of women make. It's really more flattering to go shorter with the jacket." She drew Diane back toward the dressing room. "You try it on, and I bet you'll agree."

Cassie looked through a rack of necklaces while the rustle of clothing came from the dressing room. There was a long few moments of silence, then Diane's voice said in a sort of stunned quiet, "Cassie?"

"Yes?"

"Come in."

Cassie parted the curtains and was pleased to see that she'd been so right. Diane looked incredible. The rose was wonderful for her and gave her beautiful skin heightened color while accentuating her startled brown eyes.

Everything was perfect. The V-neck and the peplum did just what she'd promised they would. Diane looked one, maybe two, sizes smaller, and the suit lent her a distinction that fit her well.

Diane put both hands to her mouth just as Rosie had done. Cassie half expected her to say "I look pretty." When she didn't, Cassie did it for her. "You look gorgeous, Mrs. Nelson." She went up behind her to tug on a sleeve to smooth it. "This is a perfect color for you. We're all going to have our hair done the morning of. Why don't I add you to the appointment?"

"Okay," Diane replied, still distracted by her refection. "Grady won't believe it's me."

"Well, this is what you're capable of. You don't have to look like this all the time, but isn't it nice to know you can?"

Diane's eyes caught Cassie's in the mirror. "I don't feel like myself."

Unsure if that was good or bad, Cassie suggested, "Well, we can keep looking and find something that'll make you more comfortable."

"That's not what I meant." Diane stepped closer to the mirror then turned to look at the back of the suit. "I mean, I've never looked this good. When I was married, my life was all about teaching, and I loved it, but it didn't require that I look…special. Then my husband became ill, so I spent most of my time at home." She expelled a breath and stood back, still studying her image. "It's a little unsettling to discover there's someone inside you that you didn't know was there."

Startled to hear the same thought she'd had about herself last night, Cassie nodded. "I know the feeling. So, what do you think?" Belatedly she looked at the price tag. It was a little "spendy" but not outrageous.

"I think I may wear it every day. I'll take it."

Purchases made, Cassie insisted Diane join her and her family for coffee.

They stood together on the corner, waiting for the red light to change to green and talking about finding the right shoes to go with Diane's suit. Cassie noticed a young man across the street in a long, dark blue raincoat. He stood near the bakery, watching her. Had he had a camera in his hand, she'd have thought the paparazzi had found her, albeit an unusually elegantly dressed paparazzo. Maybe he just recognized her as a model. Or maybe he knew Diane.

"Do you know that guy in front of the bakery?" Cassie asked Diane as the light changed and they began to cross the street. "He's staring at us."

Diane smiled at Cassie, a new ease about her. "I think he's staring at you, Cassidy." As they reached the other side of the street, the guy turned and walked away.

Cassidy paused before following Diane into the bakery, watching the man as he continued to walk, now a whole block away. She didn't care so much if the press knew where she was, except that she didn't want to subject her family to their ruthless intrusions. And she didn't want anything to upset Corie and Ben's wedding.

"WORKING OUT OF an office sounds better and better," Grady said as he and Ben watched the ambulance take away an intoxicated woman who'd driven into a thicket of blackberries. She'd been sick and they'd had to wrestle her out of her vehicle. They were both smelling ripe. "And when we're our own bosses, we won't show up for meetings and end up covering someone else's shift."

"Yeah, we might. But we're almost off shift now," Ben said. "I think we've both got wedding overload. A nice shot of Glenfiddich sounds really good right now."

They drove back to the station. Grady toweled off and pulled on sweat bottoms and an old gray hoody that felt wonderful after the freezing Pacific Ocean. He would shower at home.

"Did you have a chance to look at that office space online?" he asked Ben, who was lacing up a pair of brown boots he'd owned forever. "Imagine being right down the hall from the Beggar's Bay Bistro."

"I did." Ben stood, straightened his jeans and pulled on a thick blue sweater. "It looks good to me. I'd like to actually see it in person, but there won't be time before the wedding. I'll just trust you on it. If you think it's the spot, we'll do it."

"I do," Grady said with confidence. It had everything they needed, and it was affordable. "It's a great location, I'll pay first and last, and we can work out the split later. You just focus on the wedding. I can't believe you couldn't get off the rest of this week. I mean, I understand why I couldn't; it's not my wedding. But you?"

"Captain's shorthanded for the holidays.

Corie and the family are doing everything, anyway. All I do is stand around and agree with whatever she wants."

Grady nodded. "Probably a good idea."

"How's it going with a woman in your house? And such a gorgeous one, at that?"

"Fine. She's easy enough to live with. And, you know, after Celeste, I feel sort of off balance. I'm stepping back for a while. How're you doing with the kids?"

"I think we're doing all right. Probably have to brace myself for trying times when they get a little older. Corie's good with them, though. Has lots of experience with kids from helping out at the foster home for so long. It's just life, you know. Can't protect yourself from everything. Nothing's ever as organized or predictable as we'd like it to be."

Grady knew that for a fact. After choosing a life path grounded in reality, he'd followed a supermodel who'd asked him for help and was now happily ensconced in his house, turning it into some sort of bridal dreamscape.

"True." Grady stuffed his still soaking uniform into a plastic bag to carry to the dry cleaner's. He had several uniform shirts at home and, fortunately, a second set of slacks. "See you tomorrow."

"Right."

He stopped at the edge of the lockers and turned back to Ben. "You probably can guarantee predictability if you just don't get involved with women."

Ben pulled a backpack out of his locker then pushed the door closed with a clang. "I guess, but who wants to pay that price?"

CHAPTER NINE

"THERE'S A BOX by Grady's door," Sarah said, the index finger of her right hand on the steering wheel pointing to the coffin-size box on the mat. "Is that the fabric?"

"Must be." Cassie, her seat belt already unbuckled, turned to send a smile to Helen, Corie and Rosie in the back seat. "Thanks for such a fun shopping trip, guys. I won't bother you for the next few days 'cause I know you'll all be busy, but call me if there's anything I can do." She smiled at Sarah. "Thanks for the chauffeur service, Sarah."

"Anytime. I have a meeting most of the day tomorrow, but call and leave a message, or call Jack if you need me."

Cassie leaped out and started up the walk as Sarah turned around in the driveway. She opened the door, then stepped inside and turned around to drag the box in after her. Though the box was huge, the contents were lighter than the size suggested. Tulle was like gossamer.

Still enjoying the internal glow of having had a morning with her family, and hopefully having made a friend of Grady's mother, she dropped her purse and jacket on the sofa, along with a white sack containing a cherry fritter she'd bought for Grady at the bakery. She hurried into the kitchen for a box knife she'd seen in a pencil cup on the counter, then hurried back to the great room and carefully opened the box. The scent of Josie Bergerac's studio permeated the yards of tulle Louise had carefully packed for her. It took her right back to a Paris garden.

Cassie caught the edge of the fabric and stood, letting it unravel off the bolt. It was relatively unwrinkled, unlike the many yards of ribbon wrapped around a card. It would have to be ironed. While carefully winding the fabric back onto the bolt, she wondered if Grady owned an ironing board and an iron.

She remembered catching a glimpse of a mop and a broom in a utility closet off the kitchen. It was likely that if he had an ironing board, it would be there. She went to investigate.

The closet was small and dark, so she reached a hand in to find the light switch. She flipped it and nothing happened. With the light from the kitchen behind her, she spotted a flashlight on a shelf inside the room and took a step in, reaching for it.

Without warning, the door closed behind her. She yanked on it but it wouldn't give. Struggling to keep her breathing even, she groped for the flashlight but couldn't seem to put her hand on it. Panic tried to take hold.

Then a very logical thought occurred to her. Someone had closed the door. Someone was out there. "Grady!" she shouted with all the air in her lungs. Forcing herself to breathe in and out, and in and out again, she shouted a second time. "Grady!"

The door opened suddenly and Grady stood there, clearly surprised to find her in the closet. And to make the incident that much more awkward, he wore nothing but a towel wrapped strategically around his hips. She couldn't help that her eyes went to it to make sure it was in place. The sight of a powerful chest, wide shoulders and long, strong legs made her more breathless than the closed door had.

"What are you doing?" he demanded, obviously as confused as she was. "You're supposed to be shopping with your family and my mother."

"Grady!" she said, her pulse dribbling back to normal but her breath still a little hard to draw in. "Why did you lock the closet?"

"I didn't. It sticks."

"I'm back because we all found something to wear." Her eyes dipped again. "Except for you, apparently. What are *you* doing?"

He caught her wrist and drew her out of the closet and into the hallway. "Ben and I ended up on the road, covering someone else's shift. A drunk woman got sick all over us." He seemed annoyed that he had to explain. "I took a shower. What are you looking for?"

She became annoyed that Grady was annoyed with her. She folded her arms and said dryly, "Your silver, stocks and bonds, art objects, jewelry…"

"Stop it," he said in a gentle tone out of

sync with the words. "What's the matter with you?"

She wasn't sure. Maybe it was the sweet morning she'd had with her family, a connection she'd dreamed of having her entire life. With strong feelings on the surface, her sudden plunge into the darkness of the tiny room had upset everything inside her. She hadn't screamed, though. She was proud of that. But then, here he was, half naked and quite spectacular. Tangled emotions seemed to have made her cranky.

DESPITE THE FACT that Cassie was almost as tall as Grady, she was so slender that whatever emotional upheaval was going on inside her made her seem fragile and on the brink of a scene like the one they'd played out in the elevator.

Then he realized what had happened and he drew a deep breath, trying to rid himself of a suddenly dark mood brought on, he guessed, by guilt. "I came out of my room and thought I'd left the utility closet door open when I threw my muddy boots in there. So I just closed it, not realizing you were in there. I'm sorry."

She waved away his apology. "It's okay." Her voice was still a little high. "But you need a new bulb in there."

"I know. I've been meaning to change it. Again, I'm sorry."

"Again, it's okay." She expelled air between her lips, sweeping her hands toward the ground as though trying to push down on her fear level. She gave him a small smile. "I was looking for an ironing board and an iron. Do you have such things?"

He smiled more broadly. "Of course I do. Unkempt policemen are frowned upon. But it's in the closet in the kitchen, and the iron is on the shelf in there. What are you going to iron?"

"My fabric and ribbon arrived. The tulle's fine, but the ribbon is wrinkled."

She shifted her weight uncomfortably, her eyes darting everywhere but below his shoulders. It surprised and maybe even flattered him a little that she was traumatized by the towel.

"I thought," he said, unable to resist teasing her, "that you were used to being half naked when you're being fitted for clothes."

"I am used to being half naked." She

studied his collarbone. "I'm just not used to seeing men half naked."

"Really? But Sarah and Corie were saying when we learned you were coming to Texas that the press was full of stories about how you've dated a long line of jocks, celebrities and corporate geniuses."

"Contrary to what you might think," she said with an angle to her chin, her eyes meeting his, "for me, dating doesn't necessarily mean 'seeing each other naked.' And while you have great shoulders, nice knees and kind of big feet, I'm not especially anxious to see anything more, so would you put some clothes on, please, while I get the ironing board?"

She walked away. He smiled as he watched her go, thinking that the look in her eyes betrayed a lively curiosity, despite her claim otherwise. He wondered if it was healthy to be as pleased about that as he was, or if it betrayed an inordinate amount of ego.

He put on jeans and a dark blue Seattle Mariners sweatshirt, and went out to the great room to see what she was up to. She'd found the ironing board and the iron and was busy pressing yards and yards of ribbon in a sort of tropical blue. He peered into the open box and saw a lot of white fabric.

He had the strangest feeling his life would never be the same once she was no longer in it. It would be hard to find the balance of caution and commitment to security that had defined his life, until he'd met Celeste, fallen in love and then learned in no uncertain terms to avoid the pain and humiliation of trusting where trust wasn't warranted. His life had to be about keeping his head.

But then, he'd helped Cassie escape the paparazzi who'd found her in Texas. Just because she'd asked him to. Maybe he just couldn't trust *himself*. From that day to this, his control over anything had been iffy at best.

He hadn't died from that, he thought philosophically. Was he comfortable with it? Definitely not. She was beautiful, usually fun to be around, but possessed of a certain volatility in several areas that made it impossible for him to relax completely and feel free of all the dangerous possibilities. And that was unheard of for him. It seemed unreal.

So why did he hate the thought that she'd be gone in a few days? It didn't make sense. And he always tried to make sense.

"Do you need something to eat?" he asked.

"Uh, oh." With a groan, she set the iron down on its heel. "I forgot to get groceries. I did bring you back a cherry fritter, though. Your mom told me they're your favorite."

He arched an eyebrow in surprise. "She did? Thank you. Did you help her find a dress?"

"It's a suit, and she looks beautiful in it." He was happy that she seemed pleased. "I tried to convince her that her curves are beautiful. I said that your father must have loved them, and she sort of closed down on me. She has a bad self-image. I apologize for asking, but is he responsible for that?"

He shook his head, remembering how difficult the last few years of his father's life had been for his mother. "I don't think he did it deliberately, but he hardly noticed what she did for him during his illness. Just getting from day to day was so hard for him that all he saw was his own struggle—except when she had him take medications he hated and then she became the enemy."

"I'm sorry," Cassie said. "Well, we all love her. And I think she likes me a little better now that she understands I'll be going home. I am sorry about the groceries."

"Not a problem. I'll order pizza." His cheerful expression dimmed. "Anything you don't like on your pizza?"

"Anchovies." She crossed her eyes and made an ugly face that made him smile. "Anything else I don't like, I can pick off."

"Got it. I'll place the order when you're finished."

"Do you have a ladder tall enough to reach the loft?"

He had started away and walked back to her as she returned to ironing ribbon. "I do. To hang the bunting?"

"Yes." Her looked seemed designed to reassure him. "You don't have to do anything, if you can just get me the ladder."

He looked up at the loft railing then back at her. "It's fifteen feet to the bottom of the railing." Grinning wryly, he asked, "Are your legs insured by Lloyds of London?"

"Nothing's going to happen to my legs. While I might not be as cautious with whom I let in and out of my life as you are, I am physically careful. I learned to be that way in photo shoots where the photographer sometimes forgets that models are not all black-diamond skiers or parasailers, or even runners. I'll be fine."

"I'll get the ladder on the condition you let me help you."

"But it's fussy. You'll hate that."

"Did you not hear a thing I just said about being open to whatever you want to do for the wedding? I can deal with it."

She made an apologetic face. It was no wonder, he thought, that she was in such demand as a model. It wasn't just her beauty; she had mobile features, able to project what she felt from moment to moment. And she could go from sadness, to joy, to concern in a heartbeat. "I really didn't know I was going to get you so deeply involved in my life when I asked you to help me escape Texas. I apologize for that."

"You didn't hold me at gunpoint. I left with you because I wanted to. And at this point, your family is composed of most of my friends. We're like one big urban family, so it's hard for one life to not be affected by what happens to another."

Her eyes widened. "I don't want to alarm you, but that's not a very cautious attitude. You might be setting yourself up for a lot of fuss and drama in your life."

"You've already done that for me. I'll get the ladder."

IN THE INTEREST of simplicity—and of not making Grady spend more time two-thirds of the way up a twenty-foot ladder—Cassie didn't swag the fabric, but bunched it loosely and tied it to every third baluster so that the impression was achieved without all the measuring and draping. She worked on her stomach on the floor of the loft, reaching her arms through the balusters to help Grady place the fabric, then tying it with the blue ribbon.

When that was finished, she stood side by side with Grady in the great room, looking up to assess their work.

"It looks amazing," he said. "What's sparkling?"

"The fabric is called Sparkle Tulle. Isn't it beautiful? I thought it would pick up the light and sprinkle it around."

He looked up at the railing and nodded, smiling. "Imagine what it'll look like when the chandeliers are up. It's going to turn this place into a sort of hunting-lodge palace."

"Diametrically opposed terms."

"Life's like that."

He didn't seem to mind. She didn't want to say any more about it for fear he'd notice that glamour was taking over his life. At least for now.

"If you can help me with the stair railing at the top few steps coming down," she said, "I can handle the rest, and you can go order our pizza."

"Works for me."

It occurred to her that he was really getting into this, probably without realizing that he'd crossed over into the fussy side. She said nothing, afraid of alarming him with his own enthusiasm. Although, he had admitted to being pumped.

They worked in harmony, relaxed with pizza when their work was finished and watched an old movie on television. She fell asleep halfway through.

GRADY COVERED HER with the throw on the back of the sofa, put a pillow under her head and pulled off the boots she wore with everything because the shoes she'd ordered still hadn't arrived. He wondered if they'd come in time for the wedding. What would she do if they didn't?

He watched her beautiful face in peaceful repose and knew she'd come up with some solution that was bound to be glamorous and clever. She really was remarkable. It had to be difficult to live her life with such an unpredictable issue always hanging over her head. She couldn't know when someone would sweep her onto an elevator in L.A. or Paris—or inadvertently close a door on her in a room without a light.

Yet she dealt with all of it with good grace, if secretly. She was warm and kind and just about everything a man would want in a woman. Except that she was on the cover of international magazines, in the national news, and her bank account was probably astronomical.

Nobody knew *his* name, except derelicts and perps, and his bank account kept him comfortable but he would never be rich.

He closed his eyes and scrunched down on the sofa so he could lean his head against the back. He tried to make mental notes about supplies for the new office, where to find furniture at a reasonable price, but coherent thought fragmented and drifted away before it could form.

He awoke to being kissed. A small table lamp was lit and there was a glow from the television and the low murmur of dialogue. For an instant he felt confused, disoriented. What was he doing in the living room and why…?

Then he realized that a woman's lips were working gently against his, seemingly trying to get his attention, elicit a response. The woman smelled like a bouquet. Cassie.

It all came back to him, the admission that they held completely different views about life and love, the courtesy they extended one another, anyway, the looks they aimed at each other's backs that said they wished the situation was different.

Every impulse to be careful, to use his head instead of his heart, to remember to think about the future, came to the fore and he caught her arms and held her away. "Cassie," he said softly, the sound loud against the quiet background of the television. "What are you doing?"

She was still under his hands, half sitting in his lap, her hair disheveled, her eyes soft with surprise. "I figured it out," she whispered, her face lighting up with whatever it was. She was like a candle flame in the dimly lit room.

"What?" he asked.

"The thing that's missing in my life. The thing my heart's looking for."

"Yeah?" He hadn't a clue, even while her eyes roved his face with greedy desire and accelerated his heartbeat.

"You," she said simply, straining against his hold to lean forward and kiss his lips. Against them, she whispered, "You're what's missing, Grady."

That was crazy. It couldn't be. Her life was everything his was not. He could not be the missing piece because he couldn't fit into it anywhere.

Somehow that didn't seem to matter. His body responded as though they were perfect for one another. For now, alone in the softly lit living room, he wanted to believe there was a way to be a part of her life and make her part of his. He wanted to argue with himself that that wasn't possible, but he simply hadn't the will.

She lay in his arms, a soft, fragrant bundle of all the wonderful things a woman should be. All the other things about her that were diametrically opposed to everything he believed held no significance at that point in time. His life had been turned into a place of glamour and fuss where there were chandeliers that stood on the floor, fabric that sprinkled light around the room, where his best friend was about to be married to Cassie's sister, and any portent of doom was unrecognizable.

He cupped her head in his hand and returned her kiss, reveling in the delicious softness and artful enthusiasm of her lips, enjoying her ardor and her exploratory nibbles on his bottom lip then his earlobe.

He lay her down on the cushions and showed her every emotion inside him, the piercing heat he'd held back for days now because he knew the danger of playing with fire. He kissed her breathless, letting her know his feelings had depth and breadth and would push both of them beyond the relationship they'd tried to keep in a comfortable place.

As her hands bracketed his face, he felt a love so strong it both frightened him and filled him with a scary sense of happiness entirely new to him. Heaven help him. He was in love with Cassidy Chapman.

And she'd told him he was what her life needed.

She put both hands against his chest and pushed back. Staring into his eyes, hers were wide blue pools of turbulent emotion he couldn't quite define.

"Is this crazy?" she asked, looking as though reality was beginning to descend on her.

He knew about reality. Or, he had once. It was the killer of moments like they'd just shared.

"Yes," he had to admit.

"Then…it's stupid?"

"What is?"

"You and me. Us. Together."

Again he had to be honest. "No."

She blinked and smiled, clearly surprised by his answer. "You don't mind that you're the missing piece of my life?"

"No, I don't mind."

"You kissed me like I'm the missing piece of yours."

"I kissed you," he said carefully, thinking hard, maintaining honesty, "because I love that you want me."

She thought about that a minute and sat up, pushing him back as she did. "But not because *you* need *me*?"

"I love having you around, Cassie. I love your warmth and your sense of humor, and the fact that you love everyone and everything."

"But you don't love *me*? I mean, I know it's only been days but…there it is."

"I don't know," he admitted candidly. "Has it even been a full week yet since you fainted in my arms in Texas? Love comes from the confidence of knowing someone and having experience with how they act and react."

She sighed and her glow seemed to collapse in on itself and disappear. "And knowing they're not going to turn your home and your life into a crazy place."

"You make everywhere a crazy place. You can't help it." He was coming down from the high of finding her in his arms in the middle of the night. He remembered what she'd done to the life he'd once found so comfortable. Did he still miss that life?

He wasn't sure. He couldn't think straight. But just to be safe he said, "And I'm a little more closed off than you are. Maybe it's selfish, I don't know. But it's me. And you've just found your family and your whole life is opening up. You can afford to believe in magic, or miracles, or whatever it is."

Her gaze held depths of wisdom. "So can you. It's not like your life is over, but you're trying to live it as though you're moving into Sarah's assisted-living facility. As though it's time to put all adventure aside and let someone else take charge of the rest of your days."

That hurt a little, but he tried to make light of it. "If I touched you, Jack and Ben would put me in the hospital and possibly I would end up in a nursing home. I'm not sure three days before your sister's wedding is the time for life-altering discoveries."

"I think life-altering discoveries come in their own time." She swung her legs off the sofa, gracefully dodging him as she did so. "But what do I know? You're probably right. What man in his right mind would want to get mixed up with the daughter of a woman who was a drug addict and died in jail? Who fears small, dark places and humiliated herself in a video that's been seen all over the world?"

He stood and caught her arm as she tried to walk away. "This has nothing to do with any of that, and you know it. And, anyway..." He spread both arms in exasperation, feeling as upset as she seemed to be. "If you're afraid of darkness and confinement, why on God's earth would you want to be in love?"

CHAPTER TEN

GRADY AND BEN walked out of the station, heading for their unit while arguing about breakfast. "I'm stuffed," Grady insisted. "And you just snagged a maple bar from the break room. How can you still be hungry after the huge breakfast we had?"

Ben took offense. "You might be sharing digs with a great cook who is so grateful for a place to stay that she offers to send you off to work with a big breakfast, but I live with a woman who's learning to cope with two lively children and is getting married in two days. I get nothing to eat unless I bring it home or steal it from the kids."

"And you're not still full from last night?"

The entire family had filled Grady's great room the night before. His mother had apparently called Cassie just to chat and learned about the impromptu dinner, so she'd volunteered to drop by a dessert. Cassie had been thrilled.

Raspberry cheesecake had always been his favorite and apparently was now everyone else's, too. There hadn't been a crumb left.

He loved the Palmer-Manning family, and the two children Ben and Corie had brought home with them, but he'd been a little unsettled by their constant presence in his home—often all of them, sometimes various combinations of them.

Last night, though, he'd noticed a sort of warm easiness in himself as the big group gathered to eat around a Ping-Pong table Jack and Sarah had brought over. Cassie had spread a fresh bedsheet over it and served dinner after gathering every chair in the house to seat them all.

He'd grown up with a family far less animated, and with less reason for laughter. Or, so it had seemed. It occurred to him for the first time that it was possible the reason for general grimness was not matters from outside but lack of proper attitude inside.

He'd been surprised by how lively his mother had been, already fast friends with Helen Palmer and on cozy terms with Cassie. She'd helped her serve and when Cassie ran out of Parmesan cheese, his mother would have gone home for her own if Cassie hadn't stopped her. He didn't remember her ever being this connected to anyone except her immediate family and her three sisters.

It worried him a little to see his mother and Cassie getting on so well, but in another way, he was glad they liked each other. His mother looked so happy, and Cassie hadn't had a mother. They wouldn't have each other for long, but for a few days, it would be a good thing.

"Dinner last night was outstanding," Ben replied. "But I have a high metabolism."

"Relax. I'll buy you another maple bar."

"Now you're talking."

During their lunch break, Grady and Ben met the Realtor to sign papers for the office rental.

They stood as Melanie left, then Ben turned to Grady and offered his hand. Surprised, Grady reached out to shake it.

"I appreciate what a good friend you've been," Ben said with a gravity that was unusual for him. "I'm so grateful that you went to Texas to help me out, and that you let Cassie stay with you. I know that isn't easy for you."

"What?"

"You know. All the folderol that goes with a houseguest. Especially one who's planning a wedding. I know you hate upheaval. Although you seem more relaxed with it than you usually are. When we had to provide security for the Beggar's Bay Beauty Pageant, I thought you were going to explode on me. Fuss normally gives you hives, but you're taking all this like a champion."

"I promised," he said, rolling up his copy of their contract. He stood and glanced at his watch. "You ready to go?"

"You have a thing for Cassie?" Ben asked, getting to his feet and elbowing him. "You can tell me."

Grady opened his mouth to deny it but after Ben's declaration of friendship, he couldn't lie. "Yeah," he admitted. "But I don't want to talk about it." He headed for the car.

"Why not?"

"Because it's personal."

"I'm like your brother."

"Don't say that. It makes her like my sister. Because if she's Jack's sister and he's your brother, and *I'm* like your brother…"

"Yeah. Complicated. But there's no blood involved—at least on your part—just a strong…connection. What are you going to do about it?"

They'd reached the car and he gave Ben an impatient look over the roof. "Nothing."

"Why not? You are an uncivilized so-and-so, but she can help you with that in no time."

"Hey."

"No, you're right," Ben replied as Grady got into the car. He ducked down to look at him before he continued. "Your problem is that you're too civilized. You've taken all the risky stuff out of the equation for your future. That's not very appealing to a woman."

"How would you know?" Grady demanded as Ben got in behind the wheel. "You've got one woman, and that only happened because you're related to her. Sort of."

Ben frowned at him. "One woman is all

we're allowed, man. You marry two and you go to jail."

Grady let his head fall back as he pleaded with the heavens for patience. "I meant you're not exactly the voice of experience. Anyway, I can't imagine a way Cassie and I could ever be together. Not just geographically but...*any* way."

Ben made no effort to start the car. He stared out the windshield and said, "You'll have to explain that to me."

"No, I won't. Let's just get back to work. Call Dispatch."

"*Would* you explain it to me?"

Completely exasperated, Grady swore. "What are you not getting? She's worth a small fortune. She's experienced international acclaim. She has the kind of...I don't know...presence, I guess it is, that suggests she has the confidence of a woman of the world."

"That all sounds like pluses to me."

"I'm a cop in a little coastal town in Oregon. My bank account often borrows from my savings account when I overdraw. I traveled around Europe as a kid 'cause of my parents, but not as an adult. I've been to Mexico and Canada, but who hasn't?"

Ben turned in his seat to face him. "And you have the presence of a public servant who cares about everyone around him—unless it's a woman, then you run. Why? Is it that you don't want to be hurt again like Celeste hurt you? Because I hate to tell you this, but pain is universal."

Grady yanked off his BBPD ball cap and ran a hand through his hair. Ben was making his head hurt. "I know there's no hiding from pain. But isn't it a betrayal of intelligence to lose yourself in the same game you lost the last time?"

"Well, see, that's where there is a question, because all women are not the same. Even the beautiful ones. To some it isn't a game, it's real. You're the one that's always talking about wanting your life to be real. Well, the *real*ity is, some women play with your affections, like your ex-girlfriend, and some women just want to love you and be loved by you."

Ben shook his head as though unable to find the words to clarify his position. "For all Cassie's wealth and fame, she seems genuine. She loves all the same people we love. So what if she knows all about elegant stuff we've never heard of, and she can command those chandelier things, and fabric from Paris, and flowers from God knows where? She can do that, but she doesn't act like a goddess because of that. She just looks like one."

Exhausted though he'd hardly spoken, Grady said quietly, "But she lives in Paris and New York."

"Wouldn't you like to get to know those places better than the glimpse of Paris you got as a kid?"

"I live *here*. And...I can't see her living here."

"Maybe you shouldn't decide that for her. She seems to like it fine in Beggar's Bay."

"For a lifetime?"

Ben smiled. "So, you *are* thinking in those terms?"

"I'm going to tase you in a minute. *For the sake of argument*, do you think she could live a lifetime in Beggar's Bay?"

"Maybe she could. Her entire family is

here, and if she had a husband and children…"

"Really? Do you see me as a husband? And she has a career that spans continents. Why would she give that up? I mean, she can hop on her father's plane to visit her family here anytime she wants."

"Don't try to read her mind. And don't close yourself off to what following her around could do for your own life."

"What about our business? We aren't even open yet and you're trying to get rid of your partner?"

"No. I'm just saying, if you have to go with her until she fulfills her contracts, it won't kill you to see new places and new things. Meet new people. Loosen you up."

Paris and New York. For long periods. He couldn't see himself there. Though he'd known she was going back some time after the wedding, he just hadn't taken the trouble to think deeply about what it meant. Actually, it didn't require much depth of thought. It meant absence. Loneliness. Loss.

"I think the perfect scenario," Ben said, cutting into his thoughts, "would be that you follow her until her contracts are fulfilled, learn to speak French, buy a beret, consult knowledgeable Frenchmen about how to love a woman. Conventional wisdom is, they're the ones who know. Then, when her contract is met and you're now this accomplished man of style and wisdom, you can come back and resume your place as my partner. We'll clear those trees behind your property, build some homes back there where the elk hang out so that we have a Palmer-Manning compound and be the happiest damn tribe the world has ever seen. We can leave the elk some salmonberry bushes."

Pipedream, Grady thought, but aloud he said, "Manning-Palmer-Nelson compound. And there has to be room for my mom."

"Of course."

CHAPTER ELEVEN

CASSIE STUDIED HER REFLECTION. She was wearing the little black dress she'd bought along with her dress for the wedding. She'd gotten that princess feeling she used to get as a little girl when she was all dressed up for a birthday party, or for church.

Despite the glamorous clothes with the high price tags, her work didn't really give her that. She could make herself look the part, but that princess feeling had to come from inside, from feeling happy.

It still amazed her that she was reunited with her siblings. The happiness that knowledge gave her was impossible to describe. She'd made a decision during a sleepless night that she would fulfill her contracts with Josie and Eterna, and work like a fiend at whatever she could during that period to make enough money so that her foundation would be self-supporting.

Then she was coming back to Beggar's Bay. This was home now. She loved Paris, felt connected to the lifeblood of New York City, but her heart would now always be here. She wondered how her father would feel about life in Beggar's Bay.

She heaved a sigh and clasped a necklace she'd bought at the boutique around her neck. It held three charms—a fleur-de-lis, a heart and a pretty little sparkly crystal. They fell to just below her breasts. She added a pair of one-carat posts she wore all the time, and used a small black Ferragamo makeup bag as a purse.

Mercifully, her shoes had arrived. She hoped Grady wasn't offended by the fact that she might stand as tall as he did, maybe taller.

Grady. She experienced an upsurge of emotion in her chest and swore she saw the crystal sparkle. She put a hand there to push down on sadness at having to leave him. She could stay here and commute to Paris or New York from Salem every few weeks, but she had to drive a couple of hours to get there. And the small airport did make travel more complicated.

She was taking the risk that he'd fall in love with someone else during her absences, but that was a chance every lover took. Of course, the sticking point was that he didn't love her. But she was hoping to change that.

Of course, there was the possibility that he'd lose his appeal for *her*.

She laughed at herself. No, there wasn't. She'd never forget all he'd done to help her, all the kindnesses he'd showed…the way it felt to lean into his shoulder and have his arm close around her. It was that rightness that had been missing for so long.

And that she'd have to learn to live without if she couldn't change his mind.

She smiled at herself then grabbed a short red coat Corie had given her; one of the samples she'd made for her new line.

When Cassie told her she was surprising Grady with dinner out tonight, Corie had insisted she take it. Cassie had wanted to resist, but her sister had hugged her and said, "I'm just so happy to have something to give you."

Who could ever be unhappy with such richness in her life?

She heard the truck pull up and hurried downstairs.

GRADY WALKED IN, noticing immediately that there were no wonderful aromas coming from the kitchen. But the room carried that fragrance the fabric and ribbon had brought with them. He stopped, almost paralyzed at the sight of Cassie coming toward him. She was a vision in simple black that hugged her small but shapely bosom, her tiny waist, then flared to just above her knees, the fabric moving and swirling as she walked, a red jacket hanging from her hand.

Her hair was caught up in curly disarray on top of her head, and her makeup had an aspect of glamour tonight. Unlike the pretty, seemingly happy woman who cooked, watered the plants, moved beautiful ornaments from far-off places across the ocean, this one wore the mantle of celebrity like a second skin. Or, maybe a first one.

"Hi!" she said warmly, taking in the casual jeans and sweater he'd changed into before leaving the station. "I thought I'd take you to dinner tonight as a thank you for all the ways you've helped me this week. The wedding's day after tomorrow, and then I'm leaving on January third, so if we want to relax a little, maybe do a little dancing, tonight is it." She smiled at his look of surprise. "Do you dance?"

"I do," he replied. "In high school, before my father got sick, I took a dancing class with a bunch of friends because we thought it'd be a great way to meet and hold girls. But…" He looked down at himself. "I'm not sure I have anything dressy enough to be seen with you."

"It's just a black dress." She grinned and pointed to her feet. "You'll notice I'm not wearing boots."

"Hey!" Applauding, he went closer as she posed as though selling shoes, pointing one toe, then the other. The heels weren't very high but it didn't take more than a few inches to make her as tall as he was.

She closed the small gap between them so that they were eye to eye. Her topknot of curls gave her a slight height advantage.

"You're not going to try to push me around because you're taller, are you?" he teased.

"Come on, I don't need height to bend you to my will," she joked back. "You've adjusted to glamour and fuss to help me with this wedding. I'll bet you never thought you'd do that."

That was true.

"What about that gray wool jacket I've seen in the guest closet?" She continued, smoothing the shoulders of his sweater. "You look very nice. You just need something to pull it together in a dressy way."

He went to the closet and shrugged into the jacket. He looked at himself in the mirror on the door. All he focused on, though, was her beautiful face over his shoulder, looking on with approval.

"Perfect," she said, hooking an arm in his. "Does the Bistro have dancing?"

"They do. There's also a little supper club on the north edge of town. The dance floor's bigger, but the food isn't as good."

"Are you okay with the Bistro? Then, if you want to, you could show me your new office. But we'd have to take the stairs."

"Sure."

AN UNUSUAL SORT of easiness seemed to take charge of the evening. Because they both knew she was leaving after the wedding, the pressure was off regarding where their relationship might have gone if she'd stayed.

He was relieved that she no longer talked about him being a missing piece in a life that messed with everything he knew to be real.

She ordered scampi and salad. When he hesitated, torn between the surf 'n' turf and something more reasonable since she was paying—and that was something he had to adjust to—she ordered the steak and lobster for him, consulting him only on how he wanted the steak prepared.

"Medium-well," he said to the waiter. When the man was gone, he added to Cassie, "That might constitute pushing me around."

She shrugged it off. "Maybe. But height has nothing to do with it because we're sitting down. I'm just ordering you around on principle. So, while I'm at it, let's dance."

"Sure." He stood with her and, as he followed her to the small floor, he whispered, "But I'm leading."

As they reached the roped-off parquet floor in front of the band, she turned into his arms and wrapped hers around his neck. He credited rugged police training for the fact that his knees didn't give out.

She leaned into him, resting her cheek against his, and expelled a comfortable sigh as he wrapped his arms around her waist. The scent of lilies embraced him. She felt like a whisper in his arms.

"Your mom bought shoes today," she told him, the domestic topic far from the very non-domestic thoughts taking over his mind.

"You are a miracle worker," he said lazily. "She's worn those brown things with the weird heel for a couple of years."

"That's called a wedge." She leaned her head back to smile at him. Her eyes were always so frank, he felt as though he could see into her future. He felt the smallest twinge that it wasn't going to include him. He'd known that from the beginning, but there'd been moments... "And they're very comfortable. But she needed something black for the wedding. They have a small heel."

"Really." He tried to sound interested but he wasn't. At all. "I'm glad *your* shoes came in. Did your tennis shoes come, too?"

"They did. Walking shoes. So I can get in some exercise when the wedding's over."

"Yeah."

"You don't care, do you?"

"No. Except that I'm glad you don't have to wear boots with your dress for the wedding."

"What do you want to talk about?"

"Nothing," he said. At the slight tension he felt in her, he wished he'd thought a minute before answering. He added quickly, "I mean, our conversations usually end in an argument, and this peace is so nice."

"You're right." She rested her cheek against his again. "Let's just pretend that we get along all the time. That we're like some old married couple with nothing to worry about because we know we'll always be there for each other."

He held her a little tighter. "Okay. I like that. Where did I meet you?"

"What?"

"If we're like an old married couple, where did we meet?"

"Ah…" She thought. "In Paris. Buying macarons." There was a tightening of the shoulders on which her arms rested. That's right. Paris was outside of his reality. She added quickly, "You were a French policeman, a gendarme."

He relaxed. "*Mais oui.* That helps make it real for me."

"Maybe you arrested me because I couldn't contain my need for macarons and ran behind the counter, swept every one I could reach into a bag and ran off."

"I can see that, except that I wouldn't have arrested you. If you agreed to share with me, I'd have let you off with a warning. And what was your line of work?"

She knew he expected her to create a different persona. She didn't. This was who she was. "I'm a model. I've had my heart broken by a thoughtless boyfriend, and I'm planning to eat away my troubles."

He stopped moving and tried to read her eyes. She wanted him to know she was proud of who she was, but she didn't want him to think she considered anything his fault. "You were never my boyfriend, Grady. I'm harking back to Paul Preston. Remember? I ate away the whole humiliating incident."

It took him a moment to accept her explanation. He nodded. "Okay. So, we're on the run with macarons. Where are we going?"

"You have friends in Beggar's Bay who are like family. You know they'll protect us from Interpol. That's how we ended up here."

He laughed deep in his throat. "Interpol. Wow. Frenchmen are serious about their cookies."

"And almost everything else. Looks like our food's here." They walked hand in hand back to the table, still stuck in the gendarme/model fantasy.

They talked about frivolous things and ordered champagne with their dessert of pears Charlotte. He leaned toward her on his elbows, the glass dangling from his fingers. "Were you an organized little kid, or is this attention to detail that allows you to plan a wedding something that came to you as an adult?"

She bobbed her head from side to side. "Fifty-fifty. I've always been somewhat organized, but I did get better at it when I started modeling because I had to keep a very complicated schedule that often changed from day to day. Even hour to hour. Now I have a calendar on my phone and refer to it all the time. At least in my other life, I do. Beggar's Bay is a fly-by-the-seat-of-your-pants kind of place."

"Do you think you'd like to live here?" He wasn't sure why the question came out. He hadn't intended to ask it. But there it hung between them, seeming to echo through the room.

She looked as surprised as he felt. "Um… yes. That's my eventual plan. Finish out my contracts, then come back here to live so I can be near Jack and Corie—and all the other members of the family, of course."

She was going to live here. His heartbeat accelerated.

"What about your dad?" he asked. "Doesn't he live in Paris?"

"He told me he's selling the business. Probably won't happen right away, but two of his employees want to take it over." She frowned thoughtfully. "I think he's feeling a little old for all the traveling around."

"Yeah. That must have been frightening."

"It was."

ALL RIGHT, SHE THOUGHT. *I can ask bold questions, too.* "What about you? Do you feel any need to get around a little? See New York? Visit Paris as an adult?"

His eyes leveled on hers. This was a dangerous game they played. What if he simply said no? What would she do then?

"I'm beginning to consider it," he replied. "I could take a tour. Maybe backpack around."

A little chill of excitement ran up her spine. "If I'm between shoots, you can visit me. I'll take you to my favorite places. Buy you a macaron." She felt like it took every breath she had to speak those words. Her voice sounded pinched.

It was a nice thought. Though, as strong as her feelings now were, just an occasional visit from him made the next few years stretch out emptily, despite all she had to do.

As the evening wore on, the music began to slow and became romantic, and a little sad. Sinatra at his moodiest. The violinist tucked the instrument under his arm, held the bow aside and sang into the mike. "'You're nobody...'" His voice was scratchy and low, the music seeming to come out of him as though filtered through his own loss.

Grady stood, caught her hand and led her onto the dance floor again. "It'd be a shame not to show off that beautiful dress." This time, he danced with her as someone who *had* taken lessons, with steps and flourishes that hadn't been learned from his mother or his friends.

Cassie felt his body in contact with hers from her cheek to her knees. They fit beautifully together. Like Fred and Ginger. On a far less professional level, perhaps, but in perfect harmony, feeling the music together, connected by more than their arms wrapped around each other.

Grady stopped suddenly in the middle of the floor, his eyes lazily perusing her face. "What if I did come and visit you in Paris?"

Her heart experienced that bongo beat again. She didn't want to frighten him with excitement. "That would be nice. I think you'd like it more than you expect."

"And you're sure you're coming back?"

"Positive."

He put an arm around her shoulders and

squeezed her to him as he walked her back to the table. "Want to see our office?"

"Yes." She withdrew her credit card, placed it on the little salver and signaled the waiter.

"Do you have furniture yet?" Cassie asked Grady.

"Nothing. Except the blue thing my mother brought home from Reno." He put both hands over his face. "I have to find an excuse to hide it there."

"You don't have to hide it. It'd be perfect for supplies." When he looked doubtful, she added, "Records you won't want to have out on your desk, and the drawers with the locks would be perfect for those things you should stash, like weapons or cameras." She grinned. "Or the macarons you bring back with you from Paris."

The waiter returned her credit card and the transmittal, which she signed and handed back to him. She snatched up her purse and coat, and Grady followed her to the corridor.

She stopped in front of the elevator doors, hesitated a minute, then sighed and pushed through the door that led to the stairs instead.

"I'd like to give the elevator another try. Especially when we're only going down one flight. But I hate to ruin this beautiful evening with a screaming fit."

"It wouldn't be so alarming now that I know what to expect from you on an elevator. And in a utility closet."

She dismissed that subtle dig with a look. "I didn't scream in the utility closet. I'm very proud of that."

"You should be. And you were pretty controlled the night the power went out." He followed her downstairs. "You're going to defeat this again."

"Right or left?" she asked, opening the door onto the second floor.

"Right," he replied. "Then right again at the corridor." From there he led the way to the third door along the hall, and stopped at the oak door with a window in it trimmed in glass squares. He unlocked the door and held it aside for her.

"I love the colors," she said, walking into the middle of the room and stopping to look around. "Instead of all those landlord-beige places, this is really pretty. Blue-gray carpet. Gray walls with white trim. Is this your office?"

"This was all Ben's idea, so he should choose. Shouldn't he have the front office?"

"Usually you have to go through secretaries and underlings to get to the boss." Without heat, the offices were cold and Cassie shrugged on her jacket. "Though the front office is a little bigger. Whichever one he chooses, I'd place your desk facing the door and put your armoire at the wall behind you. It'll look wonderful with these colors." She wandered back to the front office. "And, you know that leather love seat you have under the window in my room?"

"Yeah?"

She pointed to the front wall. "Put it right there and you have a perfect place for clients to wait."

"After the wedding, I'm going to check out secondhand places for furniture. Jack got us three desks and office chairs from the old community college building he's restoring. And the Realtor wasn't sure the fridge worked, so we'll have to see about that."

"What are you going to do for computers and office machines?"

"We'll get by with our laptops and our phones for now, but I'm sure we'll want something more sophisticated eventually."

"When are you going to be officially open for business?"

"Probably February first. We'll need January to get the office together, get the word out that we're here. Ben has some personal things at home to take care of—setting up the kids' rooms and enrolling them in school."

"That's a pretty big order for him. New family, new business."

"Yeah. But he's the most together guy I know. He'll have it mastered in no time." He turned the light off in the smaller office as they passed through to the front.

"Do you think anyone really masters family?" she asked, stepping out into the hall, waiting for him to flip the front office light off and close and lock the door. "Particularly children?"

"Maybe 'mastered' was the wrong word," he agreed as they walked side by side to the stairway. "I guess I meant that he'll learn to adjust. And become really good at being a father. He has a gift for doing whatever he's determined to do."

Cassie stopped in front of the elevators. She turned to Grady, drew in a breath and then expelled it. Everyone else she knew was able to do what they were determined to do. "I'm going to try it," she said, staring at the elevator doors as though they had claws and fangs.

"Okay. I've got your back," he said. "Would holding you make it worse?"

She couldn't imagine having his arms around her would make any situation bad, but this was something over which she had little control, even though she tried hard to fight against it.

"No." She pushed the button. "If you put your arms around me, I'll put myself in Paris where I met a handsome gendarme in the bakery. It'll be my happy place."

"Let's do it."

The doors parted to reveal two elegantly dressed couples Cassie had seen in the restaurant. The couples moved back for them and Grady put an arm loosely around Cassie's shoulders.

The doors closed.

Panic came and went as though unsure how to maintain a hold on her. The doors closing tightened everything inside her, but Grady's hand on her shoulder moved gently, caressingly, and she relaxed. Still, the closed doors were right in her face, preventing her from leaving, and the space was so small, the sound of the elevator very loud.

She heard laughing conversation going on behind her and remembered that Grady said he might like to visit her in Paris. She imagined the bakery she loved so much just a few blocks from her apartment. She saw Grady in a gendarme's uniform holding a plate of colorful macarons in front of her.

The bell dinged, the elevator bounced a little and stopped, and the doors parted. The couples behind them had to walk around her. She stood there, silently congratulating herself on the accomplishment.

Grady wore a wide smile and fist-bumped her. "All right!" he said. "Well done! But, you know, we should walk out. There are people wanting to get on."

Basking in the glory of having ridden

in the elevator without screaming, Cassie had failed to notice the three young women dressed for evening, clearly on a girls' night out. They waited to go upstairs.

She apologized and exchanged smiles with them as they laughed and got into the elevator.

Then one of them gasped; a beautiful brunette with a short do and wide, dark eyes. "Cassidy Chapman?" she asked softly, blinking then leaning a little forward as she stared into her face. "The supermodel? In Beggar's Bay? Oh, my God. Oh, my God!"

Other people in the lobby noticed the commotion or heard her name and came to cluster around her as she signed one woman's shopping list, another's address book and the third's tissue.

"What happened in Ireland?" the small blonde of the group asked frankly.

Cassie related the story, leaving out the part about her claustrophobia. "I didn't know she was deaf when I shouted at her. I was tired and anxious to get home to my family. It was bad behavior, but I apologized and she accepted."

They nodded. "Of course," the brunette said. "We knew there was more to it than SAN says. Preston was such a jerk to cheat on you." She turned back to smile at Grady, her manner admiring and flirtatious. "Who's this?"

"Grady Nelson," she said. "One of Beggar's Bay Police Department's finest."

"Oh." The tall redhead with them looked him up and down. "I thought he was a model you'd brought with you from Paris."

He shook her hand. "She prefers dark-haired men," he said. "I'm her landlord. Please excuse us. You ladies have a wonderful evening." He caught Cassie's hand and pulled her with him across the lobby and out the door.

CHAPTER TWELVE

"I'M SORRY ABOUT THAT," she said as they drove toward home, neon lights in the few blocks of downtown brightening the darkness. "Even small towns have fashionistas. And the redhead and the brunette seemed to like you."

He sighed theatrically. "I know. It's the fair hair. You really don't know what you're missing with your fascination with dark-haired men. And the bod, of course, thanks to the police department's gym. All in all, my babe appeal gets to be a burden sometimes."

She was laughing before he'd finished. He pretended hurt feelings and demanded, "What? You don't think I'm cute?"

She stopped smiling to study him seriously, a light still in her eyes. "No," she said as he turned up Black Bear Ridge Road. "'Cute' is not the word I'd use. And 'handsome' isn't quite right because sometimes you have these sharp, dangerous moments when handsome just doesn't cover it."

"Dangerous?" He glanced quickly at her. "Me?"

"Emotionally dangerous," she clarified. "Like a woman could get lost in you." She paused as they drove into darkness, nothing lighting the road but the splay of his headlights. Then the almost-finished construction site of the senior retirement home appeared on the right and the school on the left. As they moved on, darkness descended again and she added quietly, "Or, maybe, find herself in you. Either way, the notion's scary."

Several heartbeats passed in the darkness. "Like I'm someone's missing piece?" He caught her hand that rested between them on the seat and kissed it. His lips were warm and dry as he kissed it again then let it go.

"Exactly like that." She spoke on a gusty breath and put her hand on his knee. "Oh, Grady."

"Almost home," he said, his voice low and tight. He turned into his driveway, screeched to an awkward halt and turned off the car.

Cassie flew sideways, wrapping her arms around his neck, finding his mouth in the shadowy confines of the truck and kissing him until she couldn't breathe. He kissed her back with the same depth of emotion, the same out-of-control need to take in as much of her as he could.

She felt one hand under her short jacket, caressing her back through her dress, the other hooked around her knee, holding her to him.

GRADY WAS ABOUT to lose his mind. He wasn't at all aware of coherent thought, ignoring the flashing *Warning! Warning!* lights in his head. He was more absorbed in the wonder of her body eagerly pressed against his, her lips wandering along his throat, to his ear, nibbling lightly on his earlobe. Her fingers caught in his hair and held as she stole every breath from his body.

She raised her head slightly, loosed her grip on his hair, and even while he tried to pull her back, she pushed against his shoulder and said in disbelief, "Oh, geez! What are they doing here?"

"Who?" he asked, not really caring, dropping kisses on her clavicle.

"My father," she replied. "And your *mother*."

"What?"

They knocked heads as she ducked to slide off his lap and he raised his head to look toward the house. He spotted his mother's Mini Cooper, which he hadn't noticed when he pulled in. And, on the other side of it was a simple coupe he also hadn't noticed. He strained to see through the windshield.

Standing under the overhanging deck, in the path of the truck's headlights that had yet to turn off, stood a tall, white-haired man in jeans and a dark gray stadium jacket. Standing next to him was Grady's mother, but he had to look twice to recognize her. Her hair was straight instead of its usual curly, and kind of fluffed out and a little punky. He wondered absently how she'd done that. And she wore a long, dark blue coat he'd never seen before, held tightly around her against the cold evening.

"Dad!" Cassie cried. She jumped out and appeared in the path of the truck's lights, running into the man's arms. The pickup lights went out and only the spotlight above the side door shone.

Grady got out of the truck, lamenting the loss of the evening's intimacy.

Cassie caught her father's arm and led him inside the house while Grady followed with his mother. The moment reminded him of the night he'd brought Cassie home. Cassie and her father stopped in the foyer, and Grady, his mother at his side, looked into the questioning eyes of Donald Chapman.

Cassie made introductions. Grady offered his hand and Chapman took it in an impressive grip. "Thank you for helping Cassie," he said. "She told me about running from Texas, then you offering her the loft for the duration of her stay."

"Mostly, it's been my pleasure. I mean, in the first place, what man doesn't dream of running off with a supermodel?" he said. Donald's ice-blue gaze said no decision had been made on his worthiness yet. "And in the second, she's an excellent cook. But then, I guess you know that."

"I do," Chapman said then questioned, "You said 'mostly' a pleasure?"

Grady smiled. "You must also be aware that she tends to…uh…take action, even when it involves someone else, without a lot of thought, and without consulting that someone else."

Chapman seemed to understand. "That's how I was hired to install a computer system for Le Sacré-Coeur School for Girls in a poor area of Paris. For free."

Grady nodded understanding. "And how is it that you're here with my mother?"

"She's brought you an orange-cranberry bread," Chapman replied. Diane dutifully held up a brick-shaped package, wrapped in foil. "I had arrived just before her with a wedding gift for Corie and Ben."

"But she has…" Grady began, about to add "a key" when his mother's eyes grew enormous and he suddenly understood the cautioning look. He thought quickly. "She has a very hospitable nature. Let me take your coats. Wine or coffee?"

She could have brought him inside, but had been reluctant to?

Donald laughed. "I'm afraid wine would put me to sleep."

"I'll put the coffee on," Cassie said and

then turned to his mother with a smile. "Orange-cranberry bread would go really well with that." Diane handed it over.

Grady led Donald into the great room and detoured to the guest closet with his coat.

"Couch is comfortable," he said when he turned to find the man standing in the middle of the room.

"How is she?" Donald asked, lowering his voice. "She told me she isn't upset about the Ireland thing, but I'm sure she has to be."

Grady encouraged him again to sit. "I think she was at first," he said, also speaking quietly, "but her brother and sister don't care. None of us does, so she's getting over it." He took the chair at a right angle to the sofa.

"Good. She works very hard at what she does and has never been one to think of herself as better than anybody. I was so happy for her that Jack found her."

"We all had a great time in Texas."

"Yes, Cassie told me you were there, too."

"I'd just been dumped by a girlfriend and Ben..." he said with a philosophical shrug. "He'd gone there to talk to Corie..."

That was true. Poorly detailed, but true. "He's my partner in the police department here. He felt sorry for me, needed help with something and invited me to Texas."

"Cassie tells me she fainted in your arms when she got there."

"And that will always be one of my fondest memories. She hadn't eaten anything before her flight out of Ireland and, despite how tough she is, she was pretty fragile."

Donald nodded, watching him but not saying anything, so he went on. "You seem to know all about how we got here. Amazing plane, by the way."

"Thank you."

"I think she's enjoying Beggar's Bay. She said you're thinking of retiring."

"I am. My work was fun for a long time, but now I need a less hectic pace." He seemed to think back. "I remember loving Beggar's Bay when I lived here with Cassie, Corie. And Jack's mom."

"Do you have somewhere to stay or would you like to stay with us? I'm sure Cassie would love that."

"Thank you. I appreciate that."

There was a moment's silence while

Donald's expression changed to one of regret. "Cassie's mother was a lovely woman when she was sober, but, for whatever reason, she couldn't manage to live that way very long. Even for her kids or for me." He looked into Grady's eyes. "Are you wondering how a drug counselor could so betray a client by falling in love with her?"

Grady leaned back. "I don't feel qualified to judge anybody. And, as a cop, I see a lot of things that defy understanding or explanation. Life's tricky."

"We just fell in love. For a while it was pretty great. She stopped using and I got to know her wonderful kids. Unfortunately it lasted just long enough for Cassie to be born, then the stress of having to cope with real life and a new baby did her in and she started using again.

"When Cassie was six months old, I told Charlene I was leaving and taking the baby with me. She called her advocate at Adult and Family Services and put on a great front of being the perfect woman and mother, and I was denied full custody.

"I left. Moved to Maine. I learned Charlene had killed her boyfriend, and the kids were being sent back to their fathers. So, I did get my daughter, though under sad circumstances."

Grady decided he liked Donald Chapman. He was mistaken about what had happened then, but it wasn't Grady's place to clarify that. "She often talks about what a happy childhood she had with you. In fact, she feels guilty about it because Jack and Corie had such a hard time for a while."

Grady's mother appeared with two plates holding slices of her orange-cranberry bread. He stared at her for a minute, thinking she looked like someone else's mother. His had never been this fashionable. She'd taken the coat off to reveal a red sweater and black slacks. The sweater had a fancy collar with wooden buttons that seemed to button nothing. Interesting concept.

"Thanks, Mom." Grady stood to pull out the rocker she usually preferred so that she could sit with her back to the fireplace. "This bread sustains the Beggar's Bay police and fire departments during the holidays," he told Donald.

"I can't sit yet," Diane said. "I'm supposed to find out if you want her caramelly coffee or the usual stuff you drink."

Donald's eyes widened. "Don't tell me she brought that dulce de leche stuff with her?"

"She claims she never travels without it."

"Then, I'll have some. I've learned to like it, too."

Grady pulled his mother back. "You sit and entertain Donald—"

"Don," Donald corrected. "Please."

"Don, with stories about Beggar's Bay. He lived here for a while. I'll help Cassie with the coffee."

He noticed that she smiled shyly at Don. The world was filled with wonders.

CASSIE UTTERED A little cry of surprise when she was suddenly spun around and inclined sideways. She gripped the arms that suspended her. Grady's. "What are you doing?" she demanded on a giggle.

"It's called a dip," he said gravely.

"And why didn't you execute this dip on the dance floor earlier?"

"There wasn't room. And I think it goes with the tango."

Still hanging from his arms, she reminded gravely, "But we haven't tangoed."

He brought her up swiftly, theatrically, so that they were face-to-face, their lips barely an inch from each other's. Her hair had fallen from its artful arrangement atop her head and was in disarray all around her.

"We have tangoed around each other," he said with a deliberately devilish quirk to his eyebrow, "since the day I brought you here. I'm tired of it."

She couldn't breathe as all her body's processes halted. But her senses worked. He smelled of that spicy aftershave he always used, held her with a strength that was exhilarating while making her feel completely safe, and he was a sight to behold—a hank of old-gold hair fallen onto his eyebrow, pale eyes with their dark rims completely focused on her, lips firmly together as though preparing to make a statement. He said, "On New Year's Day, immediately after the wedding, we're going to figure out when I'm going to visit you in Paris. I'm wild about you, Cassie." He looked into her eyes then crushed her to him. "Meanwhile, your dad's going to hang out with us for the wedding."

She hugged him back fiercely, so happy he didn't mind accommodating yet another of her family, ecstatic that he wanted to visit her. "Oh, thank you, Grady. He can have the loft and I'll sleep on the couch."

"No, he can have my room."

As he placed a hand to her cheek and kissed her, she felt that every ounce of his energy was entangled with every ounce of hers. But a little cautionary corner of her brain said to her, *"Wild about you" isn't the same as "I love you," is it?*

She reasoned that she wouldn't want him to say "I love you" if he didn't mean it.

If he's wild about you, why doesn't he mean it?

She turned off the little voice in favor of living the moment. This was almost the end of the old year, and the end of her old life. Well, she might have to do a lot of the same things, but she'd be different inside. She had a father, a brother, a sister. And a man she was not afraid to admit she loved.

CHAPTER THIRTEEN

On New Year's Eve, Cassie's call to Denise confirmed that the flowers were on their way. She took the rest of the ribbon to the florist at Beggar's Bouquet. Denise showed her the small basket whose handle she would wind with ribbon for the flower girl, and told her to try not to worry, that despite the shortage of time, she'd done hundreds of weddings and all would be well.

Cassie stopped at Robertson's Party Supplies and bought napkins, paper cups, two sizes of paper plates, and plastic wine glasses. She rented a couple of white table covers.

In an uncharacteristically edgy mood, she went grocery shopping. Judging by the snack trays she'd prepared the other day from the contents of Grady's fridge, and his preference for cherry fritters, she guessed non-fat, gluten-free and dairy-free were not priorities. She was enjoying having time to cook.

She wasn't sure what was wrong with her, unless it was Grady's insistence that he was "wild about" her. She tried to be cheered by the fact that the details of the wedding were under control, but she couldn't stop thinking about the flimsy nature of that declaration. The kiss had felt very genuine, and he wanted to visit her in Paris. He even seemed pleased that she'd be coming back to Beggar's Bay to stay. She was in love—even if it had only been a week. The time between Christmas and New Year's Day was charmed, alive with miracles and magic. But was he in love, too?

She understood that his inclination toward realism was hard to fight, particularly because of who she was and how she lived.

She was the woman who'd made him leave the Texas Christmas get-together early, who'd invited herself into his life by having nowhere to go when they got to Beggar's Bay. She was the one who'd scared him with her reaction to the elevator and turned his home into a wedding warehouse. She'd put him on top of a ladder then awakened him in the middle of the night with her own desire.

He'd known that however much she wanted and needed him, she'd change his life forever. And he wouldn't want that.

She'd faced that realization several times over the past few days, but it seemed to put her in a particularly dark place today. It took her to the past.

She knew with certainty that it was impossible to make someone love you. Her own mother, for example. She didn't remember her, but she knew that drugs had been more important to Charlene than her own children. And some of her father's girlfriends had been kind to her, but others had resented her presence in his life and hadn't cared to get to know her.

She'd met some wonderful men while modeling, but none she'd considered interesting enough, or desirable enough, for closer contact. Some had wanted her body, her money, or to share her spotlight. Fortunately she'd been clever enough to see through them.

There was nothing false about Grady, but

it seemed hard for him to believe the same was true about her.

She turned onto the road that led to Grady's home, feeling grim. It wasn't like her to inhabit a bad mood for any length of time, but it had been an unusual week. She had to cut herself some slack.

She waved at the FedEx deliveryman who had just left Grady's driveway. She wondered what had arrived and found she didn't really care. Her mood was darkening further.

That was probably why the sight of the young man in the long raincoat who'd been watching her two days ago made suppressed anger rise out of her like shrapnel out of a detonated bomb. She screeched the truck to a stop as she spotted him looking out from behind a tree. He had the grace to look embarrassed as he took her photo.

She ran out of the truck and straight for him. He didn't seem to know what to do. He held the camera in front of him, apparently thinking it would give him some protection. But all the years of having to be polite to the paparazzi so they wouldn't take an ugly photo of her, or having to tolerate their pesky presence so they wouldn't report she was a harridan, came to the fore. Well, that was no longer a concern. The whole world thought she was a dragon. What did it matter now?

He watched her come at him, his mouth in a startled O as he clutched the camera to his chest. She yanked it from him and threw it to the ground. "You'll get out of here if you know what's good for you!" she shouted, backing him up against the tree he'd hidden behind.

He was slightly shorter than she was and clearly so astonished that he didn't fight back. "I'm here for my sister's wedding and if I see you there…" She smacked both hands on his shoulders to convince him that she spoke the truth. "I will personally beat you with your own camera!"

"But I…" he tried to say, sidling away from the tree. She didn't listen. She shoved him backward again. Surprised, he tripped and rolled down the slope until a fallen tree stopped him. She slid down sideways and tried to stop before she hit him, but had too much momentum. She fell on top of him and they screamed together.

"I want you gone!" she yelled at him, sitting up and ripping leaves from her hair and shoulders. She grabbed the lapels of his coat and shook him. "Nothing and no one is going to spoil this for my sister and my family! No one!" She scrambled to her knees and tried to yank him up, too, but he was too heavy.

"Miss Chapman!" he said, his voice a little shrill and desperate. "I—"

"I don't want to hear it, you camera monkey!" She tried to pull him up again, and he pushed himself against the log with one hand while trying to dislodge her hand on his coat with the other.

GRADY WAS PAYING for two coffees at the cart near the edge of town when he heard Ben shout his name. He turned and saw Ben's furious beckoning. Great. His mocha was going to get cold again. What was it this time? He wasn't going into the blackberry bushes again. It cost him thirty dollars to get his uniform cleaned and free of stickers. And he was truly sick and tired of dealing with petty disputes. Why couldn't people just learn to get along, already? Because it was a challenging world and if you didn't take a fighting stance, the other guy would hit you first.

Cassie would hate that philosophy, but he knew it to be true. He slapped lids on the cups and ran back to the car, hot coffee bouncing through the drinking holes and burning his hand.

"What?" he demanded of Ben. "Traffic accident? Domestic?"

"Um...seems to be an assault." Ben got back in the car, secured his belt and started it up. Grady placed their coffees in the console's holder and buckled up.

"On the docks?"

"No."

Grady turned to look at Ben. He was being deliberately evasive as he backed out of the parking spot and started up Black Bear Ridge Road.

"Where?" he asked. There wasn't much up this road. He knew that because he lived at the end of it. "The crew building the assisted-living facility?"

"No." Ben shot him a glance. "Dispatch gave me your address."

"What? No one's home. Cassie had errands to run and her dad's driving around with my mom."

"Well, it sounds as though Cassie's now home and beating the crap out of some photographer. A FedEx truck driver called it in."

"Oh, God."

On one level he couldn't imagine that. On another he knew her to be full of surprises.

Ben screeched to a halt just before Grady's house. The FedEx truck had pulled off the road and the driver was pointing down the slope to the creek.

Grady jumped out of the car and saw that Cassie was indeed slapping someone around near the bottom of the slope. Right off the road beside him, he saw a camera lying in several pieces atop a fern.

He crab-walked down the slope, Ben right behind him. Cassie seemed to be trying to pull the man to his feet but she didn't quite have the muscle, and the man was scrabbling in the mud, trying to fight her off. Both of them were filthy.

Grady reached for Cassie's arm and was rewarded with a backhand to his shin and then, as he leaned over, an elbow to his throat.

"Cassidy!" he shouted.

The action stopped as though a video had frozen. She looked up at him in complete shock, mud smeared across her face and in her hair. "What are you doing home?" she demanded.

"We got a call that you were assaulting someone," he said, caught between dark amusement and disbelief.

"I am!" she said, pulling herself together. She gave the man lying in shock on the ground a fist to his ribs.

He groaned and curled into a fetal position. "Miss Chapman, please listen!"

"That's enough, Cassie." Grady put both hands under her arms and lifted her to her feet while Ben lent the other man a hand up. Grady had to put himself between them to prevent Cassie from landing another blow.

"The paparazzi are not going to ruin Corie's wedding!" she shouted, reaching around Grady to stab an accusatory finger in the photographer's direction. "He's out of here if I have to put him in his car myself!"

The man in question was caked in mud from head to toe and all over his elegant coat. There was a scratch on his face and his hands were bloody, as though he'd landed a punch.

"Did you hit her?" Grady demanded of the man, turning to Cassie to look her over. She was muddy, but didn't look injured.

The man appeared exhausted. "No, I didn't. She stepped on my hand."

"Where's your car?" Ben asked.

"I don't have one," the man replied, trying to brush off his coat but succeeding only in getting his hands even muddier. "We came in a cab."

"You and the other paparazzi?"

Sighing heavily, the man shifted his weight and replanted his stance. "I'm not a photographer. I'm a lawyer. A law student, actually. Oliver Browning."

"He's lying!" Cassie accused. "He has a camera."

"It's Mrs. Manning's camera."

The Manning name stopped all of them. Cassie's eyebrows drew together. She and her siblings had all once been Mannings, but none of them used that name now. Jack was a Palmer, Corie's last name was Ochoa and about to change to Palmer, and Cassie's last name was Chapman. "What do you mean? Who is Mrs. Manning?"

He shrugged inside his coat as though trying to realign his battered body. "Eleanor Manning, my client," he said. "Your grandmother."

"I...DON'T HAVE a grandmother," Cassie said weakly.

Oliver nodded, studying her with caution. "Yes, you do. She and your grandfather lost track of your mother when you were little. She only just found you when she saw you in the news. But I should let her tell you about it. I left her by the house. She wanted photos of your meeting her for the first time, and I heard you coming. I figured it had to be you since you're the last house on the road. So I got behind the tree to get a candid shot." He put the back of his hand to the scratches on his face and just held it there. "Not such a great idea as it turned out."

They all stood in silence then Grady said, "Are you going to press charges against Cassie for assault?"

"What? No," Oliver replied. He glanced at Cassie then looked away. "Of course not. I think I understand her reaction."

"Good. That's generous of you, Mr. Browning." Grady pushed Cassie gently toward the slope. "Then let's get you to the house so you can meet your grandmother. Maybe get cleaned up a little bit. Maybe a lot."

Cassie let Grady help her up the slope because she seemed to have zero propulsion abilities on her own.

I have a grandmother, she thought in disbelief. *I thought there was no one else but Jack and Corie and me.*

When they reached the flat driveway, Cassie stopped, frightened anew. Now there was someone else who'd waited a lifetime to meet her, and what was she going to think of the granddaughter who'd beaten up her attorney?

"Relax," Grady said gently, reading her mind. "She's going to love you."

"I assaulted her lawyer."

"He's not pressing charges, and she probably didn't see all that from up here, anyway. She'll be proud of you that you..." He hesitated and she knew he was trying to put a positive spin on it. "That you can take such good care of yourself. Come on."

By the time they reached the middle of the driveway, Cassie could see a tall, slender woman in a red raincoat, knee-high boots with tack detail and a sou'wester hat. Snow-white hair was visible below the hat.

The woman took several steps out from under the cover of the overhang and smiled tentatively at Cassie. Cassie wanted to smile back but her bottom lip quivered and her face scrunched up. This was the woman once removed from the mother she couldn't remember. She was a connection to the past.

The woman opened her arms and came toward her. Cassie ran into them. Eleanor Manning didn't seem to mind the mud.

GRADY UNLOCKED HIS door and ushered both women and Oliver inside while Ben called in to the station. Cassie turned to him, her expression still startled. "Will you call Corie and Jack, and ask them to come over?"

Ben made two more calls.

When he was finished, Cassie introduced him and Grady to Eleanor Manning.

The woman hugged Ben. "You're Jack's adopted brother," she said. "I'm so happy to meet you. Is this another brother?" She extended a hand to Grady.

"Only in spirit," Ben explained with an expression of fondness they seldom betrayed to one another. "He's my partner on the Beggar's Bay police force."

She looked from one to the other, seeming a little perplexed. "So there's something between you, Grady, and my granddaughter?"

"Tenancy," Grady said. Well, it was a half-truth. "I helped her leave Texas when the paparazzi found her, and since Corie was about to be married here, it made sense that she stay with me." He pointed to the loft. "That's her space."

"I see." She looked upward. "Oh, that bunting is beautiful."

Ben took her hand. "It was so nice to meet you. Grady and I have to get back to work, but your other grandchildren are on their way. We'll probably see you tonight."

"I'll look forward to that."

"Are you going to be okay till your brother and sister get here?" Grady asked Cassie.

"I think I'll be fine. I may have to open the bottle of Gewürztraminer, though. And, oh, I forgot! I've got a truck full of groceries."

"Ben and I'll get them in. I'll check with you in a little while and see what you want to do about dinner."

She put her arms around his neck and held on for a minute. He was big and solid, and her head and her world were spinning. Then she remembered he probably wasn't comfortable with the hug. She drew back. "Sorry," she whispered.

"Did I complain? You're sure you're going to be okay?"

"I am. They'll be here soon. Go back to work."

Cassie directed Oliver to Grady's bathroom, sat her grandmother—her *grandmother*!—on the sofa and brought her a glass of wine. Then she hurried upstairs to clean herself up. She caught a glimpse of herself in the mirror and was horrified. She was a physical mess, and she thought that the mess she was inside showed through, too.

She showered, washed her hair and then wound the partially dried mass into a knot. She changed into her jeans and yellow sweater. By the time she came down, Jack and Corie were arriving in Jack's truck.

Both looked astonished and nervous as Cassie made introductions. Eleanor cried a little more, Jack and Corie moving to sit on either side of her on the couch. Even Oliver, in Grady's police department sweats, looked emotional.

"I've wanted to find you for so long," Eleanor said, composing herself. "But I had no information. And even just twenty years ago you couldn't find everything online like you can today."

"How *did* you find us?" Jack asked.

Eleanor smiled sympathetically at Cassie. "It was the news story about you," she said, reaching across the angle that separated the chair from the sofa and patting her knee. "Oh, don't look horrified. I know what happened. I talked to your friend Fabiana."

"You did?"

"I called, trying to reach you, and she explained what had really happened that night in Ireland, and how you'd heard from your siblings and gone to Texas to meet them. So, I called Texas and spoke with Teresa. She told me you'd all come here. She had your email address but not your physical address, so I told her not to tell you I was coming." She looked suddenly reticent. "You know. On the chance you wouldn't want to see me."

"What?" all three asked simultaneously. Then Jack added, "Why?"

"Because I'm the mother of the woman who was such a bad mother to you." The words were spoken with a rasp in her voice, tears held at bay.

"She wasn't all bad," Jack said, putting an arm around her shoulders. "There was a brief period of time when she was clean and sober, when she was nice to be around. And then..." He hesitated. Cassie knew the words were still hard for him to say. Corie reached across their grandmother to touch his hand. "You bear no guilt in that, Jack," she said firmly.

Eleanor covered their hands with hers. "I know she went to jail for you. When I was trying to find her, I came upon the prison record and there was an addendum attached that explained what happened, assuring the court of your innocence."

Jack accepted that with a nod. "Right. I have to make that adjustment every day. I just so wish it could have been different."

Eleanor leaned a shoulder into his. "I know, but that would require that she had been different, and she wasn't." She looked from one grandchild to another. "I can tell you about when she was a girl, if you want to hear it. Some of it good, some of it... not."

The siblings looked at one another, consent passing among them. "Please," Jack said.

Eleanor smiled at him. "I also have to make that adjustment you make every day, because she was such a beautiful child, fun, talented, happy." Eleanor seemed forlorn then brought herself back to the moment, apparently making today's adjustment.

"In high school, it was the old story. Everyone experimented with drugs and she admitted to trying them. The real trouble didn't start until she was invited to be a backup singer for a minor rock star who came to town to judge a high school talent show. She was so thrilled, and we were happy for her, not knowing that drugs were a way of life for him and a lot of his band. She left to tour with them, called us a couple of times a week, then just once a week, then finally not at all. We literally lost her in a matter of months.

"We located her once in the depths of her addiction. Her father was furious with her, but I went to her. She refused to see me. I tried over and over, and I don't know if she was embarrassed by who she'd become or if she truly didn't care about us anymore."

Grief was visible in her eyes. "Her father gave up, but I tried to keep track of her. It wasn't easy. The singer she'd connected with died in a car accident, the group disbanded and she left the business for a while. I just couldn't find her. And I had to look on the sly because your grandfather was just so hurt and angry. He passed away last year." She turned to extend a hand to Oliver, who stood to the side with a cup of coffee while they talked.

"Oliver is the son of a good friend of mine." He came to take her hand. Cassie moved aside to make room for him. "He was studying law and had to take a year off to earn his tuition, and worked for a skip tracer. I hired him to find Charlene. That's when I learned that she...died in jail."

She shook her head as though still in disbelief. Then she brightened suddenly. "We learned that she connected with men who could keep her in drugs, except for Donald, who was a drug counselor. And while that's awful, I also learned that I had grandchildren. We found the names of the men she'd been with, and the names of her children, but each search for one or the other of you led to a dead end.

"Jack's name changed when he was adopted, and we didn't know that because the adoption was closed. Corie went to live with her father, but when we tried to track him down, we learned he had died and his widow had no idea where you were and, what was worse, didn't seem to care."

She shook her head again, her expression darkening. "I couldn't believe that could happen. Then Oliver found that Cassie was fathered by Charlene's drug counselor." She shrugged at the obvious professional betrayal in that.

"He explained to me," Cassie said in his defense, "that he knew he'd been wrong, but he'd loved her very much. She must have been something when she was clean."

Eleanor wiped at a tear. "She was."

She blew out a steadying breath and went on. "We'd heard he'd moved to Maine when Charlene went to jail, but we couldn't find him. Someone in the office where he'd worked told us he'd left counseling after Cassie was sent home to him, and opened his own business, but he didn't know where. Someone thought he might have moved to Europe.

"That's when Oliver cast a wider net. There was a supermodel named Chapman, and we knew that was Cassie's last name. About the time we discovered that, I saw the news story about you. There was a close-up of your face." She dug into her purse and produced a photo that she handed

Jack. Cassie went to stand behind him and look over his shoulder. "That's your mother at seventeen."

The young woman in the photo sat on the hood of a Corvette, long-legged and coltishly slender, laughingly posing like a starlet with one hand on her hip and the other at her hair. Cassie thought it could have been her if her own hair was darker and her eyes more fearless.

"I knew I'd found you," Eleanor went on. "Then, as I said before, it was a circuitous route to finally discover where you were." She laughed. "Poor Oliver. I'm the one who suggested he get a photo of you. I'm making an album, and I wanted to start it from the very beginning. I had no idea you'd mistake him for paparazzi."

Cassie went back to sit beside poor Oliver. He looked a little like Daniel Radcliffe. She guessed he was in his midtwenties. The bruise on his face stood out on his cheekbone and, though she'd dressed the knuckles she'd stepped on accidentally, he cradled that hand in the other.

"I'm so sorry," she said for probably the fifth time that afternoon. "Why didn't you just tell me the other day in front of the bakery what you were doing?"

"Because Eleanor asked me not to make contact. To just let her know when I'd found you and she'd hop on the first plane."

"It's all my fault," Eleanor said. "I had no idea a simple camera would elicit such a reaction."

Jack and Corie began to laugh. Cassie was indignant for a moment then she saw the humor in it. When Eleanor and even Oliver joined the laughter, she did, too.

"I wanted you all to know that your mother was a great person until drugs and selfish choices set her on a path to self-destruction. I'm sorry it made life so hard for all of you." Everyone sobered. "The night her boyfriend died must have been so traumatic for you." She put a hand to Cassie's cheek. "And you girls were just babies, two and four."

Corie tucked her arm in Cassie's and leaned her cheek against her shoulder. "We were lucky to have each other. We followed Jack when he went to see what was happening and when...when we saw... Jack shooed us back to our rooms, but we hid in the broom closet."

It came upon Cassie as a complete surprise—the old fragment of a memory—the darkness, the fear, the inability to escape.

The silk against her face.

She leaned away from Corie suddenly, impressions flickering like old movies playing too fast. The silk against her face had been Corie's hair. She stared at her startled sister.

Eleanor had stopped talking.

Jack asked worriedly, "Cassie?"

The panic began to inch up her body. Her breathing became shallow and the need to race away screaming tried to overtake her.

"Cassie, what?" Corie asked gently, wrapping an arm around her with big-sister firmness. "Tell us. It's all right."

She was unsure how to explain what she felt. How, *how* did what could only be suspicion seem so right on?

"I, uh," she said, having to clear her throat. "I have...claustrophobia." Even she realized that was an odd response to what they must be seeing in her. She should explain that, but thoughts banged around in her mind. Was she wrong? She didn't think so.

"You mean you feel claustrophobic right now?" Jack asked. He had stood to come around to her but stopped.

"No. I mean I have the condition."

Jack and Corie looked at each other, and Cassie knew.

Jack sat near her on an ottoman. "You can't possibly remember that night. You were only two years old."

Cassie's panic began to recede. She could deal with this. She was among family. They'd been through it together. She pulled her arm out from under Corie's steely grip and wrapped it around her shoulder, squeezing gently.

"I don't think it qualifies as a memory." She had to think about breathing, drawing in air, pushing it out. "For as long as I can remember, I've been afraid of small spaces. Actually, it's more than fear, it's a recoil from something I couldn't remember." She smiled at her sister. "Until I just felt Corie's hair against my face."

A tear slid down Corie's cheek. "We were hiding together in the broom closet," she said. "Mom's boyfriend was beating her and Jack shoved us back toward our room and went to help her. I didn't want to leave him, so I went to the closet and brought you with me."

"You held me so tight."

"You were afraid of the shouting and I didn't want you to run out and get hurt. I watched through the louvered door."

"It was dark."

"And a very small space."

Cassie exhaled, understanding finally what had plagued her into her attacks all these years, though she remembered only the sensations and not the night.

"Then Jack shot Brauer and it was over," Corie said. "I ran out to try to defend him, sure he was in big trouble, but Mom sent us all to bed and told us to pretend to be asleep. The police would be coming and she didn't want them to know Jack did it and that I saw it."

Cassie tightened her grip on Corie, feeling her pain. Jack knelt in front of them and held them both in his arms.

After a moment Eleanor leaned into them. "Kids, I don't know what you can do with a memory that awful but put it away. You can't forget it, but you don't ever have to think about it."

They clung together then Eleanor finally straightened and said in a hearty tone of voice, "You might find it comforting to know that you come from basically good people. My parents worked for an aircraft manufacturing company, and your grandfather and I owned a small clothing store. We sold it to an employee when it was time for Bill to retire."

They drew apart, fascinated by this new information. "Where do you live now?" Jack asked.

"In the LA area."

"Are you happy there?"

"I'm sure I'll be happier now," Eleanor said. "I have everything I need, except all the people I've loved who are gone."

"Can you stay with us for a while?" Jack asked. "My parents—my adopted parents—have a guesthouse that's sitting empty."

"Why don't you ask them to come over?" Cassie stood, too. "I can throw something together for dinner. Meanwhile, how about tea or coffee and some of Grady's mom's cranberry bread?"

The assent was unanimous.

In the kitchen, Cassie prepared a tray while Jack called the Palmers. Cassie could hear the excitement on the other end. The call was over in a minute.

He hung up and told her, "Of course she can have the guesthouse for as long as she wants. And they're coming right over."

She turned to smile into her brother's good-looking face, feeling sympathy for the young boy who'd taken on the responsibility of his sisters, endured that horrible night, then had his family torn apart. She went to put her arms around him and hold him tightly.

"I'm so sorry you've been through so much," she said.

They stood apart and he shook her gently by the shoulders. "Like Eleanor said, that's over. And here we are—with a grandmother! I didn't even know she existed." He feigned a serious expression. "Thank you for not killing her attorney. That would have been hard to explain to her. She might have changed her mind about getting to know us."

"Yeah, I kind of went off on him. But I was feeling down and…you know…inadequate."

He arched both eyebrows. "No, I don't know. Inadequate? Whatever for? You're acknowledged as one of the world's most beautiful women, and you're smart and sweet and a good cook. Grady boasts about you all the time."

Now she looked surprised. "That's hard to believe. He thinks I'm not real."

"Pardon me?"

"He has this thing about reality. Like, if something's too good, or too glamorous, or changes his world too much, it's phony. You know, he wanted to be a lawyer then had to give up his plans when his dad got sick. He seems to think that dooms him to never being able to have what he wants. So now he doesn't want things."

Jack seemed to understand. "You mean he doesn't want *you*?"

She blew air through puffed cheeks then took a tin of cookies out of a cupboard.

"That's astute of you, and yes. He likes me, I think, but he considers me superficial."

"You seem very grounded to me, even though you live in a world the rest of us can only imagine. Does he know about your claustrophobia?"

She made a face. "There was an incident in an elevator the day we all got together for lunch. He was very kind about it. He helped me keep my secret."

"You don't have to hide anything from us, you know."

"I know, I know. But your finding me finally makes our family complete and I didn't want to be a disappointment."

He rolled his eyes. "As though you could be. Now, about Grady. I think he's just afraid of what he doesn't know. It sounds as though you have strong feelings even though it's been just a short time."

She pulled down a plate and arranged cookies on it. "It's been a very intense time with the three of us getting back together again. Then there was that thing in Ireland because of my claustrophobia."

"Yeah. Sarah told me why that happened."

"Anyway, I've been restless and yearning for something."

"And it turns out to be Grady?"

She winced. "Does it show?"

"No. You seem very cool and together. But the guy's like a brick. If you need solid dependability, he's your man."

"That's the irony of it. That solid, dependable man wants his life to remain just that way. And I don't fit. I mean, my life is like a miracle now—like the future is wide open. You found Corie and me, and now we have a grandmother. I finally understand myself, so I feel invincible."

She placed slices of the cranberry-orange bread on another plate and handed it to him, dismissing the heavy discussion with a wave of her other hand. "Doesn't matter. You want to take those out to the coffee table and I'll make drinks?"

"Sure. Grady will come around, Cassie."

"I don't know."

He kissed her forehead and started away with the plates. "Well, if he doesn't, you can come and live with us, and when we have children and you're not working, you can be their favorite aunt. Meanwhile, if it's okay with you, right after this snack, we'll take Grandma to my parents' place to have a rest, you can have a little free time and Grady can get ready to meet us at the Bistro for the bachelor dinner. But we'll be back after that to finish up stuff and to see the new year in."

"Definitely. Despite all the goings-on, we have to pay some homage to New Year's Eve."

CASSIE WATCHED JACK and Corie jealously as they left with their grandmother in Jack's truck. They had a grandmother!

"How's it going?" Grady asked, finally off work and dressed in jeans and a red flannel shirt. He carried what appeared to be a very heavy grocery bag. "Where's your grandmother?"

She had to shift her mind to practical matters. She explained about Jack taking her with him. "So far, so good on the plans. The florist reports that everything's ready and in her refrigerated case. Right now she's stringing some flowers for me to add to the bunting. What's in the bag?"

He went past her to the kitchen. "Champagne. Didn't want to use any of the wedding stuff and we have to toast the new year tonight."

She followed him. "That was thoughtful."

He pretended modesty. "Hey, that's me. So, *I'm* adding the flowers to the bunting?"

"Maybe we could bribe Oliver to climb the ladder. He's coming to help in the morning."

"Everybody's coming again in the morning?"

"Just for a few last-minute details. The flowers have to go up the day of, or they'll wilt. Some of the food's coming tonight. Your mom and Helen are so cute. They're working as a very efficient team."

"Yeah. They took your dad off with them this morning to show him around Beggar's Bay. They promised to get him to the Bistro tonight in time for the bachelor dinner. Isn't all this coziness bringing out your claustrophobia?"

She looked at him in surprise. "Just the opposite. All these people in my life are opening up my world. I love my work, but my friends used to be everyone in the business, and while I've gotten to see the world's most beautiful places, I didn't realize that the simplicity of small-town life is so satisfying, comforting. I love it here. Even though I don't know a lot of people, I've walked around downtown enough to recognize a few faces and earn a smile and a 'good morning.' Often, in big cities, people are too busy for that."

He wrapped her in his arms and held her tightly. "Tell me about the contracts you have to go back to Paris for."

She looped her arms around his neck. Her eyelashes fluttered against his cheekbone as she leaned into him. His heart pulsed in the same way. "My good friend Josie Bergerac is a designer of evening clothes in Paris and I do all her shows and most of her print ads. In New York, I do TV commercials for Eterna Beauty Cosmetics."

"I know you have a condo in Paris, but where do you live when you're in New York?"

"Several friends and I keep a place there, with a view of Central Park. We come and go all the time so each of us pays the rent for a quarter of the year. Works out well.

I'll let you know when I'm going to be in New York and you can come visit me."

He was in love with a woman who shared digs on Park Avenue. What was happening? Right now, he didn't care.

"I think my mother is attracted to your father," he said, needing to think about someone else's unlikely romance. "She has a key to my house. Remember when we got home from Texas, she was in here, putting food in the refrigerator?"

"That's right. I hadn't thought about that. So why did she keep them outside in the cold?"

"I haven't had a chance to ask her. But last night she stopped me from mentioning in front of him that she had a key and could have let him in."

"If she hasn't dated in a while, maybe she was reluctant to be in a house alone with a strange man. That probably wasn't done when she was a girl."

"I'm sure you've noticed this, but my mother isn't shy."

"True, but when she was alone with my dad, waiting for us, she wasn't your mother, she was a woman. Probably a lonely woman, and she was being cautious." She widened her eyes. "How would you feel if they decided they liked each other? It's completely premature, but how tidy for us."

"Tidy?"

"My brother's adopted brother is marrying my sister, my mother and your father might connect. It's kind of all in the family—even screwy as it all is."

He nodded. Screwy didn't begin to describe it. He noticed she'd carefully sidestepped their own relationship.

She seemed to read what was in his eyes. She dropped her arms from around his neck but he continued to hold her. She rested her elbows on his arms. "You realize that you and I are looking at a long-distance relationship until I come home, and then...who knows? You might have decided it's too much trouble or too...fussy to manage all that. You might fall in love with someone else."

"What about all the jocks and geniuses that populate your life in New York and Paris? Not to mention the models and movie stars. You might change your mind about me when you see them again."

She shook her head and gave him a look that melted every bone in his body. "Not a chance. None of them is the missing piece."

He kissed her again because he couldn't help himself but had to admit he felt some worry at the worrisome responsibility. He'd been his parents' stockade wall, Celeste's "lover boy," but he'd never been the person who would make someone else's life complete. He hoped he had what she thought he had, and that her feelings for him weren't just part of this cozy family reunion where anything seemed possible.

BECAUSE THEY WERE all needed to help set up tonight, there'd be no time for a serious rehearsal dinner or, for that matter, a real New Year's Eve party. Don had offered to order pizza, so a slice and a champagne toast at midnight was going to have to serve.

He quickly changed into brown pants and a beige sweater, and arrived back in the kitchen in time to admit the beautiful, fragrant, laughing chaos that had invaded his life big-time. He was hugged by every woman, which was nice, then fed a cookie here, an hors d'oeuvre there, and Helen stuffed a forkful of something into his mouth before he could stop her. Fortunately it was delicious food for the wedding. Eleanor was glowing as part of the group. Cassie, who'd also changed, hurried in to welcome everyone.

"Mushroom cap stuffed with sausage," she said. "Good?"

"Mmm," he said, his mouth still full.

"Glad you like it."

Later, on his way out to the bachelor dinner, he spotted Cassie's face in the crowd and held up his phone. That had become code for "call me if you want me to pick up something." He was a little relieved to be able to close the door behind him and join his friends at the Bay Bistro.

THE GUYS WERE in a mood very similar to that of the women. Though their laughter was deeper and louder, and they didn't smell half as good, they seemed to be exceptionally lighthearted. As befitted a wedding, he supposed, but it seemed odd to him that Ben was so relaxed.

Jack was absurdly happy lately, and

Gary had a wry wit and a ready smile. He'd known Ben to be solid but sometimes moody and it was mind-blowing to see this transformation. Oliver, who'd also been invited, watched the action with a smile on his face. He caught Grady's eye and toasted him with his coffee cup. "Most fun surveillance I've ever been on. If you discount getting beaten up and rolled down a hill."

Grady laughed. "They're a good group. A little overcome by love at the moment. And they're fiercely protective of one another."

Oliver's expression sobered as he watched. "Yeah. I'd like to be overcome by love."

"No girlfriend?" Grady asked.

"No. Had to take a year off law school to be able to pay my tuition. Not a good situation for the woman who was dating me for my money-earning potential."

"Doesn't the fact that you stopped to earn money to keep going prove you *have* money-earning potential?"

"No, it proves I don't have enough in reserve to keep going. So she's hitched her wagon to a medical student from Montauk."

Grady could imagine Cassie's reaction if something like that had happened to a man she loved. She'd be all over it, trying to make it better. "Depends on the woman," he said. "So, you're looking to make extra money?"

"Yes," Oliver said eagerly. "Why?"

"I have a car at the airport in Reno, Nevada, that I'm having trouble finding time to retrieve."

Oliver nodded. "Left it as collateral for a loan?"

"No!" Grady explained about having promised to deliver his mother and her sister for a casino vacation then agreeing to join Ben in Texas and flying out from Reno.

"Weird logistics," Oliver noted.

"Story of my life. If I send you on a bus, would you drive the car back for me? After the holiday."

"Sure."

"When are you going home?"

"Not sure. It's beautiful here. And I don't want to just leave your grandmother. She's my mom's best friend. I'll hang around, see what she decides to do."

"You can help Ben and me move furniture into our new office while you're waiting, if you'd like. And we might have some other jobs for you. Nothing glamorous but they'll all pay."

"I'm not a glamorous kind of guy."

"Yeah. Me, either."

Aware of a sudden nudge at his ribs, Grady turned to his other side and looked into Soren's confused expression. "What's the matter with everyone?" the boy asked. "Is this really love stuff?"

"I'm afraid it is. And it's going to last for a while. Maybe even get worse. The best thing to do is get into it with them. Have you ever heard the expression 'if you can't beat them, join them?'"

Soren shook his head, but gave the words some thought. "Isn't that like being a traitor? Like changing sides?"

"Not in this case. There's really no bad side to love. You can stay away from all the fun they're having because they look kind of silly, but you'd have a better time if you got into the fun."

"Are you going to be our uncle? Mine and Rosie's?"

"Sure, like one of your uncles you aren't really related to but who are good friends of the family."

"No, I mean a real uncle. 'Cause Cassie is our aunt."

"Right. But I'm not married to Cassie."

Soren frowned. "She lives with you."

"Because she's visiting and needs a place to stay."

"She looks like she's your wife."

"What do you mean?"

"She looks at you like Corie—my mom, looks at my dad. You know, Ben."

"Well…we're pretty good friends."

Soren nodded. "Corie says that friends make the best husbands and wives. She picked up our suits today. We have to wear a tie." His expression suggested he wasn't happy about that.

"Weddings are fancy. You're supposed to look nice."

"I don't like fancy."

"I hear you."

"Can I have a sip of your coffee?"

"Uh…" Grady looked up to consult Ben, but he was busy laughing with Jack over something.

"He usually lets me have a sip, but he doesn't put anything in it. I think I'd like it better with cream."

Grady passed him the cup. "Try it. If you don't like it, we can put some sugar in it."

Soren grinned at him. "Thanks. You'd make a good uncle."

"Thank you."

He turned to ask someone to pass the sugar, but stopped when he saw Jack jump to his feet, looking happy but emotional. Jack sidled out from behind the table and went to intercept Don Chapman, who'd been delivered to the Bistro by his mother and Helen. The women quickly left.

"Jack!" Don said, coming toward him. "My God! I'd say it can't have been that long ago, but…" He opened his arms to Jack and they held each other for a long moment, Don as emotional as Jack. They finally pulled apart and Jack called Ben to him.

It occurred to Grady for the first time that Jack and Donald had been part of the same family before tragedy befell the Mannings.

"This is my brother, Ben. Remember him? He was my best friend all those years ago."

Don embraced Ben, also. "I do. I remember having to stop the two of you from driving off in my car when you were about eight years old."

"We had places to go," Ben explained. "And if we walked, you'd make us take Corie with us to keep her out of trouble."

Jack slapped his shoulder. "When you were with Mom was the best time of our lives to that point. Come and sit down. We'll get you something to eat."

The party went on with a lot of reminiscences Grady hadn't heard before. He guessed even Ben hadn't heard some of them, because he was particularly attentive.

When Ben sat again, Soren leaned toward him and Grady heard him ask in a soft voice, "Was that man your dad?"

"No, he was Uncle Jack's dad for a little while. I was Uncle Jack's friend before I became his brother, so we used to hang out together."

"You can do that?" Soren asked, eyes wide. "Make a friend your brother?"

"Sometimes. It happened for us like it did for you and Rosie. My parents adopted Uncle Jack when he was little because his mom went away and his dad had died. So he became part of my family and that made us brothers. Like you and Rosie became part of Corie's and my family, and that made you brother and sister."

Soren puzzled over that and then smiled. "Corie is always saying things are complicated in our family."

Ben squeezed the boy to him. "And that's the truth."

Cassie measured a yard-long length of natural raffia Sarah had picked up, Eleanor cut it at the end of the yardstick and Corie looped it into three and handed it to Sarah. Sarah in turn tucked in a silk Gerbera daisy and tied it with a strip of raffia, leaving enough length to attach it to the back of one of the white wooden chairs they'd rented.

The women stood back to admire their work.

"What do you think?" Cassie asked.

"I like it." Between Corie's feet was a basket of silk daisies Denise had special-ordered. "Now we have only forty-nine chairs to go."

"Shall we just make them," Eleanor

asked, "and attach them tomorrow so they don't get scrunched in the meantime?" The chairs had been folded and stashed in the kitchen.

Sarah nodded, studying the ornament closely. "That's the plan. You're sure it shouldn't be fussier?"

"I like the simplicity," Corie said, folding her arms. "It's perfect."

Eleanor put an arm around each of her granddaughters. "You're such a good team. You should all find a way to work together."

"Funny you should say that." Corie, the basket now over her arm, picked up one of the flowers and twirled it between her thumb and forefinger. "Last night, when I had rampant insomnia, I had an idea."

Her companions waited.

"What if…" she began cautiously, "we all went into business together?" She touched Sarah's arm. "Well, you can't, of course. You're busy doing important things. But we could commandeer Jack to work with us when he's between restorations."

"To do weddings?" Sarah asked doubtfully.

Corie laughed. "No. Designing clothes. Showing clothes. Selling clothes. I have a few pieces made and ideas for a complete line. Cassie knows the skinny on how designers present their work, what's required to mount a show and approach retailers. Grandma ran a store and knows how to sell. Every good designer also has a shop. Jack can do anything—back us up at presentations, schmooze prospective buyers…"

Eleanor's face lit up and she pressed her hands together. "We can do that!"

"I know you'll still be working," Corie said to Cassie, "but you'll be coming back from time to time, and when you return for good, we could have a line ready to go. What do you think?"

"I think you're brilliant." Cassie wrapped her arms around her tiny sister and reached out for their grandmother. Sarah closed in to join the hug.

Loud conversation and laughter announced the arrival of the men.

"I'm making more coffee!" Grady shouted from the kitchen.

"Good," Sarah shouted back. "We need some! We've been working while you guys were partying."

Jack appeared shortly with two coffee

mugs in each hand. "Here you go," he said. "You're all working so hard…" He stopped at their obvious emotion. "What's going on?"

Sarah took two mugs from him and passed one to Eleanor. He distributed the other two.

"You're going into business with your sisters and your grandmother," Sarah told him.

He looked surprised but didn't object. "Oh, good. Tell me we're buying a gym or a bike shop."

"It's women's clothing." Corie laughed, tucked her arm in his, and explained what each of the women would be doing.

"Great." He pretended to worry. "I'm the silent partner, right?"

"Of course not, sweetheart." Sarah kissed his cheek. "It's impossible for you to be silent. You're the big brother who makes it all work. Security, companionship, encouragement. And you could restore some pretty little building for them to work in. Something with retail space on the bottom floor."

He nodded, pleased. "I can do that."

CHAPTER FOURTEEN

IT WAS AFTER eleven o'clock by the time the chairs were finished and the chandeliers had been set up in two neat rows to test the spacing. A friend of Grady's from the station had connected the hanging chandelier from the loft overhead. It was the only one that couldn't be battery powered. Pizza had been consumed and dozens of topics had been discussed over wine, coffee and chai while everyone worked. They now all stood around, eager to see the fruits of their labors.

The entire family had been there to help—Helen and Gary, Jack and Sarah, Corie and Ben and the kids, Grady's mother, Cassie's father, Eileen and Oliver, and Cassie and Grady.

Cassie set the scene. "Corie will come down the stairs and walk up the aisle we've created with the chandeliers, then stop right here under the hanging chandelier, where Father Eisley and Ben and all the attendants will be waiting."

She went to a sort of worktable that separated the great room from the smaller space under the loft. "There'll be flowers here and the wedding cake." She walked around the room and pointed to several small tables, one in a conversation area near the fireplace, one that held a lamp and one near the stairs that at the moment held mail and a potted Christmas cactus. "There'll be bouquets on all these flat surfaces and flowers strung and added to the sparkle tulle. Now, if someone will turn off the lights, I'll turn on the chandeliers and make sure it all comes together."

Grady moved to flip the switch and she went from chandelier to chandelier to turn them on.

A collective gasp went up from the family and then applause. Even she was impressed by the absolute gorgeousness of all the beautifully placed lights in the darkness. It was like a path made of star clusters fallen to earth.

Playfully, she took her bows. Corie came

to hug her and Ben to wrap his arms around both of them.

"I can't believe how hard you worked for us," Corie said, her dark eyes brimming.

"It's been my pleasure," Cassie said sincerely. "How cool that I got to do this for you after all the years of separation."

"You've been so generous," Ben praised. "We'll never be able to thank you enough."

Eleanor came to join them. "Can a grandmother get in on this?" she asked. "I can't believe that I found all of you at such a wonderful time. I'm so happy to be part of this."

Grady turned on the television. "Okay, everyone, gather 'round, I'm going to pour champagne—and apple juice for the kids. It's almost time for the countdown. Since this new year is so…significant to all of us."

Ben indicated Soren and Rosie, fast asleep on the sofa. "I think you can save the apple juice."

Ben and Jack lifted the still-sleeping children so they could sit tightly on the couch, cradling them in one arm, and accepted a glass of champagne with the other hand.

"Anyone making resolutions?" Helen asked. Gary sat on the arm of the chair she occupied. "Or is it bad luck to talk about them?"

Ben sent her a teasing smile. "I think that's birthday wishes, Mom. Are you going to lose twenty pounds again this year?"

She shrugged in mild embarrassment. "I doubt it, though that is my resolution."

"I'm resolved to be patient," Ben said. His gravity startled everyone. "What?" he asked, surprised by their surprise. He looked down at Soren, fast asleep in his arms. "Kids need that, and I'm already reminding myself that my children are people in their own right and not a smaller version of me."

Diane, now comfortable in this group, said, "That's very true." Then she admitted candidly, "I'm resolved to do a little less meddling." There was laughter and she said quickly, "Just a *little* less. Or Grady wouldn't recognize me."

"I almost don't recognize you these days, anyway," Grady said. "With your new clothes and your new 'do, you should be walking the runways with Cassie."

She blushed when everyone concurred.

Ben pinned Grady. "What's your resolution? I mean, your whole life had been turned upside down for Corie and me, you must be promising yourself that you'll never go through anything like this again. Or have you enjoyed the chaos? Sometimes when you can't control anything else, your brain and your heart put your thoughts and feelings in order instead."

Grady pretended surprise at the accuracy of Ben's observation. He didn't want anyone to know he was right on. "Wow. You're some kind of Bob Dylan, all of a sudden."

Ben ran a hand over his eyes, taking the teasing with good grace. "I know. I'm exhausted. I don't know what I'm talking about."

"Look, look!" Eleanor pointed to the television with her champagne glass. "Only two more minutes before the ball falls."

Cassie topped up champagne glasses and everyone stood, leaving the sleeping children on the sofa, and gathered in a semicircle around the television. They counted down from ten as the ball fell, toasted each other and the new year, then embraced, making sure no one was missed.

Grady took Cassie from Sarah and hugged her. Then, looking into her eyes, he leaned in to kiss her. She met him halfway, her hands on either side of his face.

"I'm learning to deal with the chaos," he said quietly.

"Good. I think I'm learning to deal with you," she returned softly. Then her grandmother stepped between them and he turned to have the wind squeezed out of him by his mother.

"I'm so glad you talked me into getting something to wear to the wedding," she said. "I love these people."

JACK WRAPPED HIS arms around Cassie. His eyes were full of things he didn't seem to be able to say. Everyone was collecting coats and preparing to leave. "I love you, too, Jack," she said, kissing his cheek. "Thank you for working so hard to find Corie and me."

"I couldn't imagine a lifetime without the two of you. Good night, Cassie."

"Good night."

Grady stood behind her, a hand on her shoulder as they listened to the laughter, quieter now that the hour was late, and watched everyone climb into their cars.

Don carried a giant salad bowl Diane had brought and placed it in the back seat of her car. They stopped to chat.

"There definitely is something there," Grady said under his voice.

"I think you're right."

"Tidy for us."

"That's what I said."

Sarah called out as Jack drove slowly away, "You two do look good together! Good night."

There was honking and waving, and Don came back to the house.

CASSIE COULDN'T RESIST the private smile at how beautiful Grady's great room looked. Corie and Ben's wedding was going to be stunning. She was so thrilled that her sister's life had come to such a happy pass. To have helped just a little to make it happen delighted her.

"Did you get any sleep on the sofa last night?" Donald asked Grady. They were carrying the standing chandelier to the back wall. "Because you can have your room back. I assure you I'll be fine. During the mess in Bangkok, I slept on the floor of a government office."

"I'm fine on the sofa. Get some sleep. Tomorrow's going to be a long day."

The job done, Donald wrapped Cassie in a bear hug. "Good going, Cass. You could go into wedding planning when you come back here to live. It's going to be quite an event."

"Actually, Corie, Jack, Grandma and I are talking about going into business together."

"You are?" Grady stopped in the act of hauling blankets out of the guest closet.

"We are. Corie's a wonderful designer, and I have a lot of contacts in fashion. Grandma knows about shopkeeping, and Jack's just good to have around."

"Wow. So, Grandma's staying?"

"I'm pretty sure." She turned to her father. "Helen told her she can stay in the guesthouse as long as she wants. What about you, Dad? Are you staying?"

He shrugged a shoulder. "Maybe. I

saw a little bar for sale on the waterfront. I know nothing about it and have no experience, but it'd be fun to do something where people come in to relax, rather than in IT where they call you because nothing's working and they have a deadline in an hour, and you have to help them make it."

Donald helped Grady spread a flannel sheet over the leather sofa. "I'm sure your workday is a lot worse than that, but sometimes I think I've had enough of people hanging over my shoulder, pointing to their watches and telling me to hurry up, to last a lifetime."

Grady tossed a pillow to the end of the sofa. "Usually, life is pretty calm around here." He grinned at Cassie, who watched them with a smile. "Until this week."

Donald laughed. "Wedding wonderland, huh? Well, it's almost over. Then your life will get back to normal." He glanced from Cassie to Grady. "Or will it?"

Grady threw a thick thermal blanket on top of the sheet on the sofa. "Normal's not what it used to be. Anything I can get for you before I go to bed?"

Donald offered his hand. "Nothing at

all. I so appreciate your hospitality. Good night."

"Good night, Don."

Donald blew a kiss to Cassie and disappeared down the hall to Grady's bedroom.

Grady wrapped his arms around Cassie. "You going to be able to sleep? Want a brandy or something?"

"No, I'll be fine." She hugged him tightly and he breathed her in, thinking what a wonderful way this was to start a new year. "I probably won't sleep much, so, if you hear me moving around, don't worry."

"You've done everything you can to make the day perfect for Corie and Ben. You should relax."

She kissed his cheek and drew away. "I'll relax when they're married. Go to bed. I have a few things to clean up in the kitchen, then I'll turn out the lights."

"Okay. Sleep tight."

Cassie finished cleaning up then went to the stairs. Grady lay on his back on the sofa, an arm across his eyes. He was already breathing evenly in sleep.

She couldn't resist going to the new switch that controlled the overhead chandelier. The tiered light came to life in the shadowy space. It was beautiful.

She suddenly remembered the extra batteries she'd bought for the standing chandeliers and went to her purse to retrieve them. She took them out of their packaging for easy access and stashed them in the little drawer in the designated wedding cake table.

She flipped off the light and went upstairs imagining Corie and Ben and the priest standing under the hanging chandelier.

Changing into her negligee, she climbed under the covers, thinking over tomorrow's schedule. Sarah was picking her up at seven to meet Corie, Rosie, Helen and Diane for breakfast before they all went to Hair's to You to be beautified.

The guys would be over in the morning to set up chairs and put up the food tables. It was all coming together. She felt reasonably certain Grady would be visiting her in Paris, and there, in the City of Lights and of romance, she could convince him that life could be unpredictable and still wonderful, that surprises weren't all bad, and that she could make his life worth the long-distance logistics. She smiled to herself and drifted off.

BEN AND CORIE exchanged vows in front of a crackling fire while loud bagpipe music played. Cassie looked on, arms folded against involvement in this wedding that was not at all what she'd planned. They were supposed to exchange their vows under the chandelier that Grady's friend had wired under the loft. It would have been beautiful. Instead there was this whining, crackling...

Cassie sat up in bed, wide awake. Her nostrils caught the acrid smell of smoke and her ear realized the whining sound wasn't a bagpipe at all but a smoke alarm. She ran to the railing to see that the great room was on fire, black smoke filling the space, the sound of the alarm about to split her eardrums.

She ran through a litany of Oh, my God!s, took a second to slip on her tennis shoes and ran down the stairs, thinking in panic that when she'd gone to bed, Grady had been asleep on the sofa and her father was in Grady's bedroom!

Halfway down the stairs she was brought up short by the darkness in the house and the thick black smoke. She could taste it, feel it burn her eyes. It wrapped around her in an evil caress, then tightened and tightened until she couldn't get free, couldn't move, couldn't see in any direction. Panic started in the pit of her stomach and inched up her torso, constricting her heart, her lungs, her throat. She opened her mouth to scream and choked on smoke.

Making herself move instead of dissolving into a sobbing puddle took more effort than she thought she had in her. But there was Grady on the sofa and her father was in the back of the house and she had to get to them.

She used the handrail to guide her down the stairs, through the smoke, screaming Grady's name the whole time. Hurrying toward the sofa, she collided with the coffee table, crying out, then using it to guide her around it to the sofa. "Grady! Grady, we have to get out!" she shouted, running her hands along the upholstery, expecting to feel his hair, his shoulders, his blankets. But she felt nothing. Just the sofa. Then her hands hit a stack of fabric. It took her a precious second to interpret that. He was already up and gone. Or somewhere in the house, overcome by smoke?

She turned to shout his name. Certainly, if he was in the kitchen or the bathroom, he'd have heard the smoke alarm.

For an instant she stared at the flames, unable to believe what she was seeing. Flames were eating up the table under the loft, had apparently ignited the bunting and an Oriental rug. Flames licked toward the edge of the sofa.

She ran around it and toward Grady's room. As she did, burning tulle fell from the loft railing, igniting a lampshade. She stepped over something that glittered in the smoke and realized the hanging chandelier had fallen.

"Dad," she shouted, feeling the walls on both sides of the corridor. They were hot to the touch. "Daddy!"

He met her at the door, his hair rumpled but his eyes clear. "My God. Fire?"

"Yes!" She grabbed his arm and pulled him with her. "We have to go now!"

Her father stopped in his tracks. "Where's Grady?"

"I don't know, but he's not on the sofa. Come on!" Cassie tried to push him in front of her, but he caught her arm instead and hurried through the kitchen and the foyer to the side door. She heard the shrill bleat of sirens as she broke free and pushed her father into the cold predawn air.

She ran back into the house, nagged by the fear that Grady might still be inside, overcome, unconscious.

Several steps into the room, she screamed his name again, the darkness and the smoke trying to overtake her. She felt that familiar constriction trying to take her down. She spread both arms and screamed in an effort to fight it as she made herself move toward the kitchen. Smoke burned her eyes and her nostrils and she had to lean against the door frame as the darkness swirled.

GRADY DAWDLED OVER his selection at the bakery. Buying doughnuts and Danish for breakfast had seemed like a good idea when he'd woken up hungry and feeling remarkably mellow. The bakery wasn't open yet, but would be, despite the holiday. Nothing stopped the production and consumption of food in Beggar's Bay.

Finally finding himself with time to wander through the future offices of Bayside Detectives, he let himself into the back of the building and climbed the stairs to the second floor. He felt a sense of excitement as he walked slowly from room to room, imagining the phone ringing, Ben talking with a client, his mother's ugly armoire filled with all the things Cassie thought it should contain. He made a list of furniture to look for, supplies they would need, and drew a rough plan of the few rooms.

Eventually he heard activity upstairs in the restaurant, the subtle aromas of breakfast preparation. It made him hungry. He closed the office, ran down the stairs and headed for the bakery.

A cherry fritter for him was an automatic decision, but he wasn't sure what Cassie or Donald would prefer. His solution was a carefully chosen half dozen assortment. He carried the bag out to the car, munching on one of the cherry fritters, then went to the gas station, the only one he knew of that still washed your windows and checked your oil with a fill-up.

He headed home, marveling at the beautiful morning. Turning up Black Bear Ridge Road, he saw the play of sunlight through the bare deciduous trees and making conical shapes in emerald out of the Douglas fir that lined the last few yards—

He braked suddenly at the sight of black smoke billowing out of his house. He held on to the steering wheel and leaned forward, unable to believe what he was seeing. Then a side window blew out and fire leaped through the opening.

"Oh, God!" he said as he floored the gas and turned into his driveway. As he bounded out of the truck, Donald in pajama bottoms and a T-shirt, his face blackened from smoke, threw himself toward the house.

"Don!" Grady shouted to stop him. "What happened? Where's Cassie?"

Don caught his forearms as he ran toward him. "Thank God you're okay. She shoved me out and went back in."

"Stay here. I'll get her."

"No, I want to go." He held Grady's arms and shook him. "She has claus—"

Grady handed him his phone. "I know. Call 9-1-1. I'll bring her out. I know the house, so I'll be faster." Without waiting for agreement, Grady rushed inside, through the corridor to the great room— and stopped for a second, shocked by how bad the fire was. Smoke billowed and rolled, and he couldn't see much of anything except a significant point of flame. He guessed it was the table under the loft.

He couldn't imagine how Cassie was functioning in this little piece of hell. Not only was it hot and hard to breathe, but the darkness caused by the smoke was pervasive—and claustrophobic. She must be terrified. He needed to save her.

"Cassie!" he shouted, covering his mouth as he ran into the room. "Cassie? Where are you?"

Hearing no sound but the crackling flames, he advanced to the stairs and collided with her before he saw her. She was headed toward the kitchen. Her face and her bare arms and shoulders were black with smoke. She coughed and fell against the newel.

"Cassie!" He framed her face in his hands just in time to hear her raspy voice say, "Grady," and to see her eyes close as she began to collapse. He swept her up against him, remembering that this was the way they'd met. He took a moment to get his bearings, then turned sideways and headed for the door, now open and admitting firefighters on the run. He sheltered her with his face against hers as he ran against the traffic.

CASSIE, GRADY AND DONALD sat on the rear bumper of the fire truck, wrapped in blankets a firefighter had given them.

Cassie had regained consciousness the minute she'd hit the early morning air and now sat silently, an arm around Grady's waist, as they all stared at the frantic activity in and around the house. The fire was out, the fire chief had told them, and the smoke was dissipating. She'd half expected to see the roof ablaze, but the flames hadn't broken through.

"I wonder what happened," Cassie asked in a small voice.

"I have no idea." Grady sat with a hand on her knee, filled with gratitude that she was unharmed. He felt sick. He'd never been one to need fancy clothes or a mansion, but he'd loved this house from the moment he'd seen it, driving up this road with Ben, answering a call about a missing dog. It represented everything he believed in—solid, unpretentious, a place in which to live a quiet, steady life.

He'd been sure he'd never be able to afford it, but the owner had moved away the year before and had been paying two mortgages ever since. He'd been anxious to get out from under this one and was selling at an absurdly low price.

Grady loved being a bachelor in this house. He'd filled the place with furniture he'd saved for, gifts from friends, folk art finds from his collector mother. He wondered with black humor if he'd be lucky enough that the blue armoire was a loss.

His poker games around the kitchen table had been fun. He realized, of course, that that was due to the men who came to play rather than the house in which they played.

Ben's wedding! Thoughts of his poker buddies reminded him that today was Ben and Corie's wedding. And his house was the venue.

He turned to Cassie and saw the pale sadness on her face.

A HIGH, SHRILL scream was going on in Cassie's brain. She held the blanket tightly around her, felt Grady's arm encircle her shoulders and her father take her hand, but she couldn't stop staring at the broken windows and the fire hoses inside. A chill the blanket and the love of her favorite men couldn't chase away set up residence in the pit of her stomach.

She'd wanted so much for her sister to have the world's most wonderful wedding, and now most of what she'd gathered to make it spectacular, and the gorgeous home itself, had burned. What could Grady do now? And what could she do to save the wedding? And him?

Half-developed thoughts bounced around in her head, trying to find a solution worth pursuing, but kept bouncing back unfinished. She couldn't think. Ben and Corie would be so disappointed!

"Do you think your friend made a bad electrical connection for the hanging chandelier?" Donald asked, leaning around Cassie to see Grady.

Grady shrugged under the blanket. "It's possible, but he's done other work here before that's been perfectly reliable. The table we were going to use for the wedding cake was fully engulfed, though. I can't imagine why. I mean, something would have had to set it on fire. The chandelier had fallen to the floor, so maybe that had something to do with it."

Cassie leaned into Grady as the early morning gave way to a beautiful, clear day, completely at odds with the destruction of Grady's home. "Grady, I'm so sorry," she said on a cough. "I feel like this is all my fault. If I hadn't suggested having the wedding here, this might not have happened."

"We don't know that." He squeezed her closer. "Maybe you don't even want to think about this now, but do you have any ideas about the wedding? I mean, it's New

Year's Day. And I don't think anyone else has a house big enough."

Ben and Corie appeared in the chaos in jeans and parkas, picking their way over hoses as the firefighters in the background walked in and out of the house, water everywhere.

"Grady," Ben said as Corie wrapped her arms around Cassie. "I was up early, listening to the scanner. What happened?"

"Not sure," Grady replied, standing to accept Ben's comforting hug. "Place was on fire when Cassie woke up. I had gone to the bakery for doughnuts." Then with an expression of disbelief and censure, "You were listening to the scanner on the morning of your wedding?"

"You know how it is. Always a cop." Ben's gaze ran over the three of them. "Thank God you're all okay." He turned to look at the house. "The roof seems to be intact."

"Yeah, the fire was contained, and they seem to be doing a good job of putting it out. When I got here and found smoke pouring out, Donald came to tell me Cassie had pushed him out the door and run back in. I went in after her."

Cassie absorbed their exchange while listening to her sister tell her she was so grateful she hadn't been hurt, then hugging her fiercely in punctuation. When she drew away, her eyes were clear and warm. "I don't want you to worry about the wedding. We can always do it in Father Eisley's rectory."

"Fifty people won't fit in there."

"I know. But we'll get married there, then if we explain about what's happened, I'm sure everyone will understand if we cancel the reception. We can send food to the homeless shelter."

Then Cassie had a sudden, completely unexpected, inspiration. It made her smile. Corie looked just a little worried. "What?" she asked.

Cassie turned to Grady. Sensing her excitement, both men stopped talking and turned to her.

Grady smiled ruefully. "Run for cover. I know this look. What?"

"What if we have the ceremony and the reception on the back lawn?"

Grady took the question calmly then asked with measured reason, "In the dark? In forty-degree weather?"

"Why not? Power's out, but we have the standing chandeliers for light…" Her smile battled with a quick frown. "Provided they survived the fire. If they didn't, there's always candlelight and your lanterns." The smile won then wavered briefly again. "How will we keep the food cold?"

Ben grinned. "My dad has a generator. I'm sure he'd be happy to bring it over."

Cassie smiled anew. "Great! We can set the tables and chairs outside, we'll all wear our coats, and it'll be great. Something to tell the grandchildren. The New Year's Day wedding, outside and at dusk, with chandeliers and the best food anyone ever tasted, thanks to Grady's mom and Helen."

"I *like* it!" Corie said on a laugh. "Ben, what do you think?"

Ben caught Corie's hand. "As long as we get married with our family and friends here, and I know we're looking at a lifetime together, I think it's a great idea."

"Yes!" Corie punched the air. "I'm going to cancel our hair appointments and we can use that time to split the invitation list and call everyone."

Cassie frowned. "No, you go get your hair done. I'll stay here and—"

"No. We'll probably have to wear hats, anyway."

"Over your veil? Oh, that'll be cute."

"Yeah, well, you almost had to wear boots to my wedding, so don't be critical."

"Corie." Cassie caught her hands as she reached into her pocket for her phone. "Are you sure it's okay? I mean, I promised you elegance and style…"

"It'll still be elegant, just outside." Corie hugged her. "How romantic is that? The New Year's Day wedding, outside, at dusk, with standing chandeliers and the best food anyone's ever tasted, just as you said. And my long-lost sister who pulled it all together and even saved it at the last minute. Who could ever want more than that?" She drew her hand away. "I'll call Helen and ask her to tell Jack and Sarah. We left the kids with her last night so we could get ready with a little peace and quiet. Grady, want me to call your mom?"

"Sure, if you don't mind." He stood as

the fire chief approached him. Ben and Grady had often met Bart Daniels at the gym. His ability to bench press three times his weight was a source of jealousy.

"It's out, Grady," the chief said, his protective mask pulled up. "I'm sorry about the water damage, but there's not a lot we can do about that. I think we saved the sofa, and all the rented materials for Ben's wedding, but that expensive-looking rug is a loss, as well as the table, and you might have to replace some balusters in your loft railing. Otherwise, except for smoke damage, it's not too bad."

Grady shook his hand. "Thanks, Bart. I appreciate how quick you were."

"Sure. You know our slogan. 'Send us to hell and we'll put it out.'" Bart grinned. "And, when the call comes from the residence of a supermodel, no matter how temporarily she's here, we do our best to come through."

Grady clapped his shoulder. "Whatever the reason, I appreciate it."

"What are you going to do about Ben's wedding?"

"Still happening. Same time. Wear a warm coat."

"All right. Come with me. I want to show you something that might give us a clue to what happened."

"Of course." Grady turned to excuse himself to his companions, but Ben and Don were in conversation and Corie was making phone calls. He started to follow Bart.

"I'd like to come," Cassie said, holding tightly to her blanket.

"Sure." Grady put an arm around her and brought her along with them. The small table had been pulled outside, several yards from the door. It had been severely burned. The drawer was partially open.

"I just had a look in here," Bart said, reaching in with his big gloves to pull out the contents. "Since you said the table was fully engulfed when you ran through, I thought it might tell us something."

He opened the palm of his glove to reveal several barely recognizable cylinders and a melted set of keys.

"I think this is the culprit."

CHAPTER FIFTEEN

CASSIE'S HEART BEGAN to thud. *No. Oh, no, no, no!* She still didn't understand what had happened in that drawer, but she'd been the only one to put anything it. Was she responsible for this? She heard Grady swear under his breath.

On the chance that it wasn't her fault, she pointed to the cylindrical things and asked innocently, "What are those?"

"Batteries," Bart replied.

She was going to be sick.

"A lot of people don't realize that loose batteries are combustible if the nodes make contact with metal for a prolonged period." Bart's thick-gloved index finger pointed out the puddle of metal in his other palm. "My guess is they made contact with these keys. That's a small, shallow drawer. If the batteries are in their packaging, they're safe, but when they're loose…this is what can happen."

"I keep an extra set of keys in that drawer," Grady said, sounding mystified, "but not batteries."

Cassie opened her mouth to say the words but they refused to come out. She had to draw a deep breath and wrap her arms tightly around herself, still clutching the blanket, almost physically pushing out the words. "I put them there."

Grady turned to her in confusion. "What? Why?" he asked.

Now that she'd made herself speak, her words tumbled out. "They're the extras for the standing chandeliers. They really eat up the battery power, so I wanted to be prepared. And I…" Her throat tightened, but she made herself say, "I took them out of the packaging to replace them quickly if I had to. I wanted things to be…perfect." She put a hand to his arm, folded with the other across his chest. "I'm so sorry, Grady." Her voice was choked. "I didn't know that about batteries. I had no idea. And I didn't know you had anything in there. I'm so, so sorry."

He didn't move his arm but she felt the

hard muscle under her fingertips react, as though he'd been touched by something hot—or unpleasant. And something shifted in his eyes. She saw fury ignite in them. He said nothing for a minute, carefully avoiding her gaze, then asked Bart, "Mind if I go inside now? Assess the damage?"

"Sure. We'll be here another hour or so, just to make sure there's nothing else to be concerned about." He patted Grady's shoulder. "I'm so sorry, man." He gave Cassie a sympathetic look. "You're not alone, Miss Chapman. We had a man who did something similar in the console in his car. He kept batteries for his kids' electronic devices in there, and they were up against a DVD. Destroyed his car, his garage and part of the house."

Of course, there was little comfort for Cassie in that story, but she smiled thinly at the fire chief, knowing he meant to help.

She followed Grady into the house, not knowing what to say, but needing him to look at her so she could try again to tell him how sorry she was.

He turned when he heard her behind him and said quietly but with such suppressed anger in his voice that she stopped in her tracks, "Don't come with me. There's… debris everywhere." He turned his back on her and walked inside.

EVERYTHING HE COULD see was in shambles. Very wet shambles. One arm of the sofa was burned, but the rest didn't look too bad. The Oriental rug was destroyed, as was the chair his mother used to like to sit in in front of the fireplace, and the small table there. The bunting on the loft railing still hung in tatters, held by the blackened remnants of the blue ribbon. The loft balusters were burned but not destroyed. The bunting on the stairway hadn't been touched by the fire, but was black with smoke and soaked from the hoses.

His mind played back Cassie's delight in that sparkly stuff—he couldn't remember the name—and wondered what she'd think of how it looked now. He felt vaguely sympathetic for her but couldn't help coming around to the old truth. If she hadn't strained so hard for glamour and style, she wouldn't be disappointed that much of her hard work—and his home—had been destroyed. Who needed battery-operated standing chandeliers? In Beggar's Bay? On Black Bear Ridge Road?

His efforts to suppress his anger were making him snarky. He could feel it. Anger was finding its way out in nasty, critical thoughts.

"Grady." He turned at the sound of an unfamiliar voice and looked into Cassie's sky blue eyes, now tortured and miserable. She folded her arms tightly together and squared her shoulders. She still wore the fire department's blanket. "You have to tell me what you're feeling," she said.

He looked away from her to the black and shredded bunting. "You won't like it," he said simply.

"I know. But I think you have to say it, anyway."

When he shook his head and tried to walk away, she caught his arm. "I know you blame me. I didn't know that could happen when I put the batteries in there, the fact of the fire is all my fault. You can say that."

"Okay." While he still struggled to maintain control over his anger, he figured he was able to confirm what she believed. "It is all your fault. I know you didn't mean to cause this…" He swept a hand at the mess before them, then dropped it to his side. "But you did. I know you're sorry, but it doesn't help much, so you don't have to say it again."

She appeared to take that with good grace, though her hands worked nervously where she clasped them in front of her. "I wouldn't have hurt you for the world."

Allowing himself that small latitude to let her know he blamed her seemed to be a get-out-of-jail-free card to the part of his anger already escaping his control.

"I know," he allowed, "but all those glitz-and-glamour things turned on you to bite *me*. I mean, who orders floor chandeliers from Paris?" he asked scornfully. Then he pointed to the threads of black tulle still attached to the loft railing. "And your sparkling stuff almost ignited the loft! This place would have been a total loss."

He let that sink in, taking some satisfaction from the wounded look in her eyes. But he couldn't stop himself from talking. "You couldn't let them have the quiet little ceremony they wanted. No, it had to be a Hollywood production with exotic lights and decorations. I didn't complain when you volunteered me to host a wedding, then took over my house like it was your own private photo shoot location, and had scores of people coming and going all day long."

He turned to the mess and shook his head, his color a little pale. "This is more than I'm willing to deal with."

THE WORDS WERE a sharp stick to the heart. While she understood his anger, she didn't quite get his inability to see that it had all been an awful accident, and her love of fashion and glamour had nothing to do with it. She had to hear the words in no uncertain terms.

"The destruction is more than you're willing to deal with?" she asked in a steady but raspy voice. "Or I am?"

"You are," he said without even having to think it over. He turned and looked directly into her eyes. "You are," he said again. "I knew it in the beginning, but I wasn't worried because all I did was promise to get you safely from Texas to Beggar's Bay. Then you had nowhere to stay, so it was the gentlemanly thing to do to invite you to stay here. I didn't think you'd end up taking over my life, my house and now, probably, my homeowner's insurance plan." The words had remained calm and quiet and therefore sounded even more lethal—and final—than if he'd shouted them.

"All right," she said, gathering up the shreds of her heart, her dignity and her fragile ego. She tightened the blanket around her. "What do you want to do about the wedding?"

"We'll have it on the back lawn as you told Corie," he said, indicating the stream of sunlight through the front window, sparkling on the many puddles inside the house. "It's a beautiful day—outside, anyway—and Ben and Corie are my friends. You should probably find somewhere else to spend the next few nights of your stay. Too much smoke in here."

"She can stay with me," Diane's voice said. Cassie and Grady turned in unison, surprised by his mother's presence. "Corie called me," she explained, looking from one to the other like a mother breaking up an argument between her children and not sure which one started it. Then her eyes went over the destruction and she put a hand to her heart. "Grady. I'm so sorry."

"Thanks, Mom. I'll survive."

"Of course, you will, sweetheart." She went to Cassie and wrapped her in a hug. "And you. You must feel awful."

"How do you know what happened?" Grady asked.

"Corie overheard your conversation with the fire chief and told me. My God, what a mess." She finally turned to Grady with a determined smile. "You can stay on my sofa, and Jack says Donald can stay with him and Sarah. They're not moving into the new place for another couple of days. So. Let's see what shape the kitchen's in."

"I walked through," Grady said. "I think it's mostly smoke-damaged. The food might smell like barbecue, but I think we can use the room."

"I understand Gary's bringing over his generator." Diane hooked an arm in Cassie's and drew her toward the kitchen.

"I love the sound of an outdoor wedding at night in January. I think it helps us start the new year with confidence and determination." She flung an arm out theatrically. "We roll with the punches."

IT WAS GOOD that Diane was a woman with a lot to say. She asked Cassie what the plan was; Cassie explained that so far it was pretty loose, but that they keep all the food in the kitchen and carry it out to the back lawn where the tables and chairs would be placed. The big indoor bouquets could be separated into smaller ones for the tables. It should be a cold but beautiful evening for a wedding reception.

Diane picked up the theme and ran with it. She volunteered a pergola she'd bought for her garden. Grady had painted it white to match her fence but hadn't been free to help her install it yet. She thought it could be used for the spot where the bride and groom would exchange their vows. "The flowers are coming this morning, right? We'll just put them on the pergola without bunting."

Bunting. Flaming bunting. Cassie felt a

clutch of pain in her chest. *You are more than I'm willing to deal with.* Grady's words replayed in her ears, echoed in her brain, caused pointed pain in her chest.

"Don't stop to think, sweetheart," Diane said, nudging her with her elbow as they stood side by side at the kitchen counter, looking out the back window. "We have a wedding to pull together. And look!" Elk munched on the salmonberry bushes in the distance. "Nature's even coming to the party."

The room was suddenly filled with Palmer women, plus Grandma and Oliver. Sarah and Helen started making the wear-warm-coats calls and Corie and Cassie ran out to greet the Beggar's Bouquets' truck as Diane left to snag Grady and Ben to pick up her pergola.

The day went on and Cassie went with it, carried on the tide of rescuing Corie and Ben's wedding. She didn't think about what would happen when the wedding was over. Whether she would go back to Paris early, or with her father, or just off somewhere else to finally let herself think things through. To understand how what had looked so promising could have fallen apart so quickly because of batteries and a set of keys.

Her mind continued to drift in that direction, but she called it back for what she was determined was the final time. She went in search of Jack.

BY LATE MORNING the men were setting up the pergola at the far end of the yard then holding the ladder steady while Sarah and Cassie draped the flowers.

"They're so beautiful," Sarah said, holding a length of the strand up, her arms wide apart. Jack placed a hand strategically on her backside so she didn't fall off the ladder. "Have you taken a close look, Cassie? The pinks are gorgeous and my dried hydrangeas are just the blue the flowers needed."

"You were absolutely right." Cassie touched a fingertip to the large flower made up of so many tiny ones. It had been dried at the peak of its fall color. What in summer was a bright blue turned shades of pink and purple and soft blue when the weather changed. They were a perfect complement to the pink roses and the Gerbera daisies.

By noon, everyone had helped haul out the rented tables and chairs, and Donald produced a catered lunch from the Bay Bistro.

"I was going to make sandwiches," Diane said when he suggested they put together two of the tables and have lunch outside.

"This probably won't be as good," he said diplomatically. "But it's easy and paper goods can be thrown away. It won't slow down your work in the kitchen for the wedding."

An old bedsheet from the linen cabinet near Grady's room covered two tables. Diane directed Soren to a stack of paper plates and plastic cups on the kitchen counter. He disappeared inside. She handed Rosie a bag of plastic utensils and napkins. "You want to put these at every place?"

Donald had brought what seemed like a sampling of the bistro's entire lunch menu. Plates were passed around, amid conversation and laughter, and Cassie took a moment to commit the scene to memory.

This was exactly what she'd longed for all her life. She'd been happy with her father, then with her many friends, but family and those pulled into the family's orbit were what set a person's place in life.

She belonged here. This group loved her and grounded her, and she loved them. She didn't want to leave—even to go back to work in Paris and New York, but these people were Grady's friends, too. No, they were now more than that. Grady and Diane had earned entry into the Palmer-Manning clan. Even Oliver had been taken in. Her own father had belonged long ago and been welcomed right back again.

She was the only one out of Grady's circle. She looked across the table and saw him in conversation with his mother and her grandmother, and felt a pointed lump in her throat. It looked as though he was being his charming self despite what he must be feeling at the mess she'd created today.

She tried to console herself with the thought that he might feel differently tomorrow, after he'd calmed down. The damage was alarming but not irreparable. She'd asked Jack to suggest a cleanup service, then a contractor who worked with log homes. She'd already made the calls and asked them to come for estimates tomorrow. Afraid Grady would balk at her taking the initiative, she hadn't asked him, but simply done it.

Now, feeling sure that these people would all be happy together, even if she wasn't among them for a while, she felt a buoying of spirit.

She glanced at her watch. Almost one. Hurrying inside for a trash bag, she ran back out to collect the paper goods and marshal her forces.

She gave everyone assignments and sent Corie and Ben home to relax and prepare for their wedding.

Jack playfully disagreed. "No, no. Why should Ben get off so easy? He should stay and help."

Ben gave him a bland look. "Funny. I have to wrangle Soren into a suit and tie. No getting off easy there."

Rosie folded her arms, looking grim. "I have a really pretty dress, and Mom says I have to wear a coat over it so I don't get sick."

"We're all going to wear coats," Cassie said, then had a thought. "Don't you still have the coat with the angels on it that Corie made you for Christmas? That was pretty amazing."

Corie had made each of the children in the foster home a coat made of pieces of other garments put together in the most colorful and creative way.

Rosie's eyes lit up as she turned to Corie. "Did we bring it from Texas?"

"We did. I know right where it is."

Rosie stood and pulled on her hand. "Then let's go so we won't be late."

Corie tried to help clean up first, but Cassie shooed her on her way. Once she and Ben and the children were gone, everyone got serious about cleaning up and getting ready, making sure everything necessary for the wedding was in place.

By midafternoon all the tables had been covered with rented white cloths and each white, wooden chair had been decorated with the raffia ribbon and a Gerbera daisy tied to the back's crosspiece.

Vases had been collected among the family to hold the flowers placed in the center of every table. By three thirty, all the women stood in a group in the middle of the yard and looked around. Ben and Grady had brought out the armoire to hold wedding presents. It should have a frivolous purpose, she thought, before it took up residence in an office.

"I think it looks pretty good," Cassie said, relieved that everything had been pulled together despite the circumstances. She took a big whiff of the cold, late-afternoon air and marveled that the Riviera rat she'd been, the one who'd loved sunshine and warmth, was morphing into a coastal Oregon woman who didn't mind the fog and the rain. Though there was none of that today. It was a golden day, just for Ben and Corie.

"Thank you so much for all your hard work." She looked at everyone and smiled. Sarah's hair was tucked under a baseball cap. Helen wore a woolly watch cap and Grandma had tied a pretty blue scarf that matched her coat around her hair. She still looked glamorous. Only Diane was without something covering her hair, and Cassie guessed it was because she'd gotten her new 'do the day she bought her suit, and loved it so much, she didn't want to cover it.

Cassie had tied her hair in a high ponytail then knotted it into a disheveled bun. "Thank you, also, for giving up your hair appointments so we could go to plan B and still make a beautiful wedding for Corie and Ben." When she called to cancel the appointments, she promised to send a check, anyway.

Sarah hugged her. "Well, of course. That's what family does. And, frankly, this has been more fun than I've ever had at a hair appointment."

"Absolutely." Helen pointed to the half circle of chairs placed around the pergola. They would later have to be moved to the tables, but for now they had been arranged with military precision. "I defy any wedding planner to do a better job than we've done." She smiled at Cassie. "Actually, we did have a wedding planner. You have been amazing!"

She couldn't take that compliment to heart. "I burned down the venue, Helen."

"It was an accident," Diane insisted.

"And look at what you've made out of a hopeless situation."

"Success," Grandma contributed. "That's my girl." She came to wrap an arm around her. "You've brought my family back into the light," she said with a sincerity that touched Cassie to her core. "I don't understand what happened with your mother, just that I continued to love her but felt as though she cloaked us in darkness. But you and your sister and brother are such miracles of love and caring. I'm so proud to be your grandmother."

"Oh, Grandma." Cassie embraced her, struck by how sad her life must have been when her daughter had become someone she could no longer understand. Cassie couldn't remember her mother, but she'd always felt a nugget of love for her.

As dusk began to settle over the backyard, there was the sound of male argument then laughter, as Jack, Gary, Oliver and her father walked out of the kitchen onto the lawn, each carrying a standing chandelier.

Corie felt instant panic. All she could think was that Grady would hate using them after what had happened. She ran to stop Jack, who was heading for the aisle between the rows of chairs.

"Jack!" she whispered, catching his arm, steadying the chandelier as he stopped in surprise. "I'm sure Grady won't want to use these."

"He's the one who told us to bring them out. They needed a little wiping off from the smoke, but they're unharmed." He looked up and down the aisle, the other men stopping behind him.

"Wouldn't it have been easier to just have the bride carry a candle?" Gary teased.

"It would have been easier to have the wedding in the house," her father added, the stand of the chandelier wrapped protectively in his arms as he smiled at her over it. "Where we could flip a switch and the lights would go on." Then he closed his eyes and shook his head. "Oh, yeah. You burned the house down. I forgot."

"Harsh, Mr. Chapman," Oliver said. "Funny. But harsh."

Grady came out of the back, carrying a chandelier, his expression carefully controlled—no smile, no frown.

"Where do these go?" he asked Cassie.

His light eyes rested on her, but they said nothing.

Picking up the challenge, she looked into his gaze, wanting to make him react to her. "You don't mind using these?"

He arched an eyebrow. "The batteries were the problem, not the chandeliers. And these things did come all the way from Paris. Shame to waste all that effort."

Was that a slam? Or was she being too sensitive? Didn't matter, she decided. He was entitled to a snarky tone.

She walked the men up the aisle and had them place the chandeliers in two rows at eight-foot intervals. Grady ran back to the house for the sixth chandelier and put it in place.

"Light them!" Sarah said as the women crowded around. "I have to see, and it's almost dark."

Each man turned the switch and Sarah ran up to light the last one.

A collective gasp confirmed what Cassie had suspected. They were even more beautiful outside than they'd been in the house.

Helen pointed into the distance behind the pergola where there seemed to be small, round, dancing lights in the distance. "What are those?"

Everyone turned in that direction, mystified.

"The elk are watching us," Grady replied. "Apparently they're coming to the wedding. Or, at least, plan to observe from a distance."

There was a moment of quiet while everyone strained to see.

"What are we going to do for lights after the wedding when people are eating?" Helen asked.

"I've got spotlights back here," Grady replied. "And we can distribute the chandeliers among the tables. I've got batteries."

Cassie glanced away from him at her watch. Would she ever hear that word again without her heart seizing? She drew a breath. "Okay. Four o'clock. We'd all better get a move on."

Everyone dispersed with shouts of "See you in an hour!" Fortunately no one had far to go home.

CHAPTER SIXTEEN

WHILE GRADY WALKED his mother to the car, Cassie hurried into the house. It hadn't occurred to her earlier to check on her dress, but now that the wedding was less than an hour away, she wondered in a little panic if the smoke and water had ruined it. There were still puddles all over the great room floor.

She held on to the railing as she walked upstairs because there were puddles there, too, and at the nearest edge of the loft floor. Mercifully, the bed and everything beyond it seemed to have been spared.

She opened the wardrobe closet and felt a small quiver of happiness at the sight of her dress, still in its plastic sleeve from Bay Boutique, dry and unharmed. Folded beside it on the floor of the closet was the dung-green raincoat Grady had lent her.

She guessed she had little choice but to wear it.

Not that she hadn't modeled summer clothing and bathing suits in downright cold conditions in her work, but there'd always been someone standing by with a warm blanket to wrap her in. And this wasn't a photo shoot.

Today was one of those *real* times Grady lived in fear of, the kind that shook you to your core and reminded you that life was risky. Anything could happen at any time, and if you didn't want to get hurt or disappointed, or ever lose anything, you stuck to a safe plan. Took no chances. Stayed with what's familiar. Didn't let yourself be vulnerable.

She blew out air and went to the railing to look down at the destruction to Grady's great room. Wouldn't it be horrid if he was right, after all? She'd thought she was being prepared and taking no chances on a perfect wedding when she'd stored extra batteries for the chandeliers in the little drawer. Chandeliers and other beautiful things *were* familiar to her. So, technically, none of this should have happened.

Maybe it was the "letting yourself be vulnerable" point that tripped her up. She'd always believed in being brave and open, but Grady hadn't, and look what it had gotten him when he'd tried it.

"Cassie."

She was surprised to hear his voice and leaned over the railing, looking for him. When he said her name again, she realized it came from the top of the stairs.

"Please don't use the electricity while you're getting ready," he said. "Considering the hanging chandelier ripped off and fell down, and that there's water everywhere, it'll be safer to use the battery-powered lantern under the bedside table."

"Okay," she said. She tried to gauge what he was thinking and couldn't. He wasn't angry. He wasn't really anything. He looked gorgeous in his dishevelment from all their hard work today, but the man who'd been so kind and considerate of her since she'd fainted in his arms less than two weeks ago didn't seem to be there.

Then he held something out to her. "Do you want this for tonight? I know it isn't at all wedding-appropriate, but I thought

you'd like it better than the green rain
jacket."

His bomber jacket hung from his hand.
The sight of it warmed her instantly. He
was in there, somewhere under the resid-
ual anger and the disappointment at seeing
his long-held but recently doubted beliefs
proved true, after all.

She wanted to run into his arms and tell
him again how sorry she was, that he'd
been right to care for her, to let her into
his life and dive into hers, but that was hard
to prove at this point.

She moved toward him with care, afraid
of alarming him, like approaching one of
the elk that had watched their wedding
preparations. She took the jacket from him
and held it against her. "Thank you. I'll
take good care of it."

"I'm sure you will," he said. "Just keep
it until you go home."

This was home. She would be going
away. "Thanks."

"Sure. Anything you need?"

You. "I think I'm good."

"All right." He turned and picked his
way carefully down the stairs, leaped over

the puddles and disappeared down the corridor to his room.

She held the jacket to her chest and bent her head over it. The smell of his spicy aftershave clung to it. There was hope, she thought. It was fragile, but it was there.

BEN AND CORIE'S wedding was unlike anything Grady had ever seen. The bride and groom exuded such love when they looked into each other's eyes that he guessed they could have been in a desert, or in shirtsleeves at the North Pole and they wouldn't have noticed. Or, they'd have noticed but they wouldn't have cared. After a colossal struggle with life, they were finally able to declare their love and promise each other that it would last forever.

There were six or seven rows of guests on both sides of the aisle. They were bundled against the clear, cold night, anticipatory smiles in place as the Wild Men sang "All You Need is Love." The air was redolent of the surrounding fir trees, the winter smell of wood smoke and the collected perfumes the wind had brought across the ocean.

Sarah came down the aisle with her warm smile and what was probably a beautiful dress covered to her hips by a gray jacket. With a pink-and-blue bouquet, she somehow looked just right.

Grady felt a punch to his heart when Cassie followed Sarah, her hair piled at the back of her head, curls falling everywhere, a pink daisy caught in them. She was heartbreakingly beautiful without much effort, with a softness about her that was almost painful. His leather jacket enhanced rather than detracted from the figure she cut walking between the ethereal chandeliers. Below the jacket, some fluffy, fussy skirt skimmed her knees, and he took in her long, gorgeous legs.

Rosie followed in a wildly bright coat, clearly feeling beautiful. She held a small wicker basket and scattered rose petals on the grass, her beautiful black hair catching the light from the chandeliers.

Soren walked beside her, uncharacteristically serious in his suit with the hated tie. His hair was slicked back but the ever-present twinkle was in his eye as he carefully balanced the ring pillow.

Corie was gorgeous. He smiled to himself as he thought the word he'd heard Cassie use so much. He'd heard the women talk about how she'd made her own dress that looked like something a lady in the Middle Ages would have worn. She wore a soft blue jacket over it that Grandma Eleanor had lent her.

Gary Palmer walked her down the aisle, looking proud and solemn.

Ben, waiting for her, smiled with a tenderness Grady hadn't seen in him before. He knew his friend to be a kind, compassionate man, but it seemed this woman had reached deeper inside him than anything or anyone ever had.

When the wedding party turned to face the priest, there was a communal gasp as everyone noticed the elk at the edge of the property, their attention turned toward the wedding guests. There was a majestic male, several females and six or seven young ones. They were a magnificent addition to a magical day.

Cassie glanced in Grady's direction with a wide smile, clearly happy that they'd come. He had to smile back, happy, too.

The ceremony was brief but poignant. When Ben and Corie were pronounced husband and wife, Ben kissed her then crushed her to him as though nothing could ever separate them.

Loud applause and cheers erupted, and the exit music was "Time of My Life" at full volume. The guests sang along. Rosie and Soren met to walk up the aisle, a more familiar elbowing and shoving going on between them. Sarah took Grady's arm, her cheeks wet with tears, and Jack and Cassie followed behind them.

Oliver and Donald carried chairs from the wedding area to the tables with the help of other guests. Diane, Helen and Eleanor were already carrying dishes to a buffet table set up under one of the spotlights, fortunately part of a different electrical system than the house.

He was surprised when Sarah stopped him and gave him a hug. "I have to get in there and help," she said, smiling up at him. "Thank you for doing this for them even after what happened today. I think for most of us, this will go down as one of the most memorable weddings we've ever attended.

As far as the family is concerned, you and Cassie are quite the heroes."

She placed her hands on his arms. "You do understand that it was all just a terrible accident? Not that you don't have a right to be completely upset, but…Cassie wouldn't hurt anyone. I've only known her for ten days and I'm as sure of that as I am that Jack is the other half of my soul."

"That's quite a claim." He tried to lighten the moment, unable to explain to her that he was confounded by his own feelings. What he felt wasn't anger at Cassie but anger at himself for ever thinking that their lives could work together. She'd always want extravagant, glamorous and fussy things that would burn down his life and everything that had gotten him this far.

She put a hand to her heart. "My faith in her, like my love for Jack, is a core belief."

The bride and groom had been drawn aside and surrounded by their guests. Jack and Cassie were right behind Grady, and Jack took Sarah away from him. "Mine, Grady," he said with a grin. "You've got your own woman." He hugged Cassie then walked away with Sarah.

Grady and Cassie stood between the last pair of chandeliers. Cassie smiled up at him, tipping her head toward her departing brother. "Sorry about that. He thinks we still…you know…have something going."

"It's all right," he said. "I'll always care about you."

EVERY FRAGILE HOPE Cassie'd had that she could somehow turn this relationship around disintegrated. When he'd smiled back at her at the sight of the elk, she'd hoped. Now bitterly disappointed, she couldn't help the impatient roll of her eyes as she started to walk away. "Never mind." She tossed the words at him over her shoulder.

He caught her arm and drew her back, obviously annoyed. *"Never mind?"* he repeated. They locked gazes, the crystals in the chandeliers moving in the night breeze.

"Never. Mind." She repeated the words slowly, deliberately. "That is the most lifeless, insipid expression of feeling I've ever heard. If that's all you have to offer, I don't want it." She tried to leave again, but he held fast.

"Hey!" he whispered, glancing around, making sure no one was listening. "You burned down my home!"

"I did not!" she whispered back at him. "I accidentally caused the fire. And I'm sorry. Actually, I didn't even burn it all down. I made a horrible mess of the great room, true, but a cleaning company is coming tomorrow, and I've hired a contractor Jack recommended to give you an estimate on repairs. I'll take care of everything."

She jabbed a finger at his chest. "And be honest with yourself for once, Grady. You're not mad that there was a fire, you're mad because you fell in love with me even though it scares you to death, and this accident was a perfect excuse to say, 'Aha!'" She took on a villainous voice. "'You led me astray from my staid and safe little life and now look what you've done. You've made me care, and I'm not comfortable with that because you messed everything up and now I have to forgive you and love you, anyway, and that's too hard. You cost me my comfort and that's what's most important to me because when my father died I had to give up everything to help my mother.'"

He looked murderous. She could only conclude that she was right on.

"You're very lucky there are so many witnesses," he said darkly, dropping her wrist.

"Really?" Her voice dripped with irreverence. She put a thumb to the side of her nose and took a fighter's stance. "Want to go a few rounds? Come on, let's see what you've got. There's a pirate ship in your bathroom, for heaven's sake! Where's your knife-in-your-teeth fearlessness? Let's duke out the safe-and-sober versus risky-and-alive life question."

Her father and Diane appeared, looking vaguely concerned. Diane wore an apron over her coat, and her arm was tucked in Donald's.

"Everything okay here?" her father asked, looking from one to the other in concern. "You're not really going to start boxing, are you?"

Cassie relaxed from her fighter's stance and patted his chest. "I would, but Grady's too much of a gentleman to get down and dirty or display any passion. Excuse me. I've got to go help in the kitchen."

THE RECEPTION LASTED for hours. No one seemed to notice when the temperature dropped and they finally ran out of food. Laughter filled the fragrant night air and the Wild Men launched into a set of romantic numbers. Couples danced, leaning on each other, the new year beginning with looks into each other's eyes and firm embraces.

Everyone gathered to throw birdseed as Ben and Corie left. Soren and Rosie stayed behind—Jack and Sarah would watch them for the night.

The women headed back to the kitchen. When the Wild Men played the first few familiar bars of "You're Nobody Till Somebody Loves You," Cassie shooed everyone back to the dancing, then hid out in the kitchen, cleaning and crying like a crazy woman.

By the time the kitchen sparkled, the music had stopped and she went out to clear tables. She thanked the musicians and then said good-night to the last of the guests.

She had a centerpiece in each arm, ready to carry them into the house, when Diane approached her. She'd removed the apron and had her purse over her shoulder. "Do you want to come with me, Cassie?" she asked. "Grady insists he's staying here, but I don't think you'd be very comfortable. Couldn't you use a nice hot bath and a cup of tea?"

That sounded divine. "I would love that. You're sure I'm not putting you out?"

"Absolutely. You get your things and I'll go say good-night to your father. He's ready to leave with Jack and Sarah and the kids."

Cassie stopped her with a hand on her arm. "You like him, don't you?"

A youthful smile grew on Diane's mouth. "I do. He's a very interesting man, and he's so proud of you. Not because you're a celebrity, but because you're such a special young woman."

"That's nice of you to say. He seems to like you, too."

Diane giggled, looking thrilled. "I know. Isn't that wonderful? He's invited me to come look at a property he's considering buying on the outskirts of town. He said he'd planned to sell his business and retire, anyway, and now he really likes it here and since you'll be coming back…" She spread her hands as though the rest was obvious.

Cassie hugged her. "I'm so happy, Diane." She pushed her gently to where her father waited. "Go say good-night and I'll run upstairs. I promise I won't be long."

Cassie dashed up to the loft and her still-damp room. She packed up her things, putting all the extra clothing she'd bought since she'd arrived into the plastic sleeve from Bay Boutique. She resisted the impulse to dawdle over memories of her first shopping trip there, of the night she'd worn her little black dress and she and Grady had danced to Sinatra, and the feeling of his arms around her when she rode the elevator without screaming. Tears fell, but she wiped them away and dug into the closet for her boots.

She spotted the raincoat and realized it was a metaphor for what she was left with. She pulled off the leather jacket she liked so much and placed it on the foot of the bed, then shrugged into the raincoat.

With a sudden lack of energy, she sat

beside the jacket and looked around at the warm, familiar room. Though she'd been here only a few days, it felt as though she'd been here much longer, as though she was a different woman from the one who'd run away from the paparazzi with Grady. She'd give anything to be able to stay, despite the broken windows and the lack of electricity. But while the house was sound enough, her emotions were not and she would either smack Grady over his attitude or burst into tears in front of him. Neither response would be productive.

With a small groan, she stood and hurried downstairs with all her possessions. She stopped short at the sight of Grady at the door.

"I'll walk you to Mom's car," he said, taking her things from her without bothering to ask. She opened her mouth to insist that she could carry them, but he said simply, "Don't."

"Why are you mad at *me*?" she demanded a little testily. She was now officially exhausted and without her customary good humor.

He gave her a look over his shoulder that

told her that was a silly question. She had to grant him that. "Okay. Apart from the fact that I'm responsible for the house fire. I'm leaving so that you don't have to look at me anymore tonight. And I'll be back in the morning to talk to the cleaners and the contractor to get your life repaired."

His mother stood by the open trunk of her car and watched as he put Cassie's bags inside. "It's my house," he said. "I'll do that."

"I've already taken care of it. And I'm going to pay for the repairs."

"I have insurance."

"There'll be things insurance won't cover."

"Tell me about it," he said, taking her by the shoulders. "Broken heart. Broken dreams."

She gasped, staring at him openmouthed at that admission. He was going to kiss her. No, he was too angry. Her insides somersaulted in confusion.

He released her to close the trunk and open the passenger's-side door. "Get in. Please."

She complied and swung her legs in, shaken by what he'd said and trying not to betray it.

CHAPTER SEVENTEEN

GRADY WALKED INTO his trashed and empty house. He retrieved the Coleman lantern from the guest closet and went into the kitchen in search of leftover champagne. There was half a bottle in the fridge, the contents still cold thanks to Gary's generator. He poured a juice glass full and went back to sit on the unburned half of the sofa.

The smell of smoke was less pervasive now that the broken windows had been allowing air in all day. Tonight he smelled the woods behind his house, the leftover fragrance of the perfume and aftershave of his guests, the ten small bouquets one of the women had artfully lined up on the stairs.

At the wall at a right angle to the stairs, Jack and Oliver had placed the six standing chandeliers in a row. Damned things. They personified for him the extravagance of Cassie's approach to life.

But they had been beautiful tonight.

He took a sip of the champagne and felt its chill in his chest. The air coming through his broken windows made the room too cold for champagne.

He lay his head against the back of the sofa and closed his eyes, combating the terrible loneliness he felt without the sound of Cassie's movements in the loft.

Still, the fire was proof that his life was never intended to handle the glamorous but impulsive way she behaved. He'd thought he could stay with her until she was free to come back to Beggar's Bay with him for good.

He knew now that wouldn't work. Geography really didn't matter. He'd still be the guy who wanted to deal in basics, and she'd always be the woman who ordered six standing chandeliers from a prop supplier in Paris.

There was a light knock on the door. He held his watch against the lantern to check the time. It was after ten. He couldn't imagine who would be coming by at this hour.

That question was answered the next moment when Donald's face appeared in the broken window. "Grady, are you still up?" he called.

"Yeah. I'm coming." Grady went to the door and yanked it open. "Don. Hi. I thought you were spending the night with Jack and Sarah." He stood aside to let him in.

"That was the plan, but I got worried about you moping around in here." Donald had changed into jeans and his stadium jacket over an argyle sweater. He held up a bottle of brandy in one hand and had palmed the bottoms of two paper cups in the other. "I've got coffee and brandy," he said. "A much better combination than coffee, cream and sugar ever was."

"Sure. Watch your step. There's still water and debris all over the floor." Grady closed the door and led the way back to the great room. They sat on the sofa by the light of the lantern. "What made you think I'd be moping?"

Donald removed the plastic lids and poured brandy into the cups, glancing at Grady as he did so. "The fact that you love my daughter and you're pushing her away."

Grady wished he hadn't opened the door,

but when he took a sip of the coffee con-coction, he was glad he had, after all.

"We're not right for each other," he said.

"Why is that? Because she's a celeb-rity?" Donald leaned back with his own cup, crossing the ankle of one leg over the knee of the other. "Because she really doesn't care about that stuff."

"Right." Grady told him briefly about his life, his father, his change of plans to be able to help his mother.

Donald nodded. "I know." He empa-thized. "Diane told me what a good son you've been and that your father was…" He glanced at Grady then looked down at his cup. "Sometimes illness takes away your ability to deal with anything but your own problems. I had that experience with Cassie's mother. She couldn't cope with her life without taking drugs, and eventually it didn't even matter that she loved me, that she loved her kids. She chose the drugs over us."

That was true for Cassie's family, but Grady remembered a kind, loving father before his illness changed him. "He'd been a good dad."

"He had to have been," Donald said. "I can see in you that you had a good role model."

Grady sipped at his cup, feeling the hot, brandied coffee slide down into his stomach. "My parents hadn't been able to save much, and they had debt. His inability to work made my mother's and my lives very basic. There was no room for frivolous thinking, no having things easy. Life was pretty hard."

"But, that was then," Donald said. "You've matured and moved on. Or is this about that other woman? Celine?"

"Celeste," Grady corrected. He gave Donald a judicious look. "You and Mom have done a *lot* of talking."

Donald laughed. "It's hard to keep up with your mother. She's worried about you, particularly after the fire. So she shared that with me."

"Okay, I appreciate that, but you're not my parent, here."

"I know. But I'm Cassie's parent. I'm working for her, as well as for you. And if you want to spend the rest of your life stuck in place, I want a different future for her."

Grady was angry that Donald had reduced his life's problems to being "stuck in place." But in making himself think before he reacted angrily, Grady realized that that described his situation very well.

"That's why I can't let this go any farther. We're two very different people."

"Who seem to have a great time together."

"We do, but…" He swept a hand around the room. "I live in a simple, sturdy, log house. And she rents standing chandeliers. How does that ever come together?"

Donald turned to him, looking a little surprised that he wasn't getting the point.

"Okay, if you want to use a log house and a chandelier as a metaphor for your lives, I think it works. Did you not notice today that the house burned and the wedding had to be moved outside where the chandeliers lit up the landscape—and made a beautiful wedding?"

Feeling a little cornered, Grady rebutted. "Don, she's the one who burned the house."

Donald nodded on a sigh. "Can't deny that, but it's important to note that her intent was beauty and not destruction. And then, with the venue up in flames, she made the proverbial silk purse out of a sow's ear. I think that was the nicest wedding I've ever been to."

"She's rash!"

"She is."

"She never thinks twice."

"Because she sees things pretty clearly the first time."

Grady rolled his eyes. "Don. She got you out of the burning house, then went back inside to...to...I don't know...probably to save her chandeliers. That's thinking clearly?"

Donald stared at him, both eyebrows raised, a small gasp of surprise coming from his open mouth. "Is that what you think?"

"It's what I know," Grady snapped. "I went in to get her, remember?"

Donald ran a hand over his face and shook his head. He put his coffee cup down and leaned back into the sofa. "Grady," he said gravely, "she went back in for you."

Grady thought about that a minute, stunned. He'd found her near the kitchen, doing what? Trying to save the food that had been brought over last night? He couldn't quite follow Donald's reasoning. "I wasn't here," he said.

"We didn't know that. You never told us you were leaving early to go to the bakery. She went to the sofa to wake you with fire all around her, and when she didn't find you, she came for me and practically shoved me out the door so she could come back in and look for you."

No. That wasn't possible. The house was on fire and filled with black smoke. He hadn't been able to see anything when he'd gone in after her. What had it been like for her, her claustrophobia dragging on her every step?

Grady sat in silence for a long moment, unable to process the whole concept of Cassie trying to save him from the fire, probably with all the symptoms of claustrophobia impeding her.

"I thought…" He struggled to form a coherent sentence. "I thought she'd gone back in to get the wedding stuff. The chandeliers."

"Did you find her moving a chandelier toward the door?"

"No. I found her in the kitchen."

"Looking for you. And you have to know how hard that was for her. She deals with her condition almost daily and without drama."

Grady was speechless.

"She is as different from you as she can be," Donald said gently, "and that could work against you if she didn't love you and truly appreciate you for the good, kind man you are."

Resting his elbows on his knees, Grady covered his face with his hands and tried to find balance in a life that was falling over. "She never told me why she went back."

"She wouldn't," Donald said. "Maybe she thought you'd realize why."

"God," Grady muttered, hands still covering his face. "What does that make me?"

"It makes you just like her," he replied, a small smile in his voice. "You ran in after *her*. Maybe you're more alike than you imagine."

DIANE'S HOME WAS small and charming, with an interesting collection of brightly painted folk furniture and knickknacks.

Diane dropped her purse on a wooden chair painted red with black polka dots and told Cassie to put her things at the foot of the stairs. "We'll take them up later. I need a cup of tea. Want one?"

"Please."

"I hope you feel good about what you accomplished today," Diane said, stopping on her way into the kitchen. She beckoned to Cassie. "That was a lovely wedding."

"It was." Cassie stopped in the middle of the room to look around at a mind-blowing collection of hand-painted signs. Signs of encouragement, signs of observation, funny signs, and all done in primitive style. "Diane, these are wonderful. I suppose you remember where you found each one?"

"I do as a matter of fact. That one—" she pointed to one painted blue with dark blue lettering "—about the risk of failure but the joy and freedom of taking the risk. Grady's father and I had come home from our teaching jobs in Italy to give birth to Grady here. I wanted him to know that freedom, but when his father got sick we were caught in a cycle where physical and emotional survival ruled our lives. I'd found this in a little shop on a side street in Boise, though I never really got to live the lesson. But isn't it perfect?"

Cassie swallowed around a lump in her throat. It was perfect. Life wasn't, but the sign was. She pushed back from the easy slope to a pity party when she remembered that she'd conquered her claustrophobia, at least for that moment, when she'd searched for Grady in the fire. Her love for him was stronger than what she was afraid of. She thought with a little twist of irony that what she now feared the most was living the rest of her life without him.

Diane pointed her to one of two chairs at a little round table in the corner. "Have a seat. How about a cookie with your tea?"

Cassie sat but put a hand to her stomach. "No, thank you. I ate too much at the wedding."

Making a face at her, Diane filled the kettle. "You did not. You hardly ate anything. I watched you. I know it had something to do with that little boxing incident your dad and I interrupted."

"Oh, it's nobody's fault. Well, the house burning is my fault, but…"

"You don't have to explain." The kettle

clanged as Diane put it on the stove and turned on the burner. "I guess in his upset over the whole thing, Grady blames you, but not because he thinks you did it on purpose."

"I know. But that would be almost easier to understand. It's because he thinks I messed up his life with glamour and fuss. He says life works best for him when it's real and on track."

Diane brought over two mugs and two black tea bags, and sat opposite her. "He thinks that because when he came out of school to help his dad and me, our finances were a mess and his father was irascible and ungrateful.

"Grady worked a lot of double shifts to make us solvent again, and remained kind and loving to his father despite getting very little back. He just put his head down and kept going when there was very little positive from day to day. When his father passed away, there was a lot to do—a lot to pay for—then, finally, things were looking up.

"Grady helped me move to this town to be with my sisters, and when he saw how beautiful it was, he decided to stay. I thought life would finally open up for him. Then, early this year, he met Celeste."

Cassie nodded grimly. "I've heard about her."

Diane made a face. "She just looked like trouble, but she fussed over him and, for the first time in a long time, he took a chance." She pretended to stick a finger down her throat. "She called him 'lover boy,' wanted to go to fancy places, do fancy things, then she got tired of him and married somebody else. He was heartbroken."

"I know."

"He took it as proof positive that he wasn't entitled to have fun and do extravagant things. He became even more of a head-down, on-track kind of man. Thanks to Ben and Jack, he manages to have fun, but not too deeply, and never for very long. But, he's such a good man. Don't give up on him, Cassie."

"*He*'s given up on *me*, Diane." It hurt to say it, but in loving him, he claimed she'd broken his heart and his dreams.

"He needs a couple of days to find his

feet. All the stuff going on with the wedding and then the fire..."

"I'm going over there in the morning to meet the cleaners and the contractor I hired, and to arrange to have the chandeliers shipped back. I'll leave an account at the bank for both of them, but I have to fly back the following day." Cassie's voice cracked and she took a minute to pull herself together. No more loft, no more Bay Boutique, no more get-togethers with Corie and Sarah, no more Jack and Ben, no more Grandma and Helen and Diane.

No more Grady. She stood to alleviate an undefined pain. "I can't bear to be here anymore."

Diane got to her feet and wrapped her arms around her. "He'll come to you in Paris."

"He won't. It's over." She patted Diane's back and moved her gently away. "I got along without Grady for twenty-five years, I can do it again. My life is busy and exciting, and I can get back into it." She paused, trying to imagine that, but it all seemed empty now that she loved a man, had family and felt at home in Beggar's Bay.

"Drink your tea," Diane said. "Life always makes more sense when you're running on caffeine."

Right. She could do this. It was just a matter of convincing herself she couldn't have Grady and she had to leave.

They talked about Diane visiting her in Paris with Cassie's father. "He says there's a bakery near your apartment that makes wonderful pastries."

Macarons.

The very thought brought back her playful discussion with Grady about her stealing all the macarons and him being a gendarme, giving chase.

She crossed her arms on the table, put her head down and dissolved into tears.

CHAPTER EIGHTEEN

CASSIE RAISED HER head at the loud knock on Diane's door. She took a napkin from the middle of the table and dried her eyes as Diane, with a who-could-that-be frown, went to answer it.

"That better be Grady coming for you," she said.

Cassie seriously doubted it. He'd thought it made good sense to tell her he would "always care for her" but never love her. What chance was there for a man who thought like that to change his mind? Why did she want a man so determined not to love her, anyway?

She didn't anymore, she told herself firmly as she stood and pushed in her chair. She squared her shoulders on the chance that it was Grady at the door; she didn't want him to see her looking as bereft as she felt.

"Cassidy Chapman?" The sound of her name in an unfamiliar male voice floated into the kitchen. Then two men in Beg-gar's Bay Police Department uniforms appeared in the doorway, Diane standing behind them, both arms extended in a ges-ture of confusion.

"I don't understand," she was saying. "Cassie Chapman is here, but you have to be wrong. I mean, she's been at a wedding all day."

The older of the two officers—Brogan, according to his badge—held up an important-looking document. "We have a warrant for your arrest."

Cassie blinked, wondering if she'd fallen asleep at the table and was dream-ing. "What?"

Brogan approached her, barring her path to the door. The other, younger, taller of-ficer came up beside him, looking severe. His badge read Kubik. Her heart picked up its beat.

"You're under arrest," Brogan said, "for assaulting Oliver Browning on Black Bear Ridge Road on December 31."

"He was stalking me," she said, aware that she looked nervous and probably guilty. Because, technically, she was. "Well, he wasn't, but I thought he was. He was working for my grandmother, but he had a camera, and I'd seen him hiding and watching me before in town, so I naturally assumed… I mean, the paparazzi are always after me."

"He has a black eye," Kubik said, "multiple contusions, his jacket was torn, and you tossed his camera at a tree and broke it in several pieces."

Well, this wasn't good. Oliver had assured her he'd understood her reaction. He'd told Grady he wouldn't press charges. Something must have changed his mind.

"I…" she began when Brogan came around to put her hands behind her back. He read her her rights as he put the plastic cuffs on her wrists.

The other officer took hold of her elbow and began to lead her away. "But I…I…" She stammered, unable to decide how to defend herself. She had hit Oliver, she had broken his camera, she didn't remember ripping his coat, but she probably had by the time Grady had pulled her off him. But what had made him decide to press charges, after all? And wouldn't this look good alongside the news story about her meltdown in Ireland?

"You can explain it all to your attorney," Brogan said. "Put her in the car, Kubik."

"My son is on the BBPD," Diane said, following them to the door. "I'm calling him right now. You have no right to take this poor woman..."

And that was all Cassie heard as Brogan handed Diane his card so she knew who to complain about and closed the door.

The night was dark and cold, and Cassie still wore her maid-of-honor dress. For once, she wished she hadn't left the green raincoat behind at the foot of Diane's stairs with her things.

"There you go, ma'am. Into the cage." The officer opened the door for her and, palming her head, pushed her gently inside the shadowy police car. Getting in was awkward with her hands cuffed behind her. She had to turn her back, sit down, then tuck her long legs into the tight space. The door closed beside her. The back of the car was dark, the cage that separated her from the front feeling as though it was right in her face. She waited for the choked feeling, the desperate need to scream and climb out of her own skin.

Weirdly, she felt nothing like that.

Taking her completely by surprise, a voice beside her said suddenly, "Oh, God! I didn't think about that."

Grady's voice. She was hallucinating. Or she'd gone insane. Or her brain had been smoke damaged, after all. Grady, sitting on the opposite side of the back seat, opened his door, climbed out, then reached in and pulled her out with both arms around her waist.

Holding her by the shoulders, he looked apologetic. "I'm sorry," he said, reaching into the pocket of his leather jacket for a knife and cutting off the cuffs. "I didn't stop to think that being in the cage could make your claustrophobia react."

Cassie looked into his penitent eyes and struggled for clear thought. Two things crowded her awareness. She should have felt claustrophobic in the back of the police car, but she hadn't. And Grady had had her arrested? If so, why had he cut her out of the cuffs? The only thing that made any sense to her was that she was freezing.

Grady pulled off his jacket and put it

on her, zipping it up then holding it by the collar.

Over his shoulder, she saw Brogan and Kubik standing side by side, wide grins on their faces.

"Mission accomplished?" Brogan asked Grady.

"Partially," he said, still holding Cassie by the jacket collar. He turned to face his friends. "The rest is up to me. Thanks for agreeing to help me, guys. And for giving up your break."

Brogan gave Cassie an apologetic bow. "Our pleasure. Sorry we had to cuff you, ma'am, but knowing what you did to the guy you thought was stalking you, we wanted to protect ourselves."

"Mmm," she said, just beginning to see a trace of light and comprehension. "Seems to be some form of collusion, here. Is this kind of thing allowed in the police department?"

Both officers smiled without answering and got into their unit.

"Grady Joshua Nelson!" Diane called from her doorway. She was fighting a smile. "Get Cassie out of the cold. You're welcome to come inside to finish out the

rest of this fiendish plan. I'm going to bed."
She turned toward the stairs, leaving the
front door open.

"I'm sorry about putting you in the
cage," Grady said. "After all you'd been
through in the fire."

In that instant in the back of the police
car, she'd made a revealing discovery. She
told him with the wonder she felt as she
understood what happened, "It's all right
because I was fine. I may have conquered
the claustrophobia."

"Seriously? Because of the fire?"

She looked into his eyes. She saw the
man she knew and loved in them and felt
peaceful about that for a moment. Until she
wondered what he saw in her eyes.

"No," she replied. "Because I've been
conditioning myself to learn to live without you, and now *that's* the hardest thing
I have to face."

He wrapped his arms around her and
held her close. "Cassie," he said heavily,
"I'm sorry I was such an idiot. I didn't realize you'd run back inside during the fire
to save *me*. I guess I thought you'd realize
I'd gone out."

She placed a hand on each side of his waist, loving his closeness and his rapt attention. "I couldn't see anything. The smoke was everywhere. I felt the sofa and there was nothing on it but what felt like a folded pile of your blankets. I thought you might be somewhere else in the house and overcome by smoke. So I got my dad out and went in to find you."

"That's what the fire department is for."

She sighed and leaned into him. "Grady, if you're in trouble, helping you is what *I'm* for." She raised her head from his shoulder to smile at him. "And, anyway, you should talk. You came in after *me*."

"I love you," he said simply. "In fact…" He pulled her up the walk toward the house, crushing her against his side. "I have to take issue with something you told our parents."

She really tried to think back, but was too caught up in how tightly he held her to be aware of anything but the moment. "I can't remember."

He stopped at the foot of the steps to the porch and held her by the shoulders, his chin taking on a stubborn line she knew well. "You said I was too much of a gentleman to show passion."

"Because you're always so careful with your feelings and reluctant to—"

That was as far as she got. He cupped her head in his hand, brought her lips to his and kissed her with a torrid attention to detail that completely falsified her claim. She couldn't breathe but that didn't seem to matter—her lips and not her lungs seemed to be in charge at the moment.

When he finally put her a step away, still holding on to her, she gasped in a frail voice, "I take it back."

"Good." He took her hand and led her the rest of the way up the steps. He stopped short of opening the door.

"I have something to ask you," he said.

She held the sides of the jacket together with one hand. "Can we go inside and sit down where it's warm?"

"No. I have to ask you now or I'll forget the words."

"Okay."

He took a breath, firmed his stance and began haltingly. *"Ah—veux tu—me...ah... étouffer?"*

OH, GOD, SHE didn't want to. He'd been such an idiot. Why did he think that his sudden enlightenment would change everything between them? He'd hurt her…

"Um…" She narrowed an eye and he began to wonder if she hadn't understood the question. That was possible, but she was supposed to be fluent in French.

"Grady," she said, putting a hand to his chest. He placed his hand over it, feeling as though it might burn through his shirt. "You just asked in really atrocious French if I would suffocate you—or join you in a New Orleans crab dish. I'm not sure which."

He groaned in frustration. He'd practiced that line while he'd waited in the cage for his friends to bring her out. He consulted a note he pulled out of his pocket and began to try again.

She took the note from him and read in flawless French *"Veux-tu m'épouser?"*

He saw fireworks in her eyes. "You know what you're asking?" She looked up at him. "I mean…you understand that you're proposing?"

"I do." He kissed her again. "I wanted to learn it in French since, you know, that's the language of love. And the language I'll be speaking when I go back with you."

Her smile was blinding. "You really want to do that?"

"Yes!" Love opened his world. "I think Oliver's going to stay to help Ben get the agency started until we come back, and I'm going to learn about the world you live in, see if I can find a way to fit in there."

"Grady, we've fitted together beautifully since the day I fainted in your arms." She wrapped hers around his neck. "My answer is *oui*."

* * * * *

*If you enjoyed this story by
Muriel Jensen, you'll also love her
other Heartwarming books:
IN MY DREAMS,
TO LOVE AND PROTECT,
LOVE ME FOREVER and
ALWAYS FLORENCE.*

All available at Harlequin.com

Get 2 Free Books,
Plus 2 Free Gifts—
just for trying the Reader Service!

Love Inspired

YES! Please send me 2 FREE Love Inspired® Romance novels and my 2 FREE mystery gifts (gifts are worth about $10 retail). After receiving them, if I don't wish to receive any more books, I can return the shipping statement marked "cancel." If I don't cancel, I will receive 6 brand-new novels every month and be billed just $5.24 for the regular-print edition or $5.74 each for the larger-print edition in the U.S., or $5.74 each for the regular-print edition or $6.24 each for the larger-print edition in Canada. That's a saving of at least 13% off the cover price. It's quite a bargain! Shipping and handling is just 50¢ per book in the U.S. and 75¢ per book in Canada.* I understand that accepting the 2 free books and gifts places me under no obligation to buy anything. I can always return a shipment and cancel at any time. The free books and gifts are mine to keep no matter what I decide.

Please check one:
- ☐ Love Inspired Romance Regular-Print (105/305 IDN GLWW)
- ☐ Love Inspired Romance Larger-Print (122/322 IDN GLWW)

Name	(PLEASE PRINT)
Address	Apt. #
City State/Province	Zip/Postal Code

Signature (if under 18, a parent or guardian must sign)

Mail to the **Reader Service:**
IN U.S.A.: P.O. Box 1341, Buffalo, NY 14240-8531
IN CANADA: P.O. Box 603, Fort Erie, Ontario L2A 5X3

Want to try two free books from another line?
Call 1-800-873-8635 today or visit www.ReaderService.com.

*Terms and prices subject to change without notice. Prices do not include applicable taxes. Sales tax applicable in N.Y. Canadian residents will be charged applicable taxes. Offer not valid in Quebec. This offer is limited to one order per household. Books received may not be as shown. Not valid for current subscribers to Love Inspired Romance books. All orders subject to approval. Credit or debit balances in a customer's account(s) may be offset by any other outstanding balance owed by or to the customer. Please allow 4 to 6 weeks for delivery. Offer available while quantities last.

Your Privacy—The Reader Service is committed to protecting your privacy. Our Privacy Policy is available online at www.ReaderService.com or upon request from the Reader Service.

We make a portion of our mailing list available to reputable third parties that offer products we believe may interest you. If you prefer that we not exchange your name with third parties, or if you wish to clarify or modify your communication preferences, please visit us at www.ReaderService.com/consumerschoice or write to us at Reader Service Preference Service, P.O. Box 9062, Buffalo, NY 14240-9062. Include your complete name and address.

LI17R2

Get 2 Free Books,
Plus 2 Free Gifts—
just for trying the
Reader Service!

YES! Please send me 2 FREE Love Inspired® Suspense novels and my 2 FREE mystery gifts (gifts are worth about $10 retail). After receiving them, if I don't wish to receive any more books, I can return the shipping statement marked "cancel." If I don't cancel, I will receive 4 brand-new novels every month and be billed just $5.24 each for the regular-print edition or $5.74 each for the larger-print edition in the U.S., or $5.74 each for the regular-print edition or $6.24 each for the larger-print edition in Canada. That's a savings of at least 13% off the cover price. It's quite a bargain! Shipping and handling is just 50¢ per book in the U.S. and 75¢ per book in Canada.* I understand that accepting the 2 free books and gifts places me under no obligation to buy anything. I can always return a shipment and cancel at any time. The free books and gifts are mine to keep no matter what I decide.

Please check one: ☐ Love Inspired Suspense Regular-Print ☐ Love Inspired Suspense Larger-Print
(153/353 IDN GLW2) (107/307 IDN GLW2)

Name _____ (PLEASE PRINT)

Address _____ Apt. #

City _____ State/Prov. _____ Zip/Postal Code

Signature (if under 18, a parent or guardian must sign)

Mail to the **Reader Service:**
IN U.S.A.: P.O. Box 1341, Buffalo, NY 14240-8531
IN CANADA: P.O. Box 603, Fort Erie, Ontario L2A 5X3

Want to try two free books from another line?
Call 1-800-873-8635 or visit www.ReaderService.com.

* Terms and prices subject to change without notice. Prices do not include applicable taxes. Sales tax applicable in N.Y. Canadian residents will be charged applicable taxes. Offer not valid in Quebec. This offer is limited to one order per household. Books received may not be as shown. Not valid for current subscribers to Love Inspired Suspense books. All orders subject to approval. Credit or debit balances in a customer's account(s) may be offset by any other outstanding balance owed by or to the customer. Please allow 4 to 6 weeks for delivery. Offer available while quantities last.

Your Privacy—The Reader Service is committed to protecting your privacy. Our Privacy Policy is available online at www.ReaderService.com or upon request from the Reader Service.

We make a portion of our mailing list available to reputable third parties that offer products we believe may interest you. If you prefer that we not exchange your name with third parties, or if you wish to clarify or modify your communication preferences, please visit us at www.ReaderService.com/consumerschoice or write to us at Reader Service Preference Service, P.O. Box 9062, Buffalo, NY 14240-9062. Include your complete name and address.

LIS17R2

HOMETOWN HEARTS ♥

YES! Please send me **The Hometown Hearts Collection** in Larger Print. This collection begins with 3 FREE books and 2 FREE gifts in the first shipment. Along with my 3 free books, I'll also get the next 4 books from the Hometown Hearts Collection, in LARGER PRINT, which I may either return and owe nothing, or keep for the low price of $4.99 U.S./ $5.89 CDN each plus $2.99 for shipping and handling per shipment*. If I decide to continue, about once a month for 8 months I will get 6 or 7 more books, but will only need to pay for 4. That means 2 or 3 books in every shipment will be FREE! If I decide to keep the entire collection, I'll have paid for only 32 books because 19 books are FREE! I understand that accepting the 3 free books and gifts places me under no obligation to buy anything. I can always return a shipment and cancel at any time. My free books and gifts are mine to keep no matter what I decide.

262 HCN 3432 462 HCN 3432

Name _____ (PLEASE PRINT) _____

Address _____ Apt. # _____

City _____ State/Prov. _____ Zip/Postal Code _____

Signature (if under 18, a parent or guardian must sign) _____

Mail to the **Reader Service:**

IN U.S.A.: P.O. Box 1867, Buffalo, NY. 14240-1867
IN CANADA: P.O. Box 609, Fort Erie, Ontario L2A 5X3

* Terms and prices subject to change without notice. Prices do not include applicable taxes. Sales tax applicable in NY. Canadian residents will be charged applicable taxes. This offer is limited to one order per household. All orders subject to approval. Credit or debit balances in a customer's account(s) may be offset by any other outstanding balance owed by or to the customer. Please allow 4 to 6 weeks for delivery. Offer available while quantities last. Offer not available to Quebec residents.

Your Privacy—The Reader Service is committed to protecting your privacy. Our Privacy Policy is available online at www.ReaderService.com or upon request from the Reader Service.

We make a portion of our mailing list available to reputable third parties that offer products we believe may interest you. If you prefer that we not exchange your name with third parties, or if you wish to clarify or modify your communication preferences, please visit us at www.ReaderService.com/consumerschoice or write to us at Reader Service Preference Service, P.O. Box 9062, Buffalo, NY. 14240-9062. Include your complete name and address.

Get 2 Free Books,
<u>Plus</u> 2 Free Gifts—
just for trying the Reader Service!

READERSERVICE.COM

Manage your account online!

- Review your order history
- Manage your payments
- Update your address

*We've designed the
Reader Service website
just for you.*

Enjoy all the features!

- Discover new series available to you,
  and read excerpts from any series.
- Respond to mailings and special
  monthly offers.
- Browse the Bonus Bucks catalog and
  online-only exculsives.
- Share your feedback.

Visit us at:

ReaderService.com

RS16R

Get 2 Free Books,

Love Inspired HISTORICAL

<u>Plus</u> 2 Free Gifts—

just for trying the Reader Service!